SCORPIO HATES VIRGO

Signs of Love #2

ANYTA SUNDAY

First published in 2017 by Anyta Sunday,
Contact at Bürogemeinschaft ATP24, Am Treptower Park 24, 12435 Berlin, Germany

An Anyta Sunday publication
http://www.anytasunday.com

Copyright 2017 Anyta Sunday

Cover Design: Natasha Snow
Scorpio and Virgo Art Design: Maria Gandolfo (Renflowergrapx)

Content Editor: Teresa Crawford
Line Editor: HJS Editing
Proof Editor: Devil in the Details Editing

All rights reserved. This publication may not be reproduced without prior permission of the copyright owner of this book.

All the characters in this book are fictional and any resemblance to actual persons living or dead is purely coincidental.

This book contains sexual content and an unhealthy obsession with dinosaurs.

*Carolin and Andre
to many wonderful adventures together*

Percalinary
noun / per . cal . i . nary

DEFINITION OF PERCALINARY
: a reference explaining the implied meanings of words as used by Percy Freedman and Callaghan Glover

EXAMPLE OF PERCALINARY IN A SENTENCE
My first time watching Percy and Cal interact required frequent recourse to a percalinary to understand what the hell type of flirting these two were up to.

Chapter One

Praying would not bring back his aunt, so Percy Freedman was making a pact with the devil.

If he arrived at his aunt's house and she opened the door, he might stop being sarcastic. For an entire day.

If she opened the door, he might let her cut his precious hair again under the supervision of a qualified hairdresser. Minus the bowl.

If she opened the door and she was alive and kicking, he might, *just might*, be nice to neighbor and nemesis Callaghan Glover.

He drove into the cul-de-sac. Cape Cod houses lined the small street, solid and heavy under a midnight blue sky and peppered porch lights. He parked under an old oak and wrung the life out of his steering wheel.

Seriously, though.

If she opened the door, he might cry.

He slid out of his Jeep and slunk past the paint-peeling mailbox, through weedy grass, and toward the porch suffering from broken column brackets. The house looked like it was wincing after a fight had sucker punched its teeth.

Kind of how he felt coming here again.

Music wailed through the brick and shingle. Impossible hope jackrabbited his heart.

If his aunt opened the door, he might forgive her awful taste in screeching death metal.

With a nervous twist in his gut, Percy inched to the porch. The front door rocked on its hinges, and he pushed inside, whispering against the loud music. "Abby?"

He turned on the light and blinked in the empty hall. Only the sound of untuned guitars greeted him.

He passed a ransacked hall closet and stopped outside Aunt Abby's room. "Abby?" he said again as he opened the door.

Stagnant air funneled over him, smelling faintly of Aunt Abby's hibiscus perfume. Strewn over two bedside tables and a trunk at the foot the bed were his aunt's clothes and tennis gear.

Under a row of Percy-Abby pictures mounted on the wall, his cousin Frank rifled through a mahogany set of drawers.

Frank, who he'd been staying with the last couple of days.

Frank, who'd been acting off with him since the moment Percy had shown up.

Frank, who must know a faster way to drive here through the Twin Cities.

Like the snap of a lock, Frank looked up, guilt warring with defensiveness.

Percy shut off the music blasting from an old stereo, and sighed. "Well. Isn't this peachy?"

Frank looked away from him. "Took you long enough to get here."

"Have you finished taking whatever scraps she has left?"

"No." He opened her jewelry box, grabbed a handful of worthless brooches, and tossed them on the bed. "I can't believe she left the house to you."

Percy blinked back the tender punch of grief filling his chest.

"She paid off your college loans. She gave me the house, but it's run-down and there are mortgages. She was fair."

"Fair? When my parents died, she could have taken me in. I ended up in a shit-hole with my loser uncle. You practically pranced away from your living parents, and she took you in? Nothing she did was fair."

"Are you suggesting my life has been all rainbows?"

Frank shoved past Percy, muttering, "Leave it to you to bring the gay to a fight."

Percy followed him out the front door and over the ungroomed grass. "In all fairness, with this face, I bring the gay everywhere—"

Frank whirled around and tossed keys at him. "You forgot those. I brought them to you."

Lights popped on in the neighboring houses. Percy's neck prickled at a movement across the street. If he looked, he knew he'd see Cal Glover across the road looming in the shadows.

He stared at his blotchy-faced cousin. "Why did you rifle through her things? Why didn't you just ask?"

Frank's face flickered with frustration, and he shoved Percy's chest, sending him reeling a step. "Because she loved you more. Though *why* I have no idea. You're not family material, are you?"

Percy fought against the sudden hurt pulsing in his chest. He'd opened up to Frank about his ex in *confidence*. Where was his good-natured cousin who used to playfully rib him? The one he went to hockey games with? The one who *laughed*?

A tight smile tipped Frank's lips. As if he knew he'd hit a nerve. "I'm not surprised Josh left you for someone else. You were someone to fuck around with before he settled into his real life."

It took forty-two muscles to pinch a face in anger. Four to lift an arm and slap him. Difficult math. "At least I'm not in the closet."

Frank leaned in and whispered, "At least I'm not destined to be unhappy." Percy opened his mouth to retort but his cousin beat him to it. "It will happen again. You'll get close to someone, and they'll leave you. They always do."

Frank took off, leaving Percy to swallow the golf ball in his throat. With the slam of his car door, his cousin hightailed it out of the cul-de-sac.

Percy cupped the back of his neck and stared after him. Frank might be right. People he cared about never tended to stick around.

With an achy laugh, he headed to his Jeep to unload the boxes. The creak of wood followed by clomping footsteps pulled his attention across the road. Cal stepped out of his porch shadows.

A laugh wheezed out of him. He was right. Of all the neighbors to witness his dramatic return, it would have to be his nemesis.

The lukewarm hood of his Jeep bit against the small of his back where he leaned against it.

Cal plodded toward him in flannel pajama bottoms, the ends stuffed into mud-caked boots. He carried a dictionary that flattened his inside-out T-shirt to his chest. Blue marker scribbled up one of his forearms—the work of his four-year-old sister, no doubt.

A summer breeze flustered Cal's thick wavy hair. Hair the color of wet fox.

Cal stopped in front of him, and Percy folded his arms and lifted his chin. Was it possible for a twenty-two-year-old to grow another inch? Because Cal looked taller than he remembered.

"Callaghan," Percy said and plastered on a bored smile.

"Perseus."

"Quite the cavalry you are. Waltzed over just in time."

"That's me. All hero-complex."

They sized each other up as they had every summer, Thanksgiving, and Christmas they'd met since Percy moved in with his aunt. Perseus vs. Callaghan.

Cal raised his right eyebrow, the one with a nick in the center that made it look like Cal perpetually mocked him.

Percy gestured to the dictionary Cal clasped against his chest. "Going to read Frank the definition of dickface, were you?"

"Words *are* mightier than the sword." Cal thumbed the glossy spine. "Particularly if they are in a thousand-page book and you have good aim."

Percy pushed off the hood, sharply reducing the space between them. "Have good aim?"

Cal didn't move an inch. He held his ground, drawling, "Perfect, if it means saving you."

Percy snorted at the sarcasm, opened the Jeep, and grabbed a box of his clothes. He and Cal had never been good at saying goodbye. They usually tossed out a quip, rolled their eyes, or laughed before parting ways.

So, it startled him when Cal followed him to the porch. Percy gave him a weary look and headed inside.

He schlepped into the living room, the drag of his shoe echoing. One of his most significant memories had happened in Aunt Abby's living room.

At seventeen, his parents had pushed him out, and he'd come straight to Abby. She'd taken one look at him, and wrapped him into a hug. He spent the next year—his senior year—cocooned in Aunt Abby's sugarplum walls, surrounded by Victorian furniture and a ridiculous amount of china vases.

Now all that remained were her watercolor paintings, an old clock, a broken chair and rickety table, and a stained couch.

Discarded books from stolen bookshelves crammed the one remaining bookshelf. Shards of shattered mug stretched under the kitchen archway.

His stomach catapulted into his throat. No matter how hard he swallowed, it wouldn't go down.

Cal shifted from foot to foot, as though he regretted following him inside. Percy started to tell him to go back to his cozy bed, but Cal set his dictionary on the table and cut him off. "Where can I find a broom?"

"There might be one in the utility closet. Unless someone stole that too."

Percy paced, cursing the extended family who had cut him off. Who hadn't cared enough to pitch in for her funeral, but had thoroughly sorted out her belongings . . .

Cal returned with a broom and swept broken porcelain into a pile. "Maybe they took things to remember Abby by?"

Percy folded his arms and blew air to shift his long bangs. "I'm trying to be mad here. Stop interrupting me with your annoyingly considerate reasoning." Cal scooped debris into the dustpan. "Don't do that either. It's like Coyote giving CPR to the Road Runner. Not what we do."

Cal made a gurgling noise between a sigh and a groan.

"Seriously, you can go home now—"

Cal swept the broom toward Percy's feet, propelling him across the living room to the couch, littered in unopened mail. Mail that used to sit in a nice antique pigeon cubbyhole. "Sit down."

Percy glowered and tossed himself back onto the frayed cushions. "Going to offer me tea or coffee?"

"How about a handful of Advil?"

It was almost enough to make his lip twitch.

Cal leaned on the broom handle. His gaze bounced over the room, landing everywhere but him. Percy watched Cal's mouth, waiting for whatever he would say. They were frustrating, those lips. Bottom heavy and fractionally parted, permanently poised to toss a verbal grenade.

"You finally came home."

Percy's chest seized. Home sounded warm and gentle.

He drew in a sharp breath of stagnant, dusty air. "I'm back until I sell the place."

Cal lost his balance on the broom and re-gripped it. "You're not here to stay?"

"That should make your day."

Cal glanced at the clock, stroking five past midnight. "And the day has only just begun."

A small smile begged Percy's lips to turn up, and he might have been too weak to stop it.

Cal cleared his throat. "Why come home so late?"

"To avoid an inquisition. It's working marvelously."

Cal snorted and then eyed the emptiness around them. "What are you going to do about this?"

Percy drew out a roll of fruity Mentos from the inner pocket of his pine-green jacket and popped one in his mouth. He offered one to Cal, who did the same. "I'm getting out of here as soon as I can."

"Are you selling because you need the money?"

"No. Although it would be welcome, after . . ."

Percy wasn't careless with money. After earning certification in massage therapy, he had worked thirty hours a week in a hospice and supplemented his income with freelance massage jobs. Twelve grand, he'd saved up. Before Abby passed.

"You paid for her funeral, didn't you?" Cal said as if reading his mind. His words stretched.

Percy shrugged.

He wasn't an extravagant spender, but he couldn't bring himself to bury the woman who had loved him so fiercely in a cardboard coffin. The oak casket had eaten a couple thousand. The rest had gone to the funeral director, burial, headstone, caterer, venue, and florist.

He'd wanted her to have the best. The last best he could give her.

"Want to stay at our place tonight?" Cal's voice pinched as if he had to offer.

"Us nemeses crashing together? Thanks for the laugh."

"I aim to please."

"You sure do." Percy cleared his throat, scoping the room. "Here's good though."

"Clearly."

Percy winked. He wasn't *just* aiming to be stubborn. Coming back here for the first time since Aunt Abby passed was important.

He needed time to wallow. To get used to Abby's smell without her chip-toothed grin going along with it.

Clamped between the couch cushions, the white edge of an envelope caught Percy's eye. He pulled out an unstamped letter, PERCY scrawled over the front in loopy handwriting.

Crystal's yearly horoscope. Everyone in the cul-de-sac got one. Percy opened the envelope with his thumb, eyeing Cal. "Will all your dreams come true?"

Cal chuckled, the laugh somewhat subdued. "Virgo's calm, rational feathers are to get quite ruffled, apparently."

"I'd *love* to see that." Percy unfolded the paper, and an ache bloomed in his gut. "Just one horoscope this year."

Cal crouched before him, palm sliding down the broom handle. Percy stilled. Did Cal think he had to squeeze his knee and apologize for his loss or something?

Cal's hand moved and Percy cleared his throat to read aloud. "This year is all about healing the heart, Scorpio. It's time to leave negative attitudes and stoic facades at the door and let others see the real, more vulnerable you."

Percy stopped reading. Horoscopes made him shiver. A little too accurate for his tastes.

At least Cal had dropped his hand. His facial expression had relaxed into curiosity.

"You know none of this fits me at all, right?"

"Keep reading."

Percy narrowed his eyes, and continued, "Creativity plays a big part in your summer, and a powerful connection will be forged through its imaginative expression. You may be afraid of being left alone again, Scorpio, but there will be someone close to you worth sharing your love. With the right patience, heartbreak might be a thing of the past."

Nope. He couldn't read anymore.

He stuffed the paper into the envelope and hurled it toward the end of the couch covered in his torn sheets. "Bullshit."

"Tsk, tsk, tsk," Cal said, wagging a finger. "You're supposed to leave negative attitudes at the door."

Percy itched to smooth that damn mocking brow back down. "Want me vulnerable, do you?"

Cal laughed, rolled back on his heels, and stood. "Need help moving those boxes from your Jeep?"

"I've got it. Go back to bed and let me mope in peace."

CAL DIDN'T LET HIM MOPE FOR LONG.

Percy had just finished trucking his most necessary belongings into his room when the doorbell rang. Cal stood in the porch light, T-shirt the right way out, neatly folded, electric-blue sheets stacked in his arms.

Percy hooked his thumbs into the loops of his jeans. "Miss me already, do you?"

Cal gave him a slow blink. "My heart literally weeps when we're apart. Remind me again," he asked as if he didn't want to ask but couldn't help himself. "Why are we nemeses?"

"Don't you remember the first time we met?"

"Who could forget such epic gracefulness?"

Times like these Percy wished he had glasses so he could continuously push them up with his middle finger.

The morning after Percy arrived at Aunt Abby's, and the summer before Cal left to college, Percy had borrowed his Aunt's bike to take a ride and clear his mind. He wanted to embrace the neighborhood and his new start.

At the end of the driveway, however, he yanked the handlebars too hard to the left and lost his balance. He flipped over the bike and landed on his back.

Moments later, a guy leaned over him. A face with forget-me-knot blue eyes, flushed cheeks, and a kinked eyebrow. Percy hadn't learned his name until later. Cal.

Cal had helped him up, and instead of asking if Percy was okay or needed an ice pack, he'd shaken his head and delivered the first verbal grenade, "All elegance, that was."

Percy narrowed his eyes, and Cal scoffed as he handed Percy the sheets. "Wouldn't want to sweep that one under the mat. Nemeses forever. I saw the linen cupboard had been emptied and your bed is about the same size as my last one, so these should fit."

"You're giving me your sheets?"

"No, I thought you might wash them."

They scowled extra hard at each other as Cal retreated home. Percy waited until he'd gone inside before closing his door.

He hugged the sheets to his chest and slouched to bed.

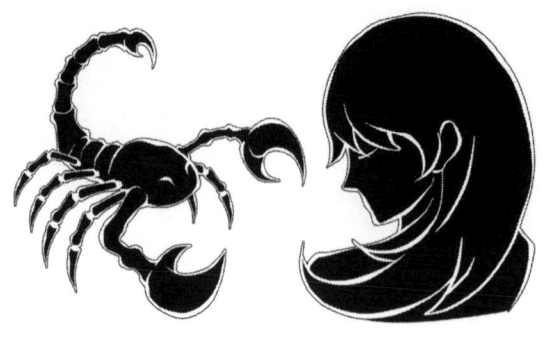

Cul-de-sac
noun / cul . de . sac

DEFINITION OF CUL-DE-SAC
: a dead-end street where Cal and Percy live
: a street end made up of very close neighbors (Percy Freedman, Cal Glover and co., the Wallaces, the Feists, the Sernas. Also, Champey Ong and Mr. Roosevelt)

EXAMPLE OF CUL-DE-SAC IN A SENTENCE
Welcome to our little corner of the world; our charming and delightful cul-de-sac.

Chapter Two

"Sorry I didn't call the police last night," Crystal said the moment Percy stepped onto her porch. "I thought that was *your* dreadful choice in music."

He'd woken to yawning wood, and after eating an expired can of apricots on the kitchen counter, decided to get on with selling the place.

Having no idea where to start, he found himself on his neighbor's porch. Before he could ask for advice though, Crystal had wrapped him into a tight hug, and she still hadn't let go.

"Sorry about the noise," Percy said, breathing in a lungful of sweet perfume. Sugary and soft, and when he closed his eyes, he imagined she was his aunt for a second.

Crystal squeezed him as though she could juice the bad out of his life. Percy was inclined to let her try.

"Champey called me wondering what was going on. She wanted to call the police—I can't believe I convinced her not to. Told her that grief can be a tough emotion, that you were drowning your sorrows in that black-hole music. I made sure no one else bothered you." She eased up on the hug and Percy clutched her another second before retreating.

"It's fine, Mrs. Wallace. Really."

She clapped him softly over his head. "Since when am I Mrs. Wallace to you? Stop that. Crystal will do."

Would she still say that when he told her he was selling?

"Last year was tough for you," she continued, not hesitating to sweep Percy's blond bangs to the side, "We all loved Abby. We're going to take care of her nephew. When you're ready to talk, come to me. Or if you'd prefer someone your own age, there's my Leos. I'll tell Leone and Theo to expect your call."

"I'm managing fine. Super."

"We're here if you change your mind. I suppose you'll be scouting for work too? My shoulders aren't the only things a little tight right now, so I can only book you every other week."

"Crystal, you don't have to—"

"We'll start this week. I'll get back to you on the specifics. Now, what did you come over for?"

Percy stuffed his hands deep into his pockets. "I need to talk about my aunt's property."

If Crystal knew why he wanted the information, she didn't let on. Maybe she thought he needed information about inheritance taxes, but he'd already dealt with that side of things. "You want to speak to Josie about that. She's out buying onesies with her dad right now."

"I heard Josie was pregnant. When is she due?"

"October. Might be a Scorpio like you. Which reminds me, the astral influences are very clear today. Don't close yourself off to company—an opportunity will present itself, and you should seriously consider getting involved in it. . ." Crystal bubbled on, then stopped herself on a third tangent and smiled. "Sorry, I get carried away. Was there anything else I can help you with?"

"Do you have a one-size-does-all toolbox? Preferably with how-to instructions?"

She huffed out a laugh. "You want the Glovers. They have a

great box of mechanical thingies, and if you ask nicely, one of them will even wield them for you."

Percy side-eyed the Glover's house across the road. Of course, he'd be directed there.

"I might try the other neighbors first."

After trying the other neighbors to no avail, Percy ended up at the Glovers' door.

He expected Cal to throw it open and levy that studious gaze on him. Expected Cal's warring frustration and delight as they played verbal dodgeball.

Instead, Cal's younger sister—the older of the two—opened it.

Ellie Glover bit her lip and hugged her chest over the #9 soccer shirt she wore with jeans. Dark hair curtained half her face, and she didn't so much as say hello. Fourteen was a tough age. Ellie looked like she wanted it over.

He couldn't blame her.

"Hey, Ellie," Percy said, "your dad home?"

She hunched her shoulders and mumbled, "He's not here."

Percy filed that reaction for later deliberation. "Okay, cool. Do you know where your toolbox is? I've got a leg that's a few screws loose of a chair."

Ellie nodded and left him on the doorstep.

Bubbly laughter swept down the hall and Percy glimpsed Cal ushering his longtime girlfriend—smart, sassy Jenny—into the living room. He wanted to follow them and listen to their conversation. How did Cal talk to her? Did they play word games too? Or was he genuine and sweet—and what did that sound like?

Ellie returned with a yellow toolbox. Someone had scribbled smiley faces onto the ends—Ellie, he bet, because the same black marker decorated the bottom of her jeans.

"You're a lifesaver, El."

Crystal was right. The toolbox held lots of mechanical thingies.

He stared at the broken chair he'd upturned on Aunt Abby's table, the amputated leg stretched perpendicular on the tabletop. A tube of heavy-duty glue and masking tape waited in line.

This was going to be fun.

Time to make a drink.

Cradling a chipped glass of lavender tea, Percy peered out the bay window at the other houses.

Mr. Feist, the cul-de-sac giant, wore flannel and overalls and hosed drooping agapanthus as his wife admired him from their porch hammock; Mr. Roosevelt balanced a thermos of coffee on a teetering pile of paper as he headed for his car. His basset, known by the neighbors as Rooster for his insane six-o'clock yapping, pranced at his heels.

Champey's ivy-choked house was quiet, but he pictured the older Cambodian woman curled over the picnic table in the backyard, writing one of her romances.

Percy set his glass on the windowsill just as Cal and Jenny exited the Glovers'. They walked to a parked Dodge, and Jenny set a cardboard box spilling with clothes on the sun-faded roof. Combing a hand through his sun-glittered hair, Cal said something that made her laugh.

Percy hugged the windowpane, eyes glued to Cal's bottom-heavy, secret-spilling mouth. Damn, he wished he could lip read. Did the box of clothes mean something?

He waited for them to kiss. It didn't happen.

Jenny rocked on the balls of her strappy heels and lunged at Cal, toppling him into a hug. His arms encircled her and he rubbed her back, face curling into her gathered hair.

Jenny pulled away, stuffed the box inside the Dodge, and rounded to the driver's side. She wound down the window and waved at him as she peeled away from the curb.

Cal's shoulders slumped as he watched her leave, and Percy sensed he might not be seeing Jenny careening into their street anytime soon. If it was a breakup, it looked like an amicable one. Not the drama he unleashed on his ex when Josh broke up with him two days before Aunt Abby's funeral.

Cal's gaze skipped over the road, and Percy shrank away from the window.

There was an art to prying into people's secrets, and it involved feigning nonchalance. And sucking on Mentos, apparently.

He stuffed the candy roll back into his pocket and picked up his phone. He found internet instructions on how to fix the chair and rummaged through the toolbox for a chisel.

A knock sounded at the door, and Percy opened it. Typical of Cal, he wore canvas shorts and a T-shirt with an image of a T-rex stretching out his short arms followed by the phrase "*Good luck reaching* first base."

Percy tempered the first grin he'd had all day. "What's up, Callaghan?"

Cal's gaze lingered on the chisel. "Having fun with my tools there?"

Percy changed his grip on the wooden handle. "Trust me, if I were having fun with your tools, you'd know."

Cal turned an endearing shade of kill-me-now, blue eyes darting every direction but Percy's.

Percy backed toward the living room, fascinated by Cal's word-choked side. "Why don't you come inside and watch me use them?"

Glowering, Cal trudged to the living room after him.

Percy pointed the chisel toward the couch, and Cal reluctantly folded himself on the end. He leaned forward, elbows resting on parted knees.

"Tea or coffee?" Percy asked. He didn't bother to tell him it would come in a glass.

Cal shook his head and let out an exhausted laugh. "Have any Advil left?"

Percy tossed him his Mentos roll. "Best I can do until I get to the store."

Cal peeled back the paper and pinched a lemon candy, his probing gaze hot as Percy inelegantly chiseled loose splinters from the chair leg.

"You're really going to sell the place?"

The chisel slid off the wood. "Didn't your dad tell you I was thinking about it?" Percy asked.

Cal picked invisible lint off his jeans. "Dad's gone away for a while."

Percy absorbed Cal's tight reaction, then busied himself slathering glue to the chair leg and wrestling masking tape around it. He hammered a couple one-inch pin nails into the joint, narrowly avoiding a whack to his thumb. "How long is a while?"

"What did you tell him?"

"He emailed me about cleaning up the yard, and I asked him if he thought the cul-de-sac would be okay with me privately selling her house."

"You don't need permission."

"Nevertheless." Percy pulled out what looked like a clamp from the toolbox. "You were all close to Abby, and you'll all have to live with whoever buys the place."

Cal frowned. He gestured to the clamp. "Do you know how to use that?"

"Are you questioning my masculinity?"

Cal eyeballed him, starting from Percy's brown-and-navy shoes and working up to his snug jeans. Cal studied him like a paleontologist chiseling mud for dinosaur fossils. Analytical. Focused on every tiny detail.

A sudden laugh churned in Percy's chest and he lost his

damn grip on the clamp. He snapped his hips forward and caught it between table and crotch. *Smooth, Percy. Real smooth.*

Cal hitched his eyebrow. "No question about that."

Percy pushed the offending clamp to the side. "Why are you here, anyway?"

Cal stood and set the half roll of Mentos on the table. "Ellie said you'd borrowed my tools. I thought it prudent to check you could use them."

"Wouldn't want me accidentally slaying myself?"

"Not unless it's at the end of pointed words."

"I don't know. I think I'd rather go using your tools."

Cal managed to retain his blush to his collar.

Percy bathed in Cal's awkwardness a few moments before throwing him a raft. "How's Ellie doing? Another summer and she'll be taller than me."

"She's okay. Bored, I guess. Her BFF is in Europe for the summer."

"BFF?"

"Kid is all about the acronyms. I wish she had a few more though."

"Acronyms?"

"Friends, Perseus."

"It's good that you're home," Percy said. When Cal's eyes sparked on the edge of a quip, he hurriedly clarified. "Ellie must love that. When did you arrive?"

Cal shoved his thumbs into the tops of his pockets, lean fingers cupping his thighs. "I moved back at Easter and don't plan on leaving anytime soon."

"You've been home two and a half months?" Percy fumbled with the clamp. Again. "I thought you only returned for summers."

"Not this time."

"Why?"

Cal rooted his gaze to Aunt Abby's broken chair. "I wanted to help with Ellie and Hannah. You need to place those clamps at least an inch apart."

"Did you quit mid-masters?"

"The drill should be charged. Screw at a fifteen-degree angle."

"But you love college."

"You might need two holes."

"Callaghan!"

Cal walked over and held the wobbly chair leg in place. "I don't love it as much as I love my family, okay?"

Percy stumbled over a response. He'd wanted a sincere answer, but he hadn't anticipated one. Questions filled his chest, weighted with unfamiliar and urgent importance. "Why do you need to stay home?"

Cal sighed and met his gaze. "Why do *you* need to *leave*?"

Callaghan
Biographical name / Cal . la . ghan

DEFINITION OF CALLAGHAN
: the name of Percy Freedman's neighbor and nemesis (see definition). Used in full form by Percy to denote fake annoyance. Almost always expressed in full in dialogue, often with sarcastic overtones

EXAMPLE OF CALLAGHAN IN A SENTENCE
Percy smirked. "Real suave, Callaghan. You'll have people falling over their feet for a piece of you."

Chapter Three

"Rip the Band-Aid off," Percy murmured to himself outside his aunt's room. He had to clear out her clothes, the brooches Frank had deemed worthless, and the tennis gear she had used weekly.

Percy rolled his forehead against the knotty-pine door. Maybe if he bored hard enough, he wouldn't have to turn the handle. He'd plow into the room that smelled like the hole in his heart.

One hand closed around the cool doorknob, and he channeled his inner Scorpio. Part lobster, part spider, part worst-fear-of-your-life.

A scorpion could handle this.

Or not, apparently.

He hiked to his room and collapsed at a vinyl desk bookended by half his unemptied boxes.

With a shiver that echoed, he opened his laptop, found Josie Serna's number, and called her.

He couldn't sell this house fast enough.

~

Josie popped by later that afternoon and, after an hour poking around, handed him a foot-long list of To-Dos. Percy pinned them to the fridge, then crawled into his bed and let the internet coddle him.

The ding of his phone indicated a new email.

To: percyfreedman, wilhelmroosevelt, callaghanglover, ellicglover, champeyong, kelvinserna, josieserna, nathanfeist, jemmafeist, crystalwallace

From: @cul-de-sac

Subject: Hello Neighbors

Summer is here. To kick it off, we'd like to invite you to join in a game of Sherlock Gnomes. Become a gnome and secretly treat your neighbors. Guess the stealthy gnomes treating you in return. Prizes awarded mid-July to participants who correctly guess all gnome identities.

A new event for our cul-de-sac families based on the much-loved Secret Santa. We hope you have fun. Sign up anonymously with your gnome name <u>here</u>. This forum offers a board to pin notices and tidbits you want to share. Come to the chatroom for general chatter and investigation.

Happy Sherlock Gnoming!

Was this the opportunity Crystal had hinted he should consider taking? Had she organized the game because the stars suggested he get involved?

He sank back against his headboard. She knew him well.

Mysteries had always been Percy's jam.

Part of him wanted to sign up, but maybe Crystal and the stars had their wires crossed. What was the point in bonding with the neighbors when he would move from the cul-de-sac soon?

Swallowing, he clicked the mail away, and busied himself in replying to a post on the Chatvica message board: **I think I might be gay, now what?**

Misery loves company, so it wasn't a surprise when he caught sight of the post: **My boyfriend left me for someone else.** Percy poured over the comments, agreeing with some he would have flipped off last year.

The discussion reminded him of a dormant thread from when he'd been in senior year, and Percy couldn't hold back from reading it once more: **Gay and falling for a (straight) guy. ~ GayDude**

Three long-winded commenters commiserated with GayDude, saying they'd all lived through the pain and knew how easy it was to overanalyze every word, action, or look. They agreed that GayDude needed to distance himself emotionally and move on.

A fourth commenter asked if GayDude was sure the guy wasn't bisexual, to which GayDude replied he'd hoped for that, but the only person his crush watched with any hint of physical attraction was one girl he'd been friends with since high school.

A fifth commenter was blunter:

> **You keep saying how nice he is like that's a sign he feels the same way. He's nice to you because he's a nice guy. Get over your fantasy. If he's straight, he likes girls. Move on. And if—on the very small chance—Mr. Straight is flirting with you, don't go counting 'he loves me, loves me not' rose petals. He might just be curious. His experimentation will leave you heartbroken. Unless a fling is enough for you, *don't give in to temptation.***

Don'tDeludeYourself really laid it out there, and he was right. Straight guys were best avoided. Especially the curious ones.

He logged off and walked back to Aunt Abby's room—and right past it.

Doors groaned, and the floor creaked underfoot as he made for the kitchen.

Halfway through making dinner using an odd assortment of pots and pans, a hollow chime rang through the bones of the house. Percy answered the door.

Cal. Because one visit a day wasn't enough.

He stood on the other side of the threshold, hands stuffed in his khaki pockets, foot grinding against the porch like at any moment he might hoof back across the street. His short hair stuck up, frazzled and wet. Percy had to refrain from sniffing Cal's rather appealing scent of aloe vera and lotion.

Percy lifted both brows in a wordless question, and Cal straightened his shoulders. "I'm not here of my own volition."

Percy scanned the porch. "Did someone shove you across the road?"

Cal made a frustrated sound in his throat and let himself into the house. Percy swallowed a sudden burst of misplaced amusement and followed him into the kitchen.

"I mentioned your run-in with Frank to Mom," Cal said, peeking inside the pots on the stove. He flung open the cupboards and nodded as though completing a mental checklist.

Percy didn't wonder what Cal was doing. Cal was always studying things. A tic he had when he was nervous. Or was around Percy.

"She's concerned." Cal gripped the doors, staring at the few pieces of dishware left. "Have you spoken to him? Cleared the air between you? Or is there a chance he'll come back?"

"I'll never speak to him again after this. If he tries coming back, I'll handle him." Percy jerked a thumb toward the overflowing bookshelf in the living room and waggled his brows. "I've whole thesauruses in there."

Cal looked torn between a smirk and a frown—the frown won out. "You'll never speak to him again? I know he was a real dick, but isn't he the only family you have left?"

"Right in the gut, Callaghan. Nice."

Cal closed the cupboards and faced him. "I just mean I hope you work it all out. Until you do, we're worried about you being on your own."

"We're?"

"*Mom*'s worried."

Percy studied Cal's darting gaze, then grabbed the bowls and dumped pasta shells and a good helping of sauce into them. "Tell your *mom* it's nice she's so worried about me, but I'll be fine."

Cal took one of the bowls and ate in the kitchen, leaning against the counters. He watched Percy as he ate, verbal grenades oddly absent. Trapped behind mouthfuls of Percy's decidedly average pasta, perhaps.

Cal shoveled in one last forkful and set his bowl in the dishwasher. His gaze caught the to-do list on the fridge, and a shadow simmered across his face. He turned toward Percy. "Are you done eating?"

"Nope."

Cal waited, folding his arms, shifting impatiently. Amused, Percy finished the last of his bowl deliberately slowly. "Why are you squirming like a guy on a first date?"

"What would it take to get you over to my house?"

Percy's brow shot up.

Cal huffed. "Mom doesn't want you spending the evening alone."

"Your mom seems awfully concerned for me."

"Don't ask me why"—Cal squinted hard at him—"but there's something about you she likes."

A smile split Percy's face—the biggest he'd had all day. Hell, all month.

"I might have missed your mom too." Percy scraped the last of his *delicious* pasta from his bowl. "I've thought of her every week I wasn't around."

"You did?"

"How could I not? She keeps me thoroughly entertained."

Percy snorted and busied himself wiping down the bench again. Cal's gaze burned the back of Percy's neck, and Percy rolled his shoulders against a fast-approaching shiver. When he looked over, Cal tilted his head and stroked Percy with an analytical gaze.

Percy swallowed the laugh bubbling in his throat, and steered the conversation to less shiver-inducing territory. "You know your mom and I used to watch murder mysteries every Sunday."

A small crease cut Cal's brow as though he'd been so lost in his thoughts he'd lost the thread of conversation. He recovered quickly. "Never the Sundays I came home from college."

"Well, no," Percy said. "I wanted to watch a murder. Not commit one."

A hefty laugh shot out of Cal. "Come on, Perseus. Let's go."

"Didn't peg you to be such a risk-taker, Callaghan."

"I didn't either, Perseus. Apparently, you bring out the unexpected in me."

THEY HAD BARELY CROSSED THE STREET WHEN A DOG BARKED.

Percy and Cal looked at each other and said "Rooster" simultaneously. The brown-spotted basset towing Mr. Roosevelt scrambled around a parked Toyota toward them.

Percy reached down and petted the dog straining to jump up his leg.

Mr. Roosevelt called him to heel. "Percy! How great to have you back. Did you bring your man up with you?"

Percy bent and buried his hands in Rooster's soft coat under the chin. "Josh didn't work out."

Mr. Roosevelt nodded, all optimism and smiles. "Haven't met Mr. Right yet, huh?"

"If I had, I'd be with him right now."

Cal brushed past Percy as he stroked Rooster's long, floppy ears. "You here for Fourth of July this year?"

Mr. Roosevelt nodded. "I'm away two days next week, but I'll be around for all manner of cul-de-sac shenanigans. Oh, look, Champey's waving me over. I promised I'd help her with a character she's writing."

"Do you have someone to look after Rooster?" Cal asked.

"Champey's way of repaying me for picking my brain."

Mr. Roosevelt left them with a wide smile, and Cal didn't wait two seconds before beelining home.

Percy kicked off his shoes and followed him to the great room down the hall. Cal's mom—a.k.a. Mrs. Glover, a.k.a. Marg—pushed up from a leather armchair the moment he waltzed into view. Balled on the couch, Ellie gave him a startled look before ducking behind her long bangs.

"Percy!" Marg said, tugging down the sleeves of what looked like one of Mr. Glover's lumberjack shirts. "You're here."

"Think Cal would fail to lure me over?"

Marg reached him in three steps and wrapped him into a hug. She looked the same as he remembered: wavy, frosted brown hair haloed in gray; warm hazel eyes; lips, like her sons, parted, ready to guess who killed the preacher's wife.

He pulled back, noting shadows under her eyes and sadness lurking behind her momentary surprise. "I missed our mystery nights," he said.

She smiled and glanced at Cal, who stood watching them from behind the kitchen island. He busied himself stuffing a bag of popcorn into the microwave. "I do love mysteries," she murmured.

Ellie shifted, staring at the large TV screen. "I thought we were watching—"

"We'll finish this first, El." Marg sat down, gesturing Percy to sit on the couch. "We'll pop on *Midsomer Murders* after."

Ellie continued watching the comedy on the monstrous screen, while Percy cozied up in soft cushions like he used to. It was like going back in time—except for knowing Cal was there. That little fact sparked a hyperawareness where Percy intuitively catalogued every movement, hum, and shared look—supposedly unnoticed—that pinged between them.

Marg absently smoothed the folds at the waist of Mr. Glover's shirt. "How are you and Josh?"

Percy let out a short laugh. Would everyone bring him up? "Turns out I'm not family material."

A glass toppled over in the kitchen. Percy's attention lasered in on Cal as he said something undignified and flung a dishtowel over the mess.

"Oh, honey. When did it end?"

Percy refocused on Marg and shrugged. "Just before Aunt Abby's funeral. I may have overreacted and deflated the tires of the SUV he bought for the kids he wants to have without me."

"He didn't actually say that?"

"It's okay. I have a crazy awesome dessert routine I indulge in whenever someone leaves me."

It went oddly quiet in the kitchen and Percy forced himself not to look. Marg, however, looked. Her expression softened and the corner of her lips curved. "Well," she said, "there's someone better out there for you."

"Someone who won't leave? Might have to see it to believe it."

"Patience, love. You'll know when it's right. In the meanwhile, have you signed up for Sherlock Gnomes?"

"Not sure if I will."

Cal rounded the couch hugging a bowl of popcorn and cast him a puzzled glance. "What? It's like Secret Santa, and you've never missed one of those."

Percy screwed on a smile. "Well, you know . . . I did all the cul-de-sac games with Aunt Abby."

Marg nodded. "I understand. I'm not participating either. Decided to leave the fun to Cal and Ellie."

Cal squeezed himself between Percy and Ellie and planted the warm bowl of buttery popcorn into Percy's lap. It wasn't quite as warm as the thigh and arm that lingered his side.

"Huh," Cal said. "I get it."

That sounded rather condescending. "Get what?"

"You're afraid Aunt Abby was the mastermind."

The attempt at manipulation was blatant and close to working, dammit. "Not true, Callaghan."

"If only there were a way to prove otherwise."

Their gazes clashed in challenge, and Percy was determined not to look away first. If he wanted to opt out of participating in the community, he would. Nobody could change his mind.

Cal's pupils widened, shrinking the lighter blue of his irises. Like his posture, his expression mimicked certitude; his gaze remained thoughtful, analytical, reserved. This Cal was his Callaghan.

"Mommy." The small voice piped up from the doorway, startling them out of the moment.

Cal's little sister shuffled into the room, hugging a fleece blanket.

"It's bedtime, Hannah," Marg gently admonished, lifting a brow much like Cal did.

"I'm thirsty," she said, slinking to the couch.

When she saw Percy, she ducked nearer to her mom. Marg kissed her forehead and was about to stand when Cal slipped off the couch onto all fours. "I'll get her some water and take her back to bed." He crawled over Percy's feet and parked next to Hannah. "Hop on."

Wait, who was *this* Callaghan?

Ellie hesitantly moved to her brother. "No T-rex," she said. "That one's scary."

"No T-rex," he agreed.

Hannah clambered onto Cal's back, blanket jammed under her and trailing over Cal's butt like a tail.

"Dino big?" she asked as Cal made theatre of hauling her to the kitchen.

"I'm a plant-eater from the late Jurassic period," Cal said. "I have plates on my back and spines on my tail. I am huge, but my brain is only as big as Mr. Roosevelt's dog's."

Hannah giggled. "Faster, faster."

"Stegosaurus only moved five miles an hour."

"'Nother dino. Faster."

Ellie's show ended, and Marg set up a mystery while Cal snapped Hannah into his arms and flew her to bed, Pteranodon style.

Marg sighed and rubbed her brow. Did it weigh on her that Cal had quit his masters in paleontology to come home? It twisted Percy's gut, and Cal wasn't anyone to him . . . anyone much.

"Popcorn, Marg?" he asked, offering her the bowl.

She looked at the bowl and her face pinched. "Don't think I could stomach it tonight."

When Cal returned, he planted himself in his spot on the couch. The entire film, he kept his eyes narrowed on the screen, not looking at Percy even once.

Percy's concentration kept slipping. By the time the detective announced he'd solved the case, Percy was certain he'd pieced the mystery together. Not the one they'd watched, but the one weighting the Glovers' house.

The answer lay in Cal and Ellie's elusiveness to any mention of their father; in Marg's exhausted, sad eyes and her baggy clothes; the way she touched her shirt at the belly. How Cal had leapt to cajole his little sister to bed.

Mr. Glover had up and left his son, daughters, and pregnant wife.

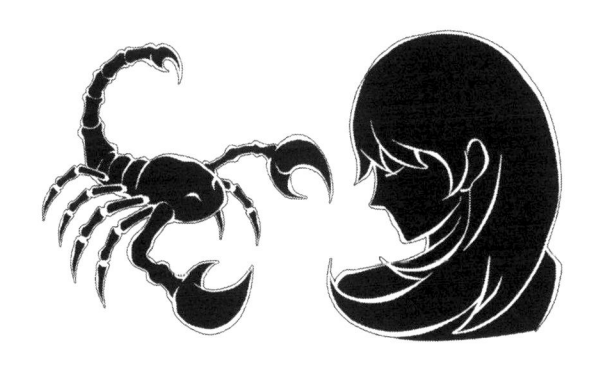

P erseus
      noun / Per . seus

DEFINITION OF **PERSEUS**
   : the name of Cal Glover's neighbor and nemesis. Used in full form by Cal to denote fake annoyance. Usually expressed in full in dialogue, often with exaggerated sarcasm

EXAMPLE OF **PERSEUS** IN A SENTENCE
   [eye roll] "Whatever would I do without you, Perseus?"

Chapter Four

Percy spooned muesli at the bay window. With the bareness of the living room, this had become his go-to spot.

It helped he could spy on the neighbors.

More specifically, the Glovers. He'd barely slept last night thinking about Cal's mom and the whole Glover family. He'd solved their mystery, but he hadn't figured out how to ask them about it. Not that it was any of his business.

He couldn't stop wondering how they were taking it. He imagined little Hannah, gazing at her mom with big eyes asking where her daddy was. Or Ellie—was this why she was so reserved? Was she crying a well of tears inside, trying to keep it together for her mom?

And Cal . . .

He shoveled another spoonful of muesli into his mouth. Fuck. He couldn't go there.

Across the road, Marg tucked Hannah into the car and waved goodbye to Cal and Ellie, who hopped toward Cal's hatchback in a dash to make it to Ellie's dishwashing job at the local diner.

Cal patted his chest and pockets as he groggily located his

keys. Last year, Ellie would've knocked her brother playfully over the head. Today, she stared at the cuff of her shirt.

They clambered into the car.

Percy was about to take his empty bowl to the kitchen when Cal's hatchback revved and stuttered before falling silent. Cal tried again.

Percy wasn't the world's handiest man, but he knew the sound of a dead engine. He sighed, found his keys, and jogged over to his stranded neighbors.

In the driver's seat, Cal closed his eyes and mouthed what Percy knew were pointed words.

He tapped at the window and Cal opened his eyes.

Another mouthed word.

Percy opened the door and leaned against it, flipping his keys over his index finger. "Need a ride?"

∽

"THIS IS WHAT A HEALTHY ENGINE SOUNDS LIKE, CALLAGHAN."

"It is also the sound of smug, Perseus."

Percy bit down on a smirk and steered the Jeep out of the cul-de-sac. He glanced at Ellie in the rearview mirror. She had pushed his boxes aside, donned headphones, and shut her eyes.

When they passed the local garage, Percy held out his hand to Cal and snapped his fingers. "Gimme your keys. I'll get Mr. Feist to jumpstart the hatchback while you're at work."

Cal stared at his hand so hard that Percy wondered if there was dirt under his nails. As hands went, Percy's were unremarkable. Everything about him was unremarkable, in fact. No freckles, moles, tattoos, or prominent veins. His skin was boring, hide-inside pale. He was fit and toned, but when Percy looked in the mirror, he was bored. Nothing special identified him.

Cal, however, held treats for the eye. One could get lost tallying Cal's uniqueness. His defined jaw smattered with faded pockmarks dusted by faint, copper-peppered stubble. Light freckles confined to the bridge of his nose. That nick in his arched eyebrows.

Percy supposed he could get tattoos, but he wouldn't know what. Also, pain. His colorful jackets and bright shoes would have to do.

"She'll need more than a jumpstart." Cal set a ring of three color-coded keys in his palm. Blue. Yellow. Green. "But have at her."

"Suppose I can get her to the garage then."

Cal pulled out his wallet and started peeling out Jacksons. Probably the closest Cal would get to telling Percy he was grateful.

Percy ignored the cash and jiggled Cal's keys before popping them into his pocket. "What's the third for?"

"Third what?"

"Blue key for the car, either the yellow or green one for your house. What's the third for? A safe stashed with secret diaries?"

Cal chuckled. "Yellow is for home. Green is the key to my heart, of course."

"Did Jenny give it back to you yesterday?" That slipped out. Percy winced.

"So, you were watching us from your window."

"What else am I supposed to do alone in Aunt Abby's house?"

"It is so good to have you back."

Percy flicked him the finger, and Cal sized up the morning traffic, a smirk twitching his cheek. It faded quickly though. "Jenny and I broke up months ago. Yesterday, I was finally giving her back some of her things."

Percy refused to show the intrigue he felt. He tapped his fingers on the wheel and kept his voice politely interested. "Didn't everyone just love her?"

"She's awesome, all right."

"Yeah, I can totally see why that would make you guys break up."

Cal swatted Percy's head, and Percy held back a surprised gurgle. Warm fingers sinking into his hair and tapping his head was a new type of grenade. "Hey, I'm driving!"

"We're stuck at an endless red." Cal swatted him once more for good measure before dropping his arm. "Jenny and I are better as friends. I'm sure we'll hang out just as much once she gets back from Spain."

"She gave you the 'let's be friends' line? Ouch."

Cal gave him a puzzled glance. "It wasn't a line. And I was the one to give it."

Percy groaned on Cal's behalf. "You didn't?"

"What? She's been a big part of my life. I want her around."

"Did she slap you? Please say yes."

"Jenny is a mature woman. She understood."

"Well, that makes someone."

"Someone who's mature?"

Percy lightly punched Cal in the surprisingly firm bicep. "Someone who understands." He inched toward the green light, slowing when it turned yellow. "Why did you break up with her?"

Cal looked away from the lights that seemed to take forever to turn red. "I'm not sure."

Percy sniffed another Glover-related mystery. "You don't know why you broke up?"

"I'm sure about breaking up. I'm just not sure why I felt so strongly about it at the time."

"When?"

"Last November," Cal said softly, almost like he knew November meant a lot to Percy. It was his birthday month, and the month Abby had her stroke.

The lights changed, and it took Percy a long moment before stepping on the gas. Cal sensed the mood shifting and changed the subject. "Do you need some work close to home?"

"I'm putting Abby's house on the market, remember?"

"You could be stuck with us a while before it sells. Maybe long enough for the hurt to pass, and for you to realize you want to stay here."

Percy glowered. "Don't assume that because I'm selling the house it's the grief talking. Else, when you're yawning, I'll assume you're famished and stuff a cheese roll in your mouth."

Cal shifted in his seat, the slightest hint of amusement rimming the frustration in his eyes. "Could you make sure there's bacon in it? I need the iron."

A traitorous laugh shot-gunned out of him, and then he glared at his neighbor.

"Let me start over," Cal said with more patience than Percy deserved. "Do you need any work?"

Percy would soon run short on cash, especially considering his lack of handy-man dexterity. Josie had said selling could happen in twenty days or six months. "In need of a massage, are you?"

"Always, after talking to you." Cal swiped the password on his phone and flipped pointlessly through screens. Sounding bored, Cal continued, "I'm happy to post some flyers up on the community noticeboard. You could offer a summer deal."

Percy bit his lip and nodded, the closest he could get to telling Cal that would be helpful. "I'll have a flyer for you by tomorrow."

Ellie leaned forward between the gap in the seats, startling Percy.

"Um, you drove past my work?" she said, and whacked her brother on the arm. "Why didn't you stop him?"

Cal blinked and scanned the street before looking at Ellie. "Guess I was distracted."

Percy made a U-turn and dropped her off.

After watching Ellie slump into work, Percy drove Cal to the community center. A block away from his work, Cal sighed and said, "Have you looked into other places to buy?"

He had emailed a guy selling a two-bedroom town house. "There's a place in Saint Paul I might check out this weekend. He might be interested in checking out Aunt Abby's property too."

"Will you have cleared out her room by then?"

"How do you know I haven't?"

Cal studied him with that probing gaze that Percy felt in his gut. "If you need a hand . . ."

"I'll be fine. It won't take long." Cal lifted his brow, and Percy nudged the conversation into another direction. "What do you do for fun, Callaghan?"

"Other than talk to you?"

"And watch me with your tools."

Cal side-eyed him. "I like kicking a soccer ball around with Ellie, filling out online surveys, reading fantasy and social commentary."

"Social commentary? Is that a pretentious way to say you binge-read your Twitter feed?"

"Fine. I binge-read my Twitter feed and get off on late-show monologues."

Percy's abrupt stop at a stop sign had the car behind them honking.

"Whoa," Cal deadpanned. "Did I say something?"

A laugh tickled Percy's chest, making his eyes sting. "Nope, no fun tidbits there at all."

Three minutes later, Percy parked outside Cal's work. He wasn't ready for Cal to leave yet though. He'd ignored the questions gnawing at him, telling himself Cal would mention his situation if he chose. But Cal saw him as a pain in the ass, so why would he unload on Percy?

Why should Percy care that he did?

"You've gone quiet." Cal unlocked his belt. He sounded frustrated at his own curiosity. "I'd like to think I rendered you speechless, but I'm probably not so lucky."

Percy fished inside his jacket pocket for his Mentos, took one, and handed the last one to Cal. "When is your mom due?"

Cal dropped the candy between his legs. He let out his breath and stared at the car ceiling. "Also, November."

November could pack a punch. "And your dad?"

"Come on, Percy. Surely you've put that together?"

"He left you."

Cal stared out the passenger window. "Mid-life crisis, I guess. I'll convince him to come back though."

Percy breathed in a deep lungful. "I'm sorry."

"The baby took him by surprise. Said he couldn't take it anymore."

"I get why you wanted to stay home."

A weak laugh. "Trying to keep the family together."

Percy's stomach twisted, and he pasted on a grin. "I still think you should continue your masters in Jurassic Park studies."

"Paleontology."

"Uh huh."

Cal shook his head and pinned Percy with tired blue eyes. "You should sign up for Sherlock Gnomes."

Percy rubbed the ribbed steering wheel. "Okay."

"Wait. Did you just agree with me?"

Percy growled. "Shut up and get out of my car."

Cal laughed, and when Percy pulled out from the curb, he forced himself not to look back.

∽

"She needs a mechanic, all right," Percy mused after three attempts jumpstarting the hatchback.

Unfortunately, Mr. Feist had been away, leaving Percy to beg cal-de-sac grouch Mr. Serna for a hand. When he'd flat-out refused, Josie—on the porch bench next to him—rubbed her baby belly and told the fetus that the grumbling old man was Grandad.

The clever play brought him to Percy's aid, albeit muttering the entire time.

After a third failed attempt, Percy removed the jumper cables and tossed them back into his Jeep.

"You're going to ask for help towing this piece of junk next, aren't you?" Mr. Serna said.

Percy peered at him over the hoods of the cars and delivered his best pretty-please smile. "Or lend me your towrope and Josie will help."

At the sight of Josie once more rubbing her belly, Mr. Serna folded his arms and glared at Percy. "I'm not sure you'd know what to do with a towrope."

"That's what the internet is for."

He grumbled. "Get a piece of cardboard and write 'On Tow,' then stick it in the back window. I'll hook up the car. Park your Jeep, we'll use my truck."

Ten minutes later, with rope securely fastened, handbrake released, and transmission in neutral, they slowly navigated the streets to the mechanic. Twenty minutes after that, Percy was gripping the overhead handle in Mr. Serna's truck as he teared back home. Fast, this time, as though Mr. Serna wanted to avoid conversation at any cost.

"Thanks for your help," Percy said.

A grunt.

"Maybe I can make it up to you sometime? Give Josie a foot massage, maybe?"

"Stop that."

"Stop what?"

"You sound like your aunt. Always trying to butter me up."

Percy swallowed, then asked, thickly. "Did it ever work?"

Mr. Serna's hard stop in his driveway jerked the seatbelt tight against Percy's chest. "No. But at least she brought me carrot muffins."

"They always said a way to a man's heart—"

"Get out."

Percy laughed—and got out.

∽

PERCY AVOIDED STAYING INSIDE AUNT ABBY'S, CHOOSING instead to design a flyer at the playground behind the Sernas' house. The same playground Percy had thrown up in during Christmas vacation senior year, the first time he'd ever gotten drunk.

Aunt Abby, the Glovers, and the Wallaces had cooked an amazing feast in their kitchen. They had also made eggnog . . .

It tasted good. Creamy and sweet, and he told Theo and Leone he could handle another one. Some crap about having a high tolerance. Cal, home from his first semester at college, was sitting across the table watching him with a raised brow. Mocking. Like Cal didn't think Percy should indulge himself quite so much, quite so quickly.

Aunt Abby, Crystal, and Cal's mom were too involved in cooking to notice Percy downing eggnog like it was water.

"Might want to slow it down there, Perseus."

Percy leaned back in his seat a smug smile on his lips before taking another slow sip.

Theo and Leone's banter about the history of nursery rhymes drowned into the background until it was just Percy and Cal staring at each other.

"For such a smart guy," Percy said, "it's strange you don't know the meaning of fun."

Cal picked up a fresh bread roll from the basket in the middle of the table, cut it open, and buttered it. "Fun. Stupid. Barbecue-barbeque." He leaned over the table and set the roll on Percy's empty plate. "Eat."

Percy scowled while ripping bits of warm roll and popping them into his mouth. He didn't want to admit it, but the room had started spinning. Quips skittered through his mind and right back out again. His belly groaned, and he was minutes away from a bout of vomiting.

Nothing he wanted anyone to know. Especially that Cal guy. They'd had a handful of encounters since he'd moved in with Abby, but each one sent shivers through his veins.

Percy forced a spirited smile and excused himself to the bathroom.

Instead, he went outside.

His stomach rioted and his throat spasmed. He'd have chucked up right then but Cal stepped out of the house toting an extra scarf, gloves, and a bottle of water. "Still having fun?"

Percy grinned as he flipped him off, then promptly swallowed a wave of nausea. "Nice night for a walk."

With that, he hiked through a fresh layer of snow, all the way to the cul-de-sac playground. The idea had been to shake Cal off, but in his stumbling state Percy was roadkill waiting to happen. Somehow, he made it to the swings, dusted off the snowflakes, and slumped onto the rubber seat.

Cal sat on the swing beside him, chains twisting as he faced Percy. Without preamble, he slung a thick scarf around Percy's neck and passed him the gloves. The chains were freezing, and Percy greedily accepted the woolen warmth. Cal offered the water, and Percy took it with forged reluctance. The cool liquid hitting his throat was a welcome relief.

Until it mixed with the eggnog, and—

Percy threw up in the dusting of snow between them. Chunks of bread made their way back up his throat, and he groaned between bouts of vomiting and choking on that damn roll. "Oh yes, eating was a superb idea. Thank you so much, Callaghan. I love to be tortured. Remind me to return the favor."

"If I indulged in that much fun, I'd deserve it."

Percy used the rest of the water to wash his mouth out and rinse the vomit away. He kicked some snow over the defiled patch of grass for good measure.

"Let's get you back to Abby's." Cal pushed off the swing and folded his arms as he waited for Percy to follow. Percy made a careful show of walking back without any more need of assistance.

Unfortunately, Percy couldn't keep from rubbing his stomach when he reentered the living room, catching his aunt's attention. She set down a steaming roast chicken and vegetables in the middle of the table and sauntered to the couch where Percy steadied himself.

Cal stood behind him like he had the entire way home, ready to catch Percy if he toppled.

"Are you okay?" she cooed, drawing him in and smoothing his hair.

Percy tensed, waiting for her to smell the eggnog and pull out her no-bullshit scolding. Which at this point, he deserved.

"He had some of your eggnog," Cal said. Percy narrowed his eyes as Aunt Abby's clutch tightened. Cal's gaze flickered briefly to his. He shrugged. "My stomach is gurgling too."

"Don't drink the eggnog!" Aunt Abby shrieked, letting go of Percy and leaping to save Crystal from taking a sip. "One of the eggs is bad."

Percy rocked unsteadily, and Cal set one hand on his shoulder. Under his breath, he tutted. "You liar."

Cal whispered in his ear. "I'm not lying. The stench of your sick is messing with my stomach." . . .

Percy scowled his way through drafting up a flyer offering massage sessions.

Before he knew it, it was time to pick up the Glovers from work.

He picked up Ellie first, waiting in the parking lot with his door cracked open to let air funnel through the sweaty heat of his Jeep.

She trudged out next to a tall, lanky Asian kid who skimmed his hands over a quarter inch of blue-and-black hair.

The breeze pushed their conversation right into his car. He wasn't opening his door wider or inching his ear nearer at all.

". . . random acts of kindness. Sounds fun."

Ellie shrugged and tapped the bulky side bag at her hip. "It is. Thanks for helping me bottle the lemonade."

"Gnomber9 for the win!" She blushed as she high-fived him back.

That's when Ellie saw Percy's Jeep. His Jeep, not his sudden shrinking back in the driver's seat.

"Gotta go, Matt."

They said nothing of the cute boy as they drove to pick up Cal, and Percy knew better than to mention it. He dropped them off, and slunk back to Abby's. He wasn't eager for another haunting night's sleep, but he was curious enough to follow through on his promise and join the Sherlock Gnomes game.

He signed into the forum under the moniker "Gnomad." A fitting choice, considering his current state.

The game officially started in two hours, when the names of the gnomes were released.

Anonymously, he ticked the box on the questionnaire that consented to gnomes entering private property during daylight hours. He'd done this with Secret Santa before. The cul-de-sac was a trustworthy bunch.

His phone buzzed in his pocket.

He pulled it out and Josh's name flashed on the screen. Hauling in a breath, he answered with a breezy, "Tell me this was a butt dial."

"Hello to you too, Percy. How're the Twin Cities?"

"Get to the point, Josh."

"You left some of your things here. Your favorite blue leather jacket."

He'd been searching for that. "Send it to me."

"Where are you living?"

"My aunt's, for now."

A long, uncomfortable silence followed. Josh cleared his throat. "I'll be up that way for Fourth of July. Maybe I could return it to you in person?"

"Mail would be faster."

Josh grunted in frustration. "I'm sorry I hurt you. I didn't want to waste our time dancing around what we both knew was a dead-end relationship."

Percy knocked his head against the wall and glared at the antique ceiling moldings. Dead-end relationship. The story of his life.

"Percy?"

"Josh?"

"It's been six months. We could've been friends if you'd stayed here."

He'd joked with Cal about the friends line hurting, but wow, it stung. As for living in Baxwell, he'd wanted to leave the moment they'd broken up, but he had to complete his work contract first. The minute he had though, he'd driven up to cousin Frank's and stayed there a couple of nights before braving it across the city to Abby's place.

"Just send the jacket," he croaked and hung up.

He tossed his phone to the side and angrily reread the thread **My boyfriend left me for someone else.** There was a new comment from Don'tDeludeYourself:

> **That's a blow to your self-worth. My suggestion: Don't rush to trust anyone in the future. Be careful with anyone who is "curious" or solely wants to "experiment." If the same thing happens, you'll feel like you can't trust anyone and you don't deserve commitment.**

When the clock struck eight, and Sherlock Gnomes officially began, Percy checked the forum.

Percy jotted down the gnome names of the ten neighbors taking part. By elimination and careful observation, he would easily match the monikers to their identities. One he knew off the bat. Others might stump him for a week or so.

He'd figure it out though. He always did.

Gnomad = Percy Freedman

Gnomber9 = Ellie Glover (Thank you, Matt.)
Mrs. Gnomer =
Gnome de Plume = Champey Ong (She is a writer, would fit)
Gnominated =
Gnomega =
Gnome More Wood =
Gnome Chomsky = Cal?
Real versus Gnominal Value =
I Don't Gnome =

He was sure Cal was Gnome Chomsky. He'd seen Noam Chomsky books in the Glovers' bookshelves firsthand. Besides, Cal was the analytical, philosophical type.

Gnomber9 was online. Percy imagined lonely Ellie bowed over her computer, hoping for a distraction.

Percy gladly gave it to her, inviting her into a private chat.

Gnomber9: Hello, Percy.

Right. Seemed he hadn't chosen the subtlest name. Now that he looked at it, the name totally gave him away.

Gnomber9: Nomad totally gives you away.

Good to know his sharp mind was on par with a fourteen-year-old's.

Gnomad: Heh. Yours is no better, Gnomber9. Or should I say Ellie?

Gnomber9: You think you gnome everything.

Gnomad: Cal might tell you otherwise, but I do. I really do.

Gnomber9: Until proven otherwise.

Gnomad: Let me ease you of any doubt. Think of a number. Keep it to yourself.

Gnomber9: Okay.

Gnomad: Add the square root of sixteen.

Gnomber9: Go on.

Gnomad: Minus two. Plus eighteen. Subtract the number you thought of. Subtract another fifteen, and add two.

Gnomber9: ?

Gnomad: Seven. See? I do gnome everything.

Gnomber9: Mrs. Wallace told me I'd be humored today.

Gnomad: Glad to be of service, El. Now spill. How many times a day do you fantasize clubbing your brother in the ears?

Gnomber9: Drive you crazy, does he?

Gnomad: Something like that. Goes both ways though.

Gnomber9: I'm sure it does.

His phone rang.

Percy checked the screen. Unknown.

He never answered unknown numbers, but Percy had a gut feeling he knew who would be on the other end. In fact, he was so sure, he answered with a smirk. "Callaghan?"

Cal's clear voice swept down the line. "Heh. Yes."

"Before you ask: Sure, I'll drop you and El off to work tomorrow." The mechanic had said he would need a couple of days.

A moment's pause. "It'll only be me."

"I consider myself warned."

∽

CAL ROCKED UP TO HIS JEEP WEARING FORM-FITTING JEANS, polished leather shoes, a matching brown satchel, and a dark jacket that covered a beige T-shirt.

"You got a meeting or something?" Percy asked, slipping his sunglasses on.

Cal opened the passenger door and looked at him over the roof. "No."

Sunlight did striking things to Cal's hair. Made it look positively copper. Not as red as his cheeks though.

A cheerful cry startled Percy, and he ripped his gaze away from Cal. Crystal was waving at them from her open kitchen window.

"Good morning," she called.

After another restless night, he could hardly call it good, but . . . "Morning."

She leaned farther out, her robe gaping a little too much down the front. "Are you out for the day?"

"Couple of hours. Taking Callaghan to work, then nipping past The Home Depot." He needed to paint the living room and bathroom, put in a new vanity, replace the door handles of the kitchen cupboards, change the faucets and showerhead, and install a new toilet seat.

"You at The Home Depot?" Cal murmured. "Sure you'll even know what to buy?"

Percy gestured him into the car. "High time I get you to work."

As he slipped into the driver's seat, Crystal called out after them, "Good to see water and earth spending time together!"

Over his sunglasses that had slipped down his nose, Percy regarded Cal. "See, this is why we'll always be nemeses."

Cal hitched his brow, and Percy turned the ignition and peeled out from the curb.

"Together we're mud."

~

When Percy returned from The Home Depot, he sensed something was different the moment he walked inside. A lingering perfume scented the air.

One step into the living room, he saw it. A TV screen sat on a wooden cabinet, and bright cushions studded the couch.

Percy fingered the silky, leaf-patterned cushions. A square card tied to the zipper bumped his fingers:

Your skill at reading between the lines will have you uncovering many truths this summer, my identity among them.
  ~Mrs. Gnomer

Between the lines. The actual lines. Hundred percent, this was Crystal. Percy heard her breathlessness as he read it. After a dramatic length of time staring, he grabbed his phone.

Theo picked up on the third ring. "Percy! Mom said you'd

call. Something about letting us share the weight of your burdens?"

Percy snorted, rubbing his fingers over Crystal's neat stitches. "How about we get to that never. Though I do need something..."

~

PERCY STARED AT THE SPARKLY NEW SHOWERHEAD HE CHOKED in his hand and then at his shower stall. The Glovers' toolbox had been dissected within an inch of its life, yet he was nowhere near ready to put the unit together.

None of the instructions online made sense.

Cal's midday message didn't help.

Callaghan: Have fun at The Home Depot?

Perseus: I always enjoy emptying my bank account. Fun times.

Installing his purchases? Even funner times.

If he didn't want to sell so badly, he'd have given up in favor of a temper tantrum.

After yelling and shoving the showerhead, toilet, and faucets into place, it was time to pick Cal up from work. A call from Frank did nothing to perk up his day.

"You're selling her house?" he yelled so loud that Percy held the phone a foot from his ear.

Cal strapped himself into the passenger seat, watching him keenly.

"Did you see the ad on Craigslist?"

"Jesus, Percy, you haven't even been back a week."

"The faster, the easier . . ." He swallowed, staring at the

parked car in front of his. Cal shifted in his seat, and Percy didn't have the balls to look at him.

Frank cursed. "Knew you were only about cashing in."

The phone almost cracked in his grip, but he kept his tone light. "You should doctor in extrasensory perception since you can read me so well."

"Was that your plan all along? Schmooze up to her, wait till she conked, and live up the good life?"

"Yes, because most of that money isn't going straight to the bank."

"I hope she's looking down on you and wishing she'd cast you out as well."

Frank disconnected a second before Percy.

"Well, this has been the best day ever," he said, pulling out onto the street, fighting the sting behind his eyes.

He tapped his fingers against the steering wheel as he drove in peak-hour traffic. "Thank you, ultra-slow drivers. Please. Take your time. Oh yes, spread out over all the fast lanes. Always wanted to join a motorcade."

Cal rummaged through the satchel resting between his feet. He pulled out a roll of Mentos and set them in the console between them.

Percy glanced at it and then at Cal, who turned his concerned gaze outside the window.

He swallowed a sudden lump in his throat. Kept his tone borderline accusatory. "Why the Mentos?"

Cal droned, "Because I ate your last one. Certainly not because you've had a rough day and I want to make you feel better."

Percy rubbed at a flutter in his chest. "In that case, pick me out a strawberry. Because I want to make it difficult for you. Certainly not because they're my favorite."

They exchanged scowls that didn't, not even slightly, turn into soft smiles.

A COUPLE OF HOURS LATER, BACK AT ABBY'S, HE WAS STARING out the bay window. He rubbed his fogged breath off the pane, glass squealing under the heel of his hand.

Across the road, Ellie moved to the Glovers' identical window and bent her head over a laptop.

There was an idea.

Percy snuck off to his bedroom, logged into the Sherlock Gnomes forum, and opened a chat with Gnomber9.

Gnomad: Carving some time for Gnomber9!

Gnomber9: Are you high?

Gnomad: On life.

Gnomber9: What brought about this chipper mood?

To be honest, he wasn't sure. It'd snuck up on him. Maybe it was seeing the TV and cushions in the living room again.

Gnomad: One of our neighbors. Wait till you're gnomed; it makes the belly flutter.

Gnomber9: Does your belly flutter a lot, Percy?

Gnomad: Hasn't for a while. This is a refreshing change. Can you hula-hoop?

Gnomber9: ?

Gnomad: I'm doing my homework.

Gnomber9: On what? Gymnastics?

Gnomad: On you. We don't know each other well. Thought I'd change that.

Gnomber9: With hula-hooping?

Gnomad: I'll take that as a no. What food do you absolutely love but never eat at home?

Gnomber9: Duck?

Gnomad: Delicious. Which one: cats or dogs?

Gnomber9: Cat videos. All the fun without the fur.

Gnomad: Fur's the best part!

Gnomber9: Not if it makes your nose swell and your eyes itch.

Gnomad: Cat videos it is. What's your favorite movie?

Gnomber9: LOTR

Gnomad: Favorite snack?

Gnomber9: Vanilla ice cream.

Gnomad: Of all the flavors in the world, vanilla?

Gnomber9: French vanilla.

Gnomad: Oh wow, that makes it so much more enticing.

Gnomber9: You're a stuff-everything-sweet-in-the-ice-cream guy, aren't you?

Gnomad: With salted caramel on top. Is there something you wish you'd said sorry for but never did?

Gnomber9: That jumped a few levels in intensity.

Gnomad: You know how I like my ice cream. We're BFFs now.

Gnomber9: There was a boy I was unintentionally mean to once.

Gnomad: Were you mean because you liked him?

Gnomber9: I'd just met him. I didn't know I liked him then.

Gnomad: But now you do? I like where this conversation is heading, Ellie, because I can help you with boy trouble.

Gnomber9: It's my turn for a question. Would you like to come over for dinner?

Dinner at the Glovers'. He couldn't deny a home-cooked meal sounded fantastic, and it'd be great trying to get Ellie to smile in real life.

Also, Cal squirming at him being there sent a rather maniacal tingle through him. They would wind each other up like jacks-in-the-box, and Percy bet his ass that Cal would pop first.

"A certain gnome invited me for dinner," Percy said thirty minutes later as the Glovers' door swung in. He'd expected Cal to answer. Expected to see arched brows and a probing blue gaze.

Instead, Marg beckoned him inside and toward the amazing smell of meatballs.

"Thanks for letting me join you."

"You're always welcome, Percy. Why not make it a thing? We cook every night anyway, and making dinner for one is a hassle."

He couldn't. The Glovers had enough on their plate, and they didn't need him bogging them down. He meant to turn her down gently. Instead, his mouth said, "Really?"

"Better than eating alone. You could take turns cooking with Cal."

Appealing. "Did Cal cook tonight? I'm having second thoughts about dinner, Marg."

She laughed as they slipped into the great room.

The girls sat at the oval mahogany table. Hannah pouted at the pickled cucumber on her plate, a streak of pink paint decorating her cheek. Ellie pinched her sister's nose and pretended to hide it, drawing out a giggle.

Ellie looked up as Percy drew out a chair next to her. She squeaked out a "hey" and turned back to her little sister. Not before he noticed her #9 soccer shirt, though. Was that her cheeky way of acknowledging their chats?

Cal carried a water jug from the kitchen and methodically filled everyone's glass. When he reached his, Percy looked up, their gazes hooking. His skin pebbled at the way Cal searched him.

A line of pink paint had dried down his neck. It spoke of an afternoon hanging out with Hannah painting sunny pictures.

Percy stroked his neck pointedly. "Looked in a mirror lately?"

"Yes," Cal said, pouring water into his glass. "I like mirrors. They have a wonderful way of not talking back."

"I wouldn't worry about them talking. Laughing, however . . ."

Cal rested a hand on Percy's chair and leaned in, his whisper tickling Percy's cheekbone. "I'd give you a piece of my mind, but I'm afraid you'd take the last piece."

Cal moved to straighten, but Percy balled his T-shirt, keeping him at eye level.

Unsure what to say, he picked up his glass with his free hand, drained the water, and said, "Refill?"

Water filled his glass, and Percy let Cal go.

Marg dished out cheesy mashed potatoes and meatballs. The gravy was amazing, and so was the hodge-podge dinner conversation. They covered kindergarten politics, cul-de-sac gossip, and the best neighborhood takeout.

"How do you like eating duck?" Percy asked Ellie. "Roasted? Fried? Boiled with a side of mouthwatering French vanilla ice cream?"

Cal made an unhealthy noise across the table and coughed, banging a fist over his chest. His eyes glittered, and when he cleared his throat, he laughed.

"Did you just choke, Callaghan?"

He sipped his water. "No, I fancy gurgling air like that."

"And pretending to cry?"

"What can I say? I'm great at multitasking."

Dinner done, Percy and Ellie cleared the table, and Cal clomped Hannah to the bathroom like a Brachiosaurus. When they returned, Marg stood up from the dining table, cradling her lower hips.

Percy slipped to her side and ran a careful hand over the small of her back. "Is this where you have pain?" She nodded. "I can help you with that."

"Really?" She sounded so hopeful.

"It'll be best if you lie on your side. Do you have a yoga mat? Otherwise, I'll grab my table."

She shook her head. "There's an old gym mat under Cal's bed."

For all the times Percy had been inside the Glovers' house, he had never set foot in Cal's room. He was surprised to follow Cal to the basement.

"You live underground. Figures."

Cal opened his door, a dimple twitching at his mouth. A shock of turquoise had Percy looking past Cal into his room.

Cal's double bed had matching striped bedsheets, clean but with adequate wrinkles to prove he wasn't freakish enough to iron them. Percy wanted to dive onto the hill of pillows towered at the headboard.

Instead, he wandered around the room, taking in the giant world map and two diagrams of a Dilophosaurus and Troodon. Dinosaurs weren't restricted to the walls, either. Miniature model skeletons sat on bookshelves, surprisingly dust-free. Behind them, the shelves overflowed with paleontology books, geology textbooks, and dictionaries galore.

Warmth simmered at his back when Cal moved closer. He glanced over his shoulder. "I bet you impress the girls easily."

"How?"

Percy tapped a finger on the shelves of smart. "A well-placed colon in a text message should do the trick."

The edges of Cal's eyes crinkled. "Maybe a well-placed semicolon. Had enough scoping my room yet?"

Percy laughed, then shook his head and proceeded to check Cal's closet.

His clothes were ironed, either hanging or folded. T-shirts and sweaters all shades of natural grays, browns, and dinosaur print. "A splash of color wouldn't hurt. You could break hearts in a little blue." He turned to the next door, which opened to a bathroom with shower. Percy walked into the navy-tiled room, blinking back his surprise. "That's handy."

He stared at the shower, unable to shake the sudden image of Cal standing inside, water cascading over his nakedness. A follow-up image included soapsuds and Cal jerking himself off. "Now I've definitely seen enough."

Cal leaned against the doorframe, watching him with that mocking brow. It did nothing to stop the unwanted tightening in Percy's jeans.

Time to get that gym mat and focus on all things Marg. Pronto.

∽

THE IMAGE OF CAL IN HIS SHOWER STUCK IN HIS HEAD LIKE A nasty thorn, following him to his place an hour later. It took a concentrated effort and a ton of porn to knock it out from behind his retinas.

It didn't help when, almost coming a second time, he realized he was sliding the soles of his feet over the sheets Cal had given him.

It knocked the generic porn-dude out of his head, and he imagined Cal's form through fogged glass. . . .

Cal stroked himself, his thick cock sliding through a slickened hand. He choked on a groan, his head rolling back. His eyes widened when he glimpsed Percy on the other side of the door watching, but his hand didn't stop. He stroked faster. His voice was mellow and dripped of sarcasm and curiosity. "Perseus."

"Callaghan." Percy entered the shower, straining and naked. He walked through the mist spraying off Cal's coiled muscles and pushed him against the wall. "You're not meant to star in my fantasies."

Cal set those measuring eyes on his, lips parting, the slick sound of his working hand growing louder. On every upward stroke, his hand grazed

Percy's stomach. "*Sex in the shower is one of your fantasies? How highly imaginative of you.*"

"*Since your favorite weapon is your mouth, I think that's what you should use.*"

"*To what?*"

"*Ruin me for any other man.*"

Cal dropped to his knees, looking up smugly. "Like my mouth doesn't do that already." . . .

Percy's toes curled and pinched the sheets as his cock unloaded hot and heavy, the orgasm wringing out every damn inch of his body.

Well. Wasn't this peachy?

S corpio
　　noun / scor . pio

DEFINITION OF **SCORPIO**
　: intuitive, self-confident, reads between the lines, passionate, wary of the idea that true love exists, hates vulnerability, sexy, immensely curious, highly imaginative
　: Percy Freedman

EXAMPLE OF **SCORPIO** IN A SENTENCE
　"What are you, psychic?"
　"Or psycho, but how about we settle on Scorpio?"

Chapter Five

In the morning, Percy dragged his ass out of bed to drive the Glovers to work. After dropping off Ellie, he continued to the community center.

Cal slouched in the passenger seat, his pressed dress shorts and T-rex T-shirt "*Good luck reaching* the stars" the only orderly things about him. His rumpled hair suggested he'd slept through his alarm, and the constant palming of his eyes hinted he'd tossed in bed all night.

The guy was a sleepy wreck.

Unfortunately, it suited him.

A yawn stretched Cal's torso, and he pushed out his chest. Percy caught the way he absently rubbed his pec.

Percy tightened his grip on the steering wheel and trained his eyes on the road, the dashboard, the tear in the upholstery of the passenger seat. "How's the hatchback?"

That didn't come out squeaky at all.

Cal shifted like he was finally waking up. "Might need till next Wednesday at the shop."

"Should be a fun week then."

Cal didn't miss a beat. "We should take some pics and make an album called Perseus and Callaghan Become Friends."

"Admit something to me—"

"I log into Hannah's Netflix account to stop the nightmares after watching scary movies."

Percy snorted and shook his head. "Good to know Dora the Explorer can take down Chucky."

"She can chokeslam like no one's business." Cal's amusement morphed to curiosity. "What did you want me to admit?"

"That you're Gnome Chomsky."

"Is that what you think?"

Percy glanced over at him, searching Cal's face for a clue. Cal had a light curl at his lips, and his brow may or may not have been slightly raised. Stupid kink. "You have a good poker face. But yes, that's what I think."

"Why's that?"

"For a start, you're fascinated with grammar like he is."

That little smile grew. "How else would I judge a potential date?"

"Right." Percy flicked on the blinker, focusing extra hard on the simple right turn. "You are incredibly smart, you stand up for what you believe in, and you are a positive influence."

"Well, I'm no Noam Chomsky."

"You might not have wide-reaching influence, but you are important to people close to you."

Though Percy tried to keep his eyes rooted on the traffic, they flickered to Cal, who was still smiling but not with cocky intensity. This smile was soft, small, and fleeting. The kind of smile that bedroom ceilings were privy to after a surprisingly good day.

When Cal glanced over, Percy refocused on the road, a small shiver curling in his stomach. "I mean like your sisters. Your mom. The neighbors."

"Do go on."

"I think I'm done. And I think I'm right."

From the corner of his eye, Percy caught Cal scrutinizing him, and the shiver intensified. Good thing they'd reached the community center. "Here we are then."

He couldn't have dropped Cal off at the curb fast enough. He was about to step on the gas again when he caught sight of a petite woman with cascading brown hair and an exaggerated smile skipping to Cal's side. Adorable came to mind.

Cal returned her smile, not once looking back at Percy as they sank into conversation and headed up the ramp to work.

Percy slammed on the radio, upping the volume until he couldn't hear himself think. He banged his palms to tunes the whole way home. When he got inside, he kicked toward his laptop that he'd left on the dining table. He would check out a few more house listings. He really, really needed to get out of this dead-end.

Two steps from the table, surprise swallowed his urgency.

Gnome magic winked at him.

Someone had brought over a waxed maple bookcase, and nicely restacked the shelves.

A sign rested on a bookend.

You can lose yourself in a sea of words.
    You can find yourself in it too.

Take care,
    Gnominated & Gnomega

Percy hunched against the bay window and stared at the shelves as he fought against the tightening in his chest.

He needed a moment out of the house.

One step onto the sidewalk, someone cheerfully called his name.

Paul Bunyan look-alike Mr. Feist strolled down the pedestrian shortcut that led to the playground. "You got a minute?" He jerked his thumb toward his Cape Cod house. "I could use a hand moving a chest of drawers."

Percy pasted on a smile. "Must be a hefty set of drawers if *you* need help."

"It'll help work those upper arms of yours. Don't ever say I don't look out for my fellow neighbors."

Percy helped Mr. Feist wrestle red-painted drawers past their ginger cat pawing at their porch hammock and down the front path. Drooping agapanthus hit the backs of his knees, making him grin. "Sad bunch of flowers you've got here. Your garden almost compares to Abby's."

"If your aunt were here, her green fingers would be all over the place. My yard too."

They trudged the drawers through the pedestrian walkway into the cul-de-sac.

"Going to the yard sale Saturday?" Mr. Feist asked as they puzzled the drawers alongside dozens of furniture pieces stored in a garage. "Might find some great bargains for your place."

My place. That made his toes curl and his breath catch.

He smacked on a smile. "Yeah, maybe. Josie says nicely placed furniture could help it sell."

"Sell? So, the rumor is true." Mr. Feist rubbed his beard. "For whatever it's worth, I hope you change your mind. My wife knows some great books for dealing with loss."

Percy kept his voice light, even managed a wink. "I'm not lost or grieving, Mr. Feist? Or should I say Gnominated? Gnomega?"

He tossed up his head and laughed. "The wife's Gnomega. There's no getting anything past you. Or possibly through to you, but that remains to be seen. If you need anything at all, just ask."

Tipping his head goodbye, Percy left Mr. Feist to it.

He mooched toward the shortcut, kicking at a stray piece of gravel. It skittered close to the gutter. He kicked it again, hurtling it a good six feet before it pinged against a hubcap.

Percy halted. At the edge of the playground, half-curtained

by a weeping willow at the side of the road, sat Cal's silver hatchback.

The hatchback that was supposed to be stuck at the mechanic.

A warm tendril of surprise unfurled in his chest as he neared the car. What was Cal up to?

Despite a healthy dose of wariness, laughter caught in his chest. Percy ran his fingertips over the sticky roof. "Interesting."

He hoofed it back to the house, this time with light feet and a smile twitching at his lips.

Oh, Callaghan, this is not good. What are we going to do about this?

∽

PERCY SAID NOTHING ABOUT THE HATCHBACK THAT afternoon or over their chicken kebab dinner. Call it a sixth sense, but something urged him to let the lie play out. It wasn't a lie of malicious intent; something else lay behind it. Something that made Percy want to laugh and simultaneously throw up, because no. Wouldn't happen. Nemeses forever.

For a moment, he was tempted to fish for information from Ellie via chat, but he held out.

Gnomber9: How many questions do you have?

Gnomad: Hundreds.

Gnomber9: Why am I the only one answering them?

Gnomad: Because I'm the inquisitor.

Gnomber9: You like to shroud yourself in mystery, don't you, Percy?

Gnomad: I do. Now tell me, what are you afraid of?

Gnomber9: These questions.

Gnomad: *snort* You're funny. Why aren't we like this in person?

Gnomber9: Friends, you mean?

Gnomad: Yeah.

Gnomber9: I wish we were.

Percy chatted with Ellie another hour, and then read online until sleep snatched him into its neighbor-filled depths. Crystal was telling him about his love horoscope, but Percy could not hear her. Then Mr. Serna was there, pushing a heavily pregnant Josie in a wheelbarrow, and then he was standing at the Glovers' door. Marg answered, rubbing her belly, and beckoned him inside.

Suddenly turquoise walls, neat bookshelves, and model dinosaurs surrounded him. The back of his neck prickled, and he whisked around, knowing he'd see Cal—

He woke with a start and checked the time. Five in the morning.

Percy showered, shoved on his clothes, and headed across the road. The Glovers were usually up at six, so it was quiet when Percy took the key hidden under the fern and snuck inside.

Downstairs, dawn leaked into the hall through the basement windows. Percy knocked against the open door, admiring Cal's long, protesting groan. "Just a minute, Ellie," he mumbled, twisting on his other side.

Percy jingled his keys and sidled around Cal's bed.

Cal looked like he'd won a wrestling match with the bed. His hands knotted the sheets, and his thighs squeezed the life out of a pillow. Cal's limbs were long and slender, and his pajamas looked good—tossed on a pile beside the bed.

Corded muscle lazily shifted as Cal snuggled into his pillow.

Percy resisted an impulse to smooth Cal's eyebrow. Even in sleep, it seemed to know too much. He mustered as much aridity as possible. "Morning, handsome."

Cal peered over the flicked-up corner of his pillow. He frowned, shut his eyes, and reopened them again.

"It's not a dream. I'm here."

A grumbling laugh. "What have I done to deserve this?"

"You woke me. Thought I'd return the favor."

Cal stretched with a deep moan, smacked his lips, and yawned. "I woke you?"

"You appeared in my dreams and startled me awake. I was too afraid to go back to sleep."

"Dreaming about me, Perseus?"

That sounded oddly smug. Percy leaned against Cal's bathroom door and folded his arms. "Look, I was thinking . . ."

Cal stuffed a second pillow under his head. "You? Thinking? Do tell."

Percy scratched his chin with his middle finger. Cal's bright grin crinkled the sides of his eyes.

"You need a ride to work?" Percy studied Cal closely, absorbing the slight twitch near his nose and the way his eyes slid away from his for a moment.

The lie was obvious.

"Ah, yes."

Percy wasn't sure if he wanted to call Cal out, laugh, or to tell him to stop.

"Didn't we arrange that last night?" Cal asked.

Oh. Yeah. "Just checking. I was . . . tired. Moving on. I want to do something nice for Ellie. Something to make her smile. What do you suggest?"

Cal looked over at the clock perched on his side table and back at Percy. "I like that you think I'll be full of great ideas at twenty past five in the morning."

"You're Cal. You're always full of ideas."

Cal rubbed his eyes. "Jeez, for a moment there I thought you were nice. What about we—I mean you two—drive to the park and kick around a ball?"

With a laugh, Percy sat on the firm bed at Cal's feet. He pinched Cal's foot, making him twitch, then slid his fingers to the arch. He rubbed small circles against a knot—a habit he acquired from his job. Before his fingers got a mind of their own, he withdrew his hands away and combed his hair.

"If I must suffer through an hour chasing after a ball, you're suffering with me."

∼

THREE TIMES PERCY TRIPPED OVER THE DAMN BALL AND FACE-planted into freshly mowed grass. Each time, both Glovers giggled louder, harder.

He would have been insulted if he weren't so keen to see Ellie's face lift in a smile. Actually, he was still insulted.

"Stupid game."

The taste of grass in his mouth, Percy picked up the offending ball and tucked it under his arm.

"And here I thought you'd be good with balls," Cal murmured as he jogged past Percy to collect the jackets they'd used as markers.

Cal's unexpected comment wiped the scowl off his face.

He grinned as Ellie chased Cal over their makeshift soccer pitch, toward the parked Jeep, kicking shredded grass at him. Cal had to turn back around to lunge for the jacket he'd dropped but Ellie got there first.

She held it up as though it were ransom. Cal mimicked her

with her jacket.

"Let's swap," he said, and his smile dropped as he looked her in the eye. "Please?"

"Too late," she said evenly. "I'm keeping yours, and you're keeping mine."

Cal growled, tackled her by the waist, and hefted her over his shoulder.

"Lemme down, lemme down." She drummed fists over his back, jacket slapping his ass in time to her laughs.

Evening sunshine showered over them and Percy gulped in a lungful of summer, surprised at how warm it felt.

Despite his two left feet, this was bearable. Maybe a little more than bearable.

Cal missed the gutter and dropped awkwardly. When he yelped, Ellie slid off him, her laughter fading to a giggle. Cal was chuckling too, but his brow was pinched, and he rubbed his lower back.

Percy watched the way Cal touched his right glute as they packed themselves into the Jeep.

Percy's phone rang, vibrating along the dashboard where he'd left it. Cal picked it up and offered it to him. "Your cousin, Frank."

Oh, fun. "Let it go to voicemail."

Cal pushed the phone toward him. "What if he wants to apologize? Make amends?"

"Doubt it."

"Perseus . . ."

"No point investing energy into a relationship with a guy who's going to leave when things get hard."

"That's a pessimistic way of seeing the world. Give him a chance? He might surprise you."

Percy glanced at the persistently buzzing phone, then stubbornly refocused on the road.

"Could we stop for ice cream on the way home?" Ellie piped

up from the back. "It's so hot."

Percy threw himself into Ellie's request, ignoring Cal's questioning gaze. "I know a place that does a decent vanilla. Not French, mind you."

He had Cal and Ellie wait in the air-conditioned Jeep while he ran into a small ice cream parlor and bought them all a cone of vanilla.

Percy handed them out and got on the road again. He was trying to give vanilla a chance. But really? Vanilla? "Yum?" he offered.

Cal licked slow swirls around the ice cream, a soft smile dancing in his gaze. "Yum," he agreed. He glanced over his shoulder at Ellie. "What do you think?"

"Mmm, nice and cold."

"I almost forgot," Cal said as he cleaned off a smudge of ice cream from his T-rex T-shirt. "Dorothy saw me putting up your flyers on the noticeboards. She lives on the floor above the center, and she told me to put the two of you in contact. She's free Friday afternoons starting next week."

"Really?"

"Yep. She runs a book club and said if you're any good, she'll pimp your services out."

"Always wanted to be pimped out."

"Good, because I'm working on it. I strung up more flyers at the local library and on Target's community noticeboards. You'll get all the work you need to keep you busy."

"Stop being so helpful," Percy said. "I'll start liking you."

"That would be a disaster."

That really would be.

Cal's lips twisted on a smile that lingered all the way home. It even reappeared when Marg asked why they were all too full to eat much of her famous beef stew.

After dinner, Ellie slunk to the couch to watch TV, while Cal and Percy did the dishes.

Cal crudely massaged his lower back as he waited for the last wet pots. Percy stole the dishtowel from Cal and wiped the suds off his hands. He breathed out heavily. "Face the window over the sink, Callaghan."

Cal blinked, confused. "Ah, what?"

Percy clasped Cal's forearm and steered him around. He pushed Cal's front up against the sink and skated his hand over the light hairs on Cal's arm, over his elbow to his lower back. Percy slid his fingers under Cal's T-shirt and massaged the smooth, cool skin, making the guy gasp.

"It hurts here, doesn't it?"

Their gazes snagged in the window reflection. The ball in Cal's throat dipped, and he looked down at the soapy dishwater.

Percy firmly worked the tops of both glutes, feeling for tightness. Cal's breath caught.

"As much as I liked the display of strength, El's too big to be throwing over your shoulder."

"I used to do it all the time. Kid grew up too fast."

Percy glided his fingers from the middle of Cal's back to his sides, eliciting another soft sound of relief. The stupid T-shirt kept slipping down, hindering proper technique. "To do this right, I need you lying down, pants off."

Cal stiffened under his touch and turned around. Percy let his fingers fall away from Cal's taut muscles.

Cal didn't quite look him in the eye. "Your fingers are . . . that felt . . . Dorothy will definitely pimp you out."

Percy suppressed the laughter singing in his veins. "If it flares up again, tell me. I'll get out my massage table and work you more thoroughly."

A slight flush crept up Cal's neck. Hard to believe this guy had cracked a joke about him being good with balls.

Hannah ran into the kitchen and threw her arms around Cal's legs. "Give me a ride to bed!"

Cal went to drop on his knees, and Percy stopped him,

squeezing his elbow. "Give your back a break."

Percy beamed at Hannah. "Your brother hurt himself. Can I help you to bed?"

"But I want a dinosaur."

"Of course!" He sank to all fours and roared, because dinosaurs sounded like lions apparently. "I'm a vegetarian dino."

Hannah didn't look impressed. One of her pigtails hit her nose as she tilted her head. "What dino?"

Uh . . . "The one with the three horns."

Cal snickered. "Triceratops."

"You don't look like 'ceratops."

Percy scoffed. "And Cal pulled off a Stegosaurus? I mean, I know he's prickly but—"

A nudge met the back of his thigh. Cal let out a soft, humored growl.

"How about we do this, Hannah?" Cal crouched in front of him and dolloped soapsuds on either side of Percy's forehead. Cal's eyes sparkled with amusement, and Hannah cheered him on.

Cal smeared the last of the wet suds on Percy's nose, shaping them into a pointed tip.

Percy nipped at Cal's hand, and Cal wagged a finger. "I don't taste any good to Triceratops."

"To this one, you do." It was out before Percy considered the words. For a moment, they stared at each other. An impractical zap of electricity shot between them.

Hannah poked Cal's shoulder, turning his attention to her. "This dino bites. He needs a leash."

Well, wasn't this getting a little twisted.

Percy could handle that.

Cal, however, turned a shade of red Percy had never seen.

"Hop on, Hannah." Percy steadied her as she climbed onto his back. "Your brother will tell us everything we didn't need to know about Triceratops as we trot to bed."

Cal let out a relieved breath and dove into all things dinosaur.

~

Gnomad: I had fun with you today!

Gnomber9: Watching you play sucker made my week.

Gnomad: !

Gnomber9: No, really. You have no idea how much I enjoyed myself.

Gnomad: Prepare for more Percy-filled afternoons! (Maybe no sucker next time?)

Gnomber9: (Might be hard if you're there.)

Gnomad: Jeez, El, you sound as smart as Cal. Speaking of, do me a favor and make sure he doesn't lift Hannah for a week?

Gnomber9: No lifting Hannah. Got it.

Gnomad: Back to question 999, and it's a deep one. Is there anything you regret not doing?

Gnomber9: Plenty.

Gnomad: Something specific come to mind?

Ellie typed for a while, piquing Percy's interest. He pulled out his Mentos and sucked on a candy as he waited. When the message showed up, a tender bloom of pain filled his chest. He drew the laptop nearer.

Gnomber9: At Aunt Abby's funeral, you looked heartbroken. Your lips were shaking so badly, you could barely hold your speech cards. I wanted to run to the podium and hold you. The whole day, I wanted to hold you and tell you how sorry I was for your loss.

Percy blinked back the heat in his eyes. Her funeral was as fresh in his mind and heart as if it had happened yesterday:

The small church with exposed beams and sunlight glowing through stained-glass arches. Ethereal. Like his aunt's spirit sat in the room with them. Rows of pews crammed with people who loved Aunt Abby. Friends, colleagues, and the entire cul-de-sac. His parents, on rocky terms with Abby, did not speak. They didn't even sit on the front pew reserved for them. Frank had looked like he wanted to sit there, but had hunched in one of the back rows instead.

It had made his heart sore, being the only one in that first row.

He looked back at the second row, where the Wallaces and the Glovers had packed themselves together. His gaze skipped over Mr. Glover and Marg hugging Hannah, lingered for a moment on Ellie sniffing into her sleeve, and then snagged on Cal, who was looking at him. Face pensive, blue eyes shinier than usual. Maybe it was the light, but for once his brow didn't seem to mock him.

Percy glanced at the empty pew and back. Cal must have read the hurt in his expression because he whispered to his mom, and when Percy walked to the podium to give his speech, the Glovers filled the front pew.

His voice cracked and shook. Ellie leaned into Cal's side,

holding him tightly. Cal kissed the top of her head, then focused on Percy, expression pained.

Percy used him as an anchor as he fumbled through his speech. Afraid if he focused on anything else, he'd crumble. Looking at Cal reached into the most stubborn part of him. Cal couldn't see him cry. He wouldn't let it happen.

But the sob appeared anyway, and Ellie confirmed how obvious it was when she ambled up to him at the reception, folded her arms, and shifted uncomfortably as she squeaked out her condolences.

Maybe she'd been on the brink of giving him a hug at that moment.

Biting his lip, Percy tapped on the keyboard.

Gnomad: Thank you for thinking of me that day. I needed it.

Gnomber9: If you ever need anything, or if you want to talk about it . . .

Gnomad: Yeah, thanks. I'm fine.

Gnomber9: Percy?

Gnomad: Yeah?

Gnomber9: Next time I see you hurting, I'm going to hold you.

∽

THE WALLACES' WRAPAROUND PORCH WAS PERFECTLY QUIET. Crystal and her husband were perusing furniture at the neighborhood yard sale, hopefully having enough fun to keep them occupied the next twenty minutes. Or however long it took Percy to do his gnoming.

Morning sunshine soaked through Percy's bright yellow T-shirt as he paced the porch, whispering into the phone.

Theo Wallace, Crystal's son, yawned down the line and smacked his lips. "Hmmm, what?"

"Where do I find the spare key to your house?"

"Oh, today's the day," Theo said, then pitched his voice to a whisper. "Check the loose board under the window closest to the fence." A rich male laughed in the near background. "Shhh, Jamie."

"Apologies," this Jamie said. "Wouldn't want anyone on this side of the country to overhear your neighbor burglarizing your home."

Sounds of a scuffle followed a huff. Laughter trickled faintly down the line as though Theo were holding his hand over the speaker. Floorboards groaned underfoot as Percy snuck to the spot Theo described, pried up the loose board, and let himself inside the house.

He breathed in the lingering scent of incense and stole past crystal cabinets to the utility closet in the hall.

Theo's breathing rustled down the line once more. "You in?"

"Yeah," Percy said, "and I see the ladder. Who's Jamie?"

"That," Theo said, sounding rather smug indeed, "would be my boyfriend."

Percy leaned too hard on the closet door and it gave way, bashing against the hallway wall.

"Say what?" Last he knew, Theo had been all about the girls. He'd been heartbroken when his longtime girlfriend had left him. "I thought you were straight?"

"Apparently, I'm bi. I was a bit clueless at first"—another humored laugh rang out in the background—"fine, a little more than that, but looking back, I was definitely crushing on my best friend."

Percy sagged against the door as he absorbed the news. Theo, who'd always come across as straight, crushing on a guy. "That's quite a story."

"You'll meet him Fourth of July. Prepare for an epic game of Zombie Apocalypse."

"If I'm still around, you'll have to tell me how you fell for this Jamie." He shook off the shock and yanked the chain hanging in the closet, filling it with light.

"What are you talking about, if you're still around?"

"Are the boxes in the attic all labeled?"

"Zombie Apocalypse is tradition."

"I'll peek inside. Everything baby or crystal related she wanted down, right? Anything else?"

"Is it because of your aunt?"

"Sorry, need two hands for the ladder. Bye." Percy brusquely shoved his phone into his pocket.

Using the paint-splattered ladder, he crawled into the spider-infested, low-angled attic. Percy used his cellphone flashlight as he balanced on beams to find the boxes.

A draft tickled over his face and made him shiver. No wonder Crystal avoided this place.

Something landed on his neck, and he slapped it off, fingers sticky with old webs. In the farthest corner, of course, he found the boxes marked baby toys, clothes, and crystals.

One by one, he stacked the boxes in the hall.

He took the shoebox of crystals to the kitchen, where he polished them and arranged them in a napkin-laced breadbasket with a note from Gnomad.

He was putting away the ladder when voices sounded on the porch. A grumbling male, the unmistakable melody of Crystal, and the dry cadence of—wait, what was Cal doing here?

Percy ducked into Theo's room as the front door opened. He peered around the doorframe down the hall. Mr. Wallace trudged inside, favoring one foot, followed by Crystal and Cal, who hefted the very dresser Percy had struggled under with Mr. Feist.

Why was Cal lifting it with his bad back? Hadn't Percy made it clear he needed to take it easy?

"Where do you want this?" Cal puffed.

Crystal set down her side of the dresser and hauled in a breath. "Let's rest a moment. We'll move it to Theo's room."

Of course.

Percy swallowed the scowl he was telepathically sending to Cal and focused on his own dilemma. Namely getting out of there. He crept to the window, pressed his palms against the cool pane, and shoved. The window rattled but didn't budge.

He curled his fingers around the metal loops set into the frame and lifted. Still, nothing moved.

Peachy.

He peered into the hall, where Cal was rubbing his lower back and wincing. He silently chastised Cal for being an idiot.

Crystal spoke to Cal at 100 miles per hour. "Today was meant to put a smile on my face, and that's because of you, Cal Glover." She dropped her voice a decibel. "Hubby says I should mind my own business, and I will, but I wanted to tell you to explore the tension."

Tension?

"Tension?" Cal asked.

"The planets suggest you shy away from trying new things. Ease out of your shell this month."

Cal looked skeptical. "Am I really like a Virgo?"

"With your fast mind and smart humor? Absolutely. You're also a perfectionist and expect far too much of yourself. That can make you overly self-conscious of your flaws. Oh, you should be kinder to yourself too. You are very loyal, Virgo. So many good traits for a long-lasting relationship. You get a bad rap when it comes to sex, but it couldn't be further from the truth. You're discreet, but among the most sexual behind closed doors. You just prefer to know your partner first."

Cal pinched the bridge of his nose. "Bit less of the sex talk please."

"That's what I like most about Virgos. You say what's on your mind and mean it. You value frankness and honesty."

Cal paused, then let out a sigh as he moved to his end of the dresser. "I would say you're right, but honesty hasn't been my forte lately." Percy practically humped Theo's doorframe trying to catch their every word.

Crystal ran her hands down the dresser, preparing to pick it up again. "You mean well. I'm sure you'll figure it out."

Cal's lips parted in response and he looked over a bending Crystal. Percy shrank back too slowly and Cal's gaze snagged on him.

Surprise flickered across his face, shadowing to a frown that swiftly morphed into mild amusement. In fact, he might have been sporting a grimace rather than a grin.

Percy heard Cal chiding him in the slight shake of his head.

Ah, crap. The last person he wanted to figure out he was Gnomad. Though, being honest, Cal had probably figured it out already. His little sister had, after all.

Whatever. That didn't mean he wanted to give in completely. If Crystal didn't know, he'd like to keep it that way.

Eyes still locked on Cal, Percy tossed him an exaggerated smile and then mouthed *Help me?*

Cal blinked, and then refocused on the dresser. "Before we drag this into Theo's room, can we grab a drink of water?"

"Thirsty, dear?"

Cal glanced in Percy's direction. "Something like that."

When Crystal pottered into the kitchen waving Cal in after her, Percy hauled ass out of there. He smiled as he heard Crystal's delight at spotting the crystals.

Once back to the anonymity of the sidewalk, Percy breathed

in the warm freedom. At the edge of the oak separating his place with Crystal's, he paused. Two neighbors were suspiciously sneaking out of Aunt Abby's house. Champey Ong and Mr. Roosevelt looked slyly from side to side, and Percy tucked himself behind the knotty trunk so they wouldn't know he knew.

At this rate, he'd sort out all the gnome identities in record time.

Once the writer and history teacher passed unaware, Percy jogged into the house.

A large rug stretched out between the couch and TV, a wooden coffee table resting atop it. A lovely lamp and cabinet perched in the corner of the living room and three more high-backed chairs circled his dining table. His no-longer-rickety dining table.

He picked up three cards. One from Gnome de Plume—Champey Ong for sure—one from Gnomber9—Ellie had helped them?—and one from Gnome Chomsky—Cal.

"Your poor back," he said aloud.

He bit his lip on a soft smile as he searched for the fourth card from Mr. Roosevelt. Unless he'd forgotten to leave one?

He grabbed himself a drink of water and was hit with another punch of hiccups when he found mugs and a matching set of dishes in his previously bare cupboards.

Maybe Mr. Roosevelt had just been helping Champey.

Or maybe not.

The coffee table screamed Callaghan Glover. The mugs too. He had watched him take stock of his cupboards.

He heeled back outside and stopped outside the Wallaces' fence, staring into the kitchen window at Cal chatting with Crystal. He called Cal's phone.

Cal set his water down and checked his phone, turning toward the window as he answered. It took him a second to spot him.

"You shouldn't be lifting things, Callaghan."

"Can't leave a neighbor in need, Perseus."

They stared at each other for a few moments. Crystal's voice chirped in the background.

"Meet you on your porch in five." Percy hung up, shaking his head at the hard stare Cal was sending his way.

Fifteen minutes later, Cal meandered up his path with a quiet, contemplative look on his face. When he spotted Percy lying on the porch bench, hands tucked behind his head, he pivoted toward him. "You're welcome, Perseus."

Percy flashed Cal his teeth.

Cal shook his head and stopped at the bench by his feet. A light tap hit the side of Percy's knee. Percy clenched against the shivers sifting through him and stubbornly crossed his ankles.

Cal rolled his eyes. Instead of retreating, he cuffed Percy's ankles, swiveled his feet off the bench, and sat down.

Percy swung up into a sitting position that brought them much closer together than he had calculated. His shorts brushed the skin at Cal's thigh where his shorts had ridden up. "Fine, I'll say it. Thank you for pulling me out of that tough spot."

Cal sank back into the bench rather smugly. "How hard was that?"

"Very."

"Crystal was thrilled to have her crystals and baby things."

"She wants to split them between your mom and Josie." Not only did Percy's gnome magic help Crystal avoid the attic, it helped Marg too. "Look, I wondered . . ."

Cal's brows shot up. "Yes?"

The front door opened, and Marg stepped out, throwing her arms up in delight. "There's my handsome one." She handed Cal a long, narrow piece of paper. "I appreciate you doing the shopping. It's the only time the hairdresser could fit us girls in."

"Sure." Cal scanned the list. "Didn't you want chocolate?"

Marg patted her sides with a soft laugh. "Read my hips and tell me."

Cal looked at his mom. "Cuddly. Does that indicate how much you and the baby love chocolate and that I should buy some? Or that you need to cut back and I shouldn't buy any?"

Charming, Cal. Virgos really did say things as they saw them.

"You're lucky I love you, son."

Side by side, they watched Marg and Cal's sisters bundle into Marg's car. When it peeled smoothly away from the curb, a chuckle filled Percy's chest and rose in his throat. He pretended to study his fingers, slyly giving Cal the side-eye. "How are you getting to the store?"

A soft blush hit Cal's cheeks, and he swallowed audibly.

Percy bit down another laugh and rocked onto his feet. He rested a fleeting hand on Cal's shoulder, urging him up. "You know, since I've been eating here most nights, I should chip in for food. Let me grab my wallet and I'll meet you by my Jeep in two."

The relieved sigh Cal released as he stood didn't go unnoticed.

Percy turned away in time to hide the knowing curl of his lips.

∼

"Stop watching them fight." Cal hooked Percy's upper arm and tugged him toward the grocery store.

"But it's happening right there."

Cal kept his head down, avoiding the fight happening right in front of the carts. Percy craned his neck to keep his eyes on the red-faced couple yelling.

"No need to gawk."

"But it's fascinating. He must have done something horrible. She's throwing Pringles in his face."

At the entrance to the store, Cal halted, scanning the parking lot.

"No carts here," Percy said. "Guess we have to go back where that couple is fighting."

Cal dragged him inside to a stack of wheeled baskets. "We'll use these." He loosened his grip on Percy's arm, the warm touch morphing to a tickle.

Percy glanced at Cal's hand. Long fingers, trimmed nails, and a light dusting of hair peeking out of his sleeve at the wrist. A vein bumped the smooth skin across the back of his hand. Strong, capable hands. Hands that lifted sisters. Fingers that flicked through dictionaries.

Their gazes snagged and Cal let him go. He fished for the shopping list, folded the paper, and neatly ripped it in two. "Let's split up. You grab those. I'll take care of the rest."

The basket was too small. Percy filled it with vegetables, fruit, and fresh bread. By the time he walked down the condiments aisle, he was cradling a carton of eggs and a bag of flour. Like a T-rex, he pawed a jar of jam off the shelf.

He towed his basket down the aisles searching for Cal. His shoelaces had come undone, and the basket wheels kept running over the frayed ends.

He was an accident waiting to happen.

Percy slowed his approach when he spotted Cal. He stood admiring Cal's long, lean figure as he scanned a shelf of stretch-mark creams. After double checking his list, Cal picked out a tube of lotion and piled it into his basket.

"Told you we should have gone back for the cart," Percy said, hand suddenly sweaty around the jam jar.

Cal took Percy in with a slow sweep of his eyes and a growing shake of his head. "Let me help." He crouched, and before Percy could gargle in surprise, Cal was tugging the tongue of his shoe. The muscles of his back flexed under his T-shirt as he tied his laces.

Cal had to know what he was doing, right?

"I'm almost done." Breath fanned over Percy's knee. "Got

everything you need?"

Percy stared at Cal's head. "Nope." He sure didn't.

Cal raised a quizzical brow. "What do you need?"

Percy shook himself to his senses. "Ah, dessert."

"Ice cream? Get some."

"I shouldn't."

A frustratingly charming smile touched Cal's lips as he stood, and Percy all but threw the groceries at him and hiked off for the frozen section.

Nemeses. They were meant to be nemeses.

It physically pained him to pass the chocolate-caramel ice cream and grab a tub of French vanilla, but it was Ellie's favorite.

At the checkout behind Cal, he placed the tub of ice cream on the conveyor. "What would you think of me stealing your sister tonight for a *Lord of the Rings* marathon?"

Cal's gaze flickered to his. The store's fluorescent lights made his blue eyes sparkle. "She'd love that."

"I know." Percy unpacked the eggs, flour, and jam from Cal's arms and set that down next.

Cal laughed. "You think you know everything, don't you?"

Percy tore his eyes away and snagged a packet of Mentos and M&Ms. When both their baskets had been emptied onto the belt, Percy placed a checkout divider halfway. "I'll get this."

Cal looked horrified. "We're a family of three and a half, and you eat like a bird."

"I haven't done any cooking. Let's split it. Crystal paid me in cash for her massage yesterday."

Cal cleared his throat. "He might have left us, but Dad makes sure there's enough money."

"I didn't offer out of pity, I just . . . Let me chip in, okay?"

Cal studied him. Maybe he read Percy's pride because he relented. "On one condition."

That stirred a laugh out of him. "What's that?"

"You hand Mom the chocolate."

Virgo
noun / vir . go

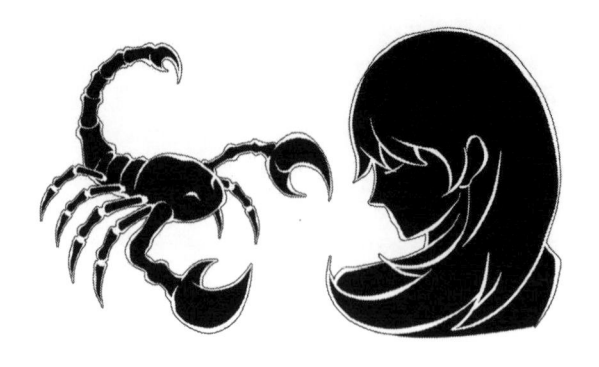

DEFINITION OF VIRGO
: precise, reserved, embarrasses easily, rational, analytical, considerate, chivalrous, highly reliable, wonderfully sarcastic, can be very critical, sexually discreet, loyal
: Cal Glover

EXAMPLE OF VIRGO IN A SENTENCE
"Never pick a verbal fight with a Virgo. You will go down."

Chapter Six

At the end of dinner, Percy invited Ellie to his place for a *Lord of the Rings* marathon. While Marg bathed Hannah, Percy fidgeted with the tablecloth and glanced at Cal. "I know you don't visit of your own volition. But if you find someone to shove you over the road . . ."

"Thanks for the warm invite. Sadly, I won't make it."

Ellie plucked plates off the table, giggling. "He has a date tonight."

Percy stilled. His belly dipped as he forced a grin. "Someone flash you some fancy words, Callaghan?"

Cal tilted his head and studied him before answering. "Not fancy so much as fascinating."

Percy's chair tipped back as he stood. He barely managed to catch it before it fell. "Well, make sure to explore the tension!"

Instead of handing his plate to Ellie, Cal stood and took the load out of her arms. "Get yourself ready, El. I'll clear these."

She left, and the room barely fit their freight load of awkwardness.

Percy grabbed a wet cloth and wiped the table. "So . . . a night out, huh?"

Cal placed the dirty dishes into the dishwasher. "I asked Michelle if she wanted to see a movie over a week ago."

The words *before you came* back flittered through his mind, but Percy didn't let them linger. "A movie? I thought your idea of a night out would be the restricted section of the library."

"It would have been but for the pesky rule that we can't apparate into Hogwarts."

"Crap."

A rumbling laugh. "I might take you to the local library though. Clearly, you need the tour."

"Better make it a date." He cursed his tongue, avoiding Cal's eyes by rinsing out the cloth. "How are you getting to this movie of yours?"

Cal fiddled with the buttons on the dishwasher. "Um, mom's car."

Percy sighed. This lie was as frustrating as it was fascinating. He let it slide.

"Can you do me a favor?" Cal rubbed his neck. "Can you fish out some ideas Ellie might like to do the rest of the summer?"

"Of course."

Cal rocked on his heels. With nothing left to do in the kitchen, he looked unsure if he should stay or go.

This nemesis thing was getting trickier to navigate.

Percy helped him out. "Hit the shower and start scrubbing up. You'll need a few hours."

"Like there's any way I'm sweeping her off her feet."

"Make sure you don't." Percy's tone should have been flatter. He cleared his throat. "You'll mess up your back."

"My back. Right." Cal's gaze stroked Percy's lips and throat.

Cal's attention shifted to Ellie sliding back into the kitchen, wearing pajama pants, slippers, and a large Crayola-blue hoody. "What is it about my things, El?" he asked.

She sank her hands into the large pouch-pocket and nuzzled

her chin under the collar. "This one's cuddly. Besides, I haven't seen you wearing it."

"Because I just bought it." Cal guffawed when Ellie gave him puppy-dog eyes. "Never mind. Have fun. Don't wake Mom when you get in."

∼

"YOU KNOW MORE *LORD OF THE RINGS* TRIVIA THAN ANYONE should."

The laugh that burst out of Ellie warmed Percy. This was what he wanted from the evening.

In fact, the evening would be perfect if he could settle down. He'd been fine during the first half of the film, but now it was approaching midnight, and Percy kept jumping up from the couch to grab them drinks and snacks from the kitchen. Restlessness thrummed in his veins.

"Cal and I try to outdo each other." Ellie shrugged. "Did you know that Orlando Bloom got knocked off his horse and broke his ribs, and he went right back to work the next day?"

"That's the hundredth Legolas tidbit you've thrown at me. I smell a crush."

Ellie shrank behind her curtain of hair. "You remind me of him, that's all. I like Samwise the best. He makes me smile."

Headlights coming down the cul-de-sac distracted him. He hopped off the couch and peeked out the bay window. Just a turning van.

Ellie laughed at something on screen and threw out another trivia tidbit. Percy caught the tail end. "... in her car, and they melted."

He hauled his ass back to Ellie and the movie. Ten minutes later, his leg started jiggling. He needed to use this energy constructively. "Here's another question for you."

She glanced at him and back to the screen. "Another?"

"Ha, I know. If you could have a day out anywhere, where would you go?"

She cuddled into Cal's hoody. "Pittsburgh."

"What's in Pittsburgh?"

A pause. "Dad. He's staying with Granddad."

Oh. Shit. "I'm sorry, El."

She shrugged. "This is a touching scene. We should watch."

One look at the screen showed Boromir taking three arrows to protect Merry and Pippin, and Percy's throat tightened. "I forgot about the ice cream!"

Percy dug into the freezer for the tub of French vanilla. He spooned two bowlfuls for them. To his scoops, he added chocolate, caramel syrup, and smashed M&M's. No Ben & Jerry's, but it would do.

A laugh coiled out of him as he handed Ellie her bowl. Vanilla. Weird girl.

With a grin, he spooned his concoction onto his tongue. Not too shabby. "You're missing out on this caramel deliciousness."

Ellie tapped her scoops of ice cream with her spoon. "Maybe I could have a couple of M&M's this time?"

Percy jumped up and brought the packet over. "Trust me, they add to the taste."

The sound of an engine twisted Percy's stomach, causing him to pivot from the couch and slink past the windows. Still no sign of Marg's car.

He dumped his bowl into the sink and forced himself to pay attention to the movie. Once *The Fellowship of The Ring* ended, Ellie excused herself to the bathroom.

Percy perched on the windowsill, resting his forehead on the cool glass. His breath fogged the pane as he squinted over the dark road.

"What are you looking at?" Ellie's boots clunked as she reentered the living room.

"Nothing!" Well, that sounded innocent. "It's a new moon tonight."

Ellie lifted her brow, a smaller version of Cal's. "Sounds like something Crystal would say."

A strangled laugh left him, and suddenly *explore the tension* was running on repeat in his mind. Thank you, Ellie Glover.

Where were distractions when he needed them?

"So, the million-dollar question." How do you think Cal's date is going? "Do you think Cal should go back to college?"

Ellie frowned and turned on The Two Towers. "Mom and I are working to convince him."

A wave of relief crashed over him. "That's good."

"You should help," she said. "Tell him to go back."

"Me?" He laughed, but it sounded fake. "Cal wouldn't care what I say."

"Are you kidding? You've been back a week, and already Cal is, like, a million times happier."

A lump tightened in Percy's throat. "He enjoys giving me shit, that's all."

"No, he enjoys shooting the shit." She pulled on the cords of Cal's hoody. "I think you coming home has made this situation bearable for him."

Her words twisted something in his chest. Since seeing Cal's hatchback under the weeping willow, Percy had suspected the reason Cal lied was because he liked their morning rides together.

He'd never thought it was something Cal needed.

As if she hadn't said something that had his eyes prickling, Ellie focused on the TV screen.

Percy stared at the Glovers' porch-lit house. Shortly before one a.m., Cal returned home. Instead of getting out of his car, he sat in the driver's seat.

The hairs on Percy's neck lifted. Percy knew Cal was looking at Aunt Abby's house. Maybe even recognized him at the window lit by the colors jumping from the TV screen.

His stomach flipped. Pulling out his phone, he sent Cal a text message.

Percy: If you want to gawk at me, at least get out of your car, so I can gawk back.

Cal: Wondered if El wanted me to watch the rest with you guys?

Sure he did.

Percy: El would like that a lot.

Seconds later, Cal was crossing the road. Percy leapt off the sill, mused Ellie's hair on his way out of the living room, and whipped open the door before Cal had a chance to knock. A waft of moisturizer hit Percy's nose and he fought not to sniff the gentle scent. "You on my porch. At night. It's becoming a habit."

"I'm sure it will be a tough one to break."

Cal's sky-blue shirt was almost the exact color of his eyes. No way Michelle didn't melt over it.

Percy beckoned Cal inside. *How was your date?* "New shirt?"

"You should see the blush to go with it."

"I think I am."

In the living room, Cal leaned over the couch right next to Ellie. She jumped and playfully slapped him. "Just in time for one of your favorite Legolas scenes." She wriggled to the right, making room for Cal in the middle.

Percy sank onto the arm of the couch, silently willing Ellie to ask about Cal's date.

She didn't ask a thing.

"I don't think you're sitting far enough away," Cal said, looking from Percy to the empty seat cushion between them.

Biting his lip, Percy sank onto the cushion, Cal's heat thrumming at his side. He focused on the movie and nothing else. Not Ellie and Cal swapping trivia and high-fiving each other on their geek-o-graphic memories; not Cal's sleeve brushing over his bare arm whenever they shifted; not Cal whispering into his ear near the end of the third movie when Ellie had fallen asleep. "This is the most exciting part."

Percy bit his lip. "Yep, I'm pretty excited too."

Cal spoke again, and Percy's eyelids shuttered. "Somehow the emotion—"

"Sneaks up on you."

"Exactly."

Percy finally looked at him.

Flickering light danced over his profile as he watched the screen. His gaze glazed; lips pressed tight and brow pushed together as if in thought. He rubbed the hand closest to Percy over his thigh, up and down, the movement sending little waves of electricity jumping over to his forearm. "Thank you for this. I mean, doing this. With Ellie."

Oh Cal, what were you doing to him? "Your sister is awesome. We might be becoming BFFs."

Cal hit him with the full weight of that blue gaze. "Really? What makes you think that?"

"We've been messaging each other via the Sherlock Gnomes forum. She makes me laugh."

Cal made a funny noise in his throat like he was about to say something and the sound made Percy shiver. Before he could think any more about it, Ellie stirred.

Cal coaxed Ellie to her feet and escorted her to the front door.

"Thanks for the movie," she said, drowsily. It was past four in the morning, so Percy didn't blame her. If it hadn't been for Cal right there on the couch keeping his senses on high alert, he'd have conked out hours ago.

"You're welcome, El."

Cal steered his sister over the porch and across the road, and Percy waited until they were behind closed doors before he locked up.

He headed off to bed, an emptiness niggling into his chest when he passed his aunt's room.

Lying in the dark, he played with his phone, swiping it on and off. His thoughts skipped from his aunt to Cal on his couch to that stupid hatchback lie that was changing everything.

He twisted onto his side and stared at the shadowy form of his stacked boxes. With a groan, Percy swiped and called.

The phone rang three times before Cal picked up. "Miss me already?"

Percy's own words tossed back at him, and despite being spoken with Cal's signature dryness, Percy heard more in them now. His chest gave a small twist. "You're literally the last person I think of at night, and the first in the morning."

Cal gave the requisite snort. "You want to know how my date went, don't you?"

"Now that you bring it up . . . I suppose you should tell me."

"Let's just say my back's not messed up, and I doubt I'll have to worry about that happening."

Percy rolled onto his back, swallowing tightly. Both their breaths huffed down the line, and Percy pictured Cal lying in his bed drinking in the dark. Cal's voice dropped close to a whisper. "Anything else you want, Perseus?"

"You." He cleared his throat. "To help me look at a potential house."

∾

THEY ARRIVED AT PETER MOLTON'S PLACE, A FORTY-FIVE-minute drive from Aunt Abby's. The small house was crammed between two less-maintained town houses. Percy wasn't too sure about it.

"This is housing at its best," Cal said. He'd spent the drive fluctuating from happy to frustrated. The farther they drove, the more pinched his expression. "Let's go."

Percy clicked his belt open, holding back a laugh at the blatant scowl Cal sent him.

"I meant let's go back home."

"I know. Now, come on."

A pokey front garden gave way to a creaky porch. "This place isn't right for you," Cal said, brushing a bug off his T-shirt. A *new* blue shirt, Percy noticed.

An amused grin pushed at Percy's lips as he knocked on the door after trying the defunct bell.

A curly-haired Peter cracked open the door, flustered and shifty-eyed. "Um, just a moment." He shut the door and yelled to someone.

"Great first impression," Cal muttered at his ear, and a shiver scuttled down Percy's spine.

The door swung open, and Peter beckoned them in with hurried sweeps of his hand. He slammed the door shut behind them.

"This way," Peter said, leading them into the dark, rusty-smelling house.

Cal bumped the back of his hand against Percy's, knuckles skating against the ticklish skin at his wrist. "If we get murdered, it's your fault."

"If we're murdered, I'll take the blame." Maybe he was already wishing they'd not come inside, but the urge to tease Cal had overwhelmed him. Also, he was fascinated by how bad the place was. Certainly looked different online.

Peter stopped in a heavily draped living room with a low-lit chandelier. "Paperwork is out back, but the grand tour starts here—"

A woman cursed from somewhere out back. Something about "that damn escape artist."

"Stay right there," Peter said tightly. "One of my pets needs locking up."

Peter hoofed off, and Cal folded his arms, clearly unimpressed, feet shuffling toward the exit. "If he comes back and tries to make us his pets . . ."

Percy snorted. "What a wildly dark imagination you have. I like it."

"Dark imagination? It's called self-preservation." Cal tiptoed to the windows and lifted the drapes. To check for bars on the windows, perhaps.

None, thank fuck.

The thick material shifted, blocking out the natural light once more. Cal pivoted but didn't turn around, his fingers still pinching the drapes. "Why'd you invite me today?" he asked.

Percy rubbed his hand where Cal's earlier touch still lingered and stared at the sunken cushions of the leather couch. "Human shield?"

A large yellow snake slithering over the couch cut off Percy's nervous laugh. Cal lurched protectively in front of him, arm outstretched, pushing against his chest.

"Clearly, you need one."

They both stumbled back a few steps, eyes not leaving the reptile.

"Maybe not quite the place I had in mind?" Percy managed with a shiver.

Cal reached for Percy's hand and squeezed his fingers as he tugged him in front of him. He planted a warm hand on Percy's shoulder, the other at the small of his back, and propelled him toward the front door.

"I draw the line at snakes, Perseus."

"Is this a bad time to crack a joke, Callaghan?"

∼

They hightailed it back to the cul-de-sac.

"Why did you freak out?" Percy said, locking the Jeep. "You're an expert on scary animals."

Cal leveled him with a look. "Extinct ones, Perseus."

They stared at each other over the roof that glinted with afternoon sunshine, neither making the first step to part ways. It was too early to invite himself to the Glovers for mystery night.

"What are you up to now?" Cal's voice dripped with boredom that Percy didn't believe for a second.

Percy clutched his keys and rounded the Jeep toward his house. "Was supposed to clean up Aunt Abby's room before Peter visited." He sighed too heavily, then overcorrected, acting too enthused. "He's spared me that task, at least."

Wincing, Percy looked away from Cal down the line of houses.

A soft scrape of shoe against pavement, and then Cal blocked the direct sunshine. Percy sensed him about to acknowledge the sad shit in his life.

He couldn't hear it. "You get back to Ellie. Take her out for ice cream or something."

Cal frowned.

Percy winked at him. "Turn that frown upside down, Callaghan. I'll catch you at dinner."

"No."

Cal's firm response threw Percy. He twisted toward Cal, who bore a pondering expression. A gentle touch played over his knuckles, and Cal gripped his hand and pulled him toward his porch.

"Let's clear her room together."

Butterflies rioted in Percy's belly. "Sound that sorry, did I?"

"Something like that." Cal squeezed his hand. "I have a brilliant plan to make it easier on you."

At the door, Cal let go. The keys jiggled less surely in Percy's grip. Somehow Percy got the damn door to work. "Plan?"

"It's hard to be in her room because it hurts, right?"

Yes. "So?"

"Let me help you sort her things. Offset the sadness by thinking how much you hate me."

"It's a . . . surprising amount."

A humored laugh.

In the hallway outside Aunt Abby's bedroom, Cal stopped. "I'm going to open this door now. You go right ahead and visualize clubbing me around the ears."

The lump in Percy's throat got decidedly larger. "Callaghan . . ." Cal twisted the knob and paused. Percy cleared his throat and looked into those deep blue eyes. "Thank you."

Cal blinked, and his throat worked a swallow. He smoothed his surprise, pushed open the door, and gestured Percy inside.

Sunlight streamed through the windows under frilly curtains. Dust motes sparkled lazily, drifting over the bed and steamer trunk.

Percy sighed, planted himself heavily onto the quilted bed, and scooped up her scattered brooches. The springs under the mattress groaned and protested. The bed had seen a few too many decades.

Cal moved to the family pictures on the wall—Abby and his dad, and Percy as a toddler, then a kid, then a teen.

"She was the first person I told."

"That you have an insane ability to drive guys crazy?"

"Or, you know, that they drive me crazy."

They shared a tempered, slightly melancholic smile.

Cal ran a finger over the picture that showed Percy and Abby holding up a flag they'd captured last Fourth of July weekend. "She was a good, no bullshit woman. Once, she caught this young kid dropping litter into the gutter, and she told him off."

"Good."

Cal laughed. "She made him pick it up, right there in public. He sure never did it again."

"How do you know?"

A sheepish smile. "That kid was me."

Percy rubbed the heels of his hands over his eyes and dropped back on the bed. It made a clicking sound and dipped deeply in the middle. Percy grappled at the quilt to regain balance.

Both ends of the bed flapped upward as he flailed helplessly, trying to sit back up. "I think this bed is trying to swallow me," he said, laughing.

Cal extended a hand and helped Percy onto his feet. Suddenly, they were an inch apart, and the air was thickening.

Cal cleared his throat and stepped back, air sweeping between them. "How about we empty the small stuff first?"

For the next hour and a half, Percy and Cal worked side by side organizing Abby's clothes, camping gear, art supplies, and half-finished knitting projects into boxes for the thrift shop. The large, sunny room had potential. If he uploaded a few photos once it was reorganized, the house might garner more interest.

"Bit of paint," Cal said after they'd shifted the boxes to the attic, "and this room would look completely different."

Percy stood, hands on hips, taking in the bare room. Only the trunk and bed remained. Percy gazed at the faded patches of floral wallpaper where their photos had been. "It'd still smell like her though."

"Not for long, judging how much aftershave you use."

Percy flipped his middle finger at him and his cheeky grin. "Would feel like her room though."

"Maybe for a little while, until you made your own memories."

"Not staying, Callaghan. It's too big. I'd need you in every room to offset the sadness."

Cal shoved his thumbs into pockets, tapping his fingers.

"Life-size cutouts, perhaps? Or, if more invasive hatred would help, I could rent out one of your rooms."

Percy's throat clamped and he let out a squeaky grunt.

"You look horrified," Cal said. "Guess I'm doing a good job distracting you."

"That you are."

Cal tapped the trunk with his foot. "Shall I help you lug this chest into the hall?"

"Unless you want me massaging your glutes the next six weeks, no lifting heavy things."

Cal looked at the trunk and hesitated like he might do it anyway—then his phone rang. He pulled the phone from his back pocket and stared at the screen. He twisted away from Percy as he answered. "Hi, Dad. You got my emails?"

Percy held his breath and scrutinized Cal. His unsteady tone, his slouched shoulders, the way his fingers pinched his pocket, the swallowing sounds he made as he listened to his Dad's update.

"Ellie needs to see you. She misses you a lot." Cal looked up, blinking rapidly at the ceiling. Percy itched to snap the phone from his hand and tell Mr. Glover to call back later. "It would be easier if you came up here, Dad."

He paced the length of the bed, brow heavy with sadness. And then . . . Cal deflated. He rubbed the bridge of his nose, glanced at Percy, and hurriedly looked away again. His voice fell flat. "Fine. Ellie and I will come to you. Mom and Hannah the following weekend. You have to face her. Get used to it."

Cal turned as he stuffed his phone back into his pocket, and Percy's stomach churned. He crept around the side of the bed, clearing his throat as though it might help him know what to say. He stopped directly in front of Cal. "Look at me."

Cal swallowed his emotion and looked. Light tingles flowed through Percy as their gazes connected. Cal's lips tipped up in a half-smile. "Huh. This offsetting thing works both ways."

Percy cocked his head, humming. Before he could think better of it, he inched a half-step and reached for Cal's pocket. Cal didn't flinch, but his throat jutted as Percy wedged a finger inside. The warmth of Cal's thigh leaked through the material, and Percy hurriedly pinched the phone and wiggled it free.

He traced Cal's triangle on the screen to unlock it, dragging a surprised sound from Cal.

"I pay attention," Percy said. He opened the camera app and took a selfie, staring right at the camera the way they always did with each other. "There." He snuck the phone back into Cal's pocket. "For whenever you need offsetting."

Cal made a strangled sound and sat on the end of the bed. "Why is this so—"

With an echoing snap, the bed frame gave way and Cal fell backward. Percy grabbed him, one hand latching onto his wrist, the other the T-shirt at his waist. The mattress bowed in the middle, and Cal's legs jerked out, thrusting Percy off balance.

He collapsed on top of Cal with an *ooof*, the additional weight forcing the old mattress to press them in from both sides. Percy's mouth practically suctioned onto Cal's throat, their chests plastered together, so close Percy felt Cal's heart thumping, warm thighs cushioning his legs. Their crotches aligned in a way that was one small shift from compromising.

Cal's resigned laugh rumbled through Percy. He removed his hand wedged between their hips and pushed against Cal's chest. They looked at each other and Cal stopped laughing.

"Why is this so, what?" Percy asked.

Cal shifted under him, expression flustered. "Why is this so . . . hard?"

Percy wasn't sure Cal was referring to the situation with his dad. He bit his lip and torturously struggled off Cal and the bed. "I'm sorry there aren't more happy endings."

Cal fought free from the clutches of the mattress. "Give it to me," he said, fingers beckoning.

Percy's pulse jumped wildly. He rocked on the balls of his feet and bumped into Cal. The gap between the bed and the wall was far too narrow. "Um, what?"

"Your phone. So I can put my picture on it."

Oh, right. He handed over his phone. Cal took a snapshot and gave it back to him. The picture captured Cal in soft light. His hair looked as soft on screen as it did in real life. He didn't outright smile, but something about Cal's lips held a grin anyway. And damn, his all too analytical gaze . . .

"Is it all right?" Cal asked.

Percy shut the app and rolled his eyes. "Beautiful, Callaghan. How will I ever stop looking at it?"

∽

How would he ever stop looking at it?

No matter what angle he held his phone, Cal's eyes followed him. The more he studied the picture, the more Cal appeared life-like, observing him and shimmering with a knowing smile when Percy sat back against his bed pillows and palmed his aching dick through his night shorts.

Percy muttered gruffly as he rearranged himself. "Nope, not going to do it."

He stuffed the phone under his pillow, grabbed his laptop, and logged into his Chatvica account. It took him less than a minute to dig up the thread he wanted: **Gay and falling for a (straight) guy. ~ GayDude**

No matter how many times Percy read the comments, they still boiled down to one thing: Keep an emotional distance.

Percy opened a comment box and typed.

GayDude: Thank you for the replies. I know it's taken me a while to respond. I guess I find the truth frustrating. I'm writing back now because I am

struggling with the whole "keeping an emotional distance" thing. I tried. I mean, I am trying. For years we've had a feigned nemesis thing going on, and I encourage it to avoid anything real. It's enough I find him attractive, I don't want to *like* him on any deeper level. Not when I know nothing could come of it. (I know I'm not family material. Know he would leave eventually—I have twenty tiramisu containers that say the same thing!)

That aside, I think he wants us to be . . . well, not nemeses anymore. He needs someone in his life to hang out with and talk to. And so do I. I think I can navigate it so no lines are crossed. I mean, I'm a rational guy.

He could totally do this.

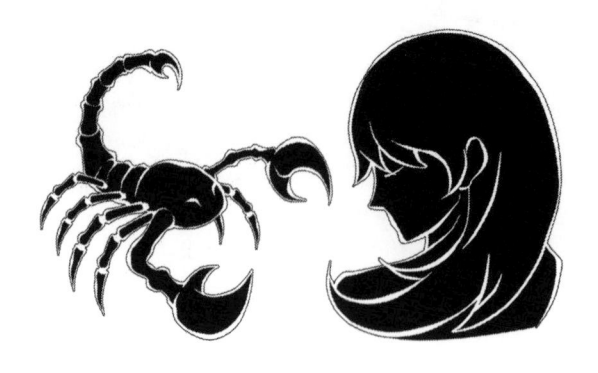

S arcasm
    noun / sar . casm

DEFINITION OF **SARCASM**
: a mode of satirical wit often used by Perseus and Callaghan toward each other
: the native language of Callaghan Glover and Perseus Freedman

EXAMPLE OF **SARCASM** IN A SENTENCE
"What, no sarcasm today, Callaghan? Someone hit you over the head or what? Seriously, who was it? I need to know who to thank."

Chapter Seven

When Wednesday rolled around, the hatchback charade couldn't be prolonged.

Percy dropped Ellie at work, then continued to the community center. Rain drizzled, and he flicked his wipers on full speed.

Cal's eyes followed as they swished back and forth. "You tell those little drops who's boss."

Percy adjusted the speed to the slow clap of window wiping. "Will your car be ready today?"

"Ah, yes. I'll pick her up from the garage this afternoon."

Sure you will.

Percy took a detour through the city to prolong the time before they arrived at Cal's work. He tapped his thumbs over the steering wheel, working himself up to address the lie. He'd suggest they continue carpooling regardless whether Cal's car was in working order.

Cal rubbed his palms over the passenger seat, making the leather squeal. "Maybe we can share a set of wheels when you're in town for clients? You know, it makes sense. For the environment."

Percy suppressed the need to grin wildly. "I definitely want to keep the . . . *environment* strong and healthy."

Cal feigned interest in straightening a kink in his belt strap.

Percy soaked it up, his mood an octave more upbeat. "So, Fourth of July . . ." Even if he found someone to buy the house, he could drop by for a visit. "I say we kick Theo and his boyfriend's butt at Zombie Apocalypse."

"I'd heard Theo was with a guy."

Percy slated him a look. "And you kept that piece of gossip to yourself?"

"It wasn't any of my business to go around blurting to just anyone."

Just anyone? Percy shook off a curl of disappointment and chuckled. "Were you surprised?"

"Not really?"

Not really? But it was Theo. He'd only had girlfriends. "Well, I was surprised." Percy peeked over at Cal, hands gripping the wheel. "He made a good point about sexuality being fluid . . ."

Cal hummed and looked out the passenger window. What did that hum mean? Yes, sexuality was fluid, and he knew from experience? Or was it a simple murmur of agreement that had no bearing on his own sexuality and Percy needed to stop thinking about this?

He pulled up to the center, and Cal climbed out of the car. "Oh, and regarding the Fourth, I'll be hosting the street barbecue again this year. You're invited, of course."

"Never expected anything less." Percy leaned over the console and called after him. "Can't wait to admire your grill, Callaghan."

Cal flashed him a large, toothy smile. "Admire away, Perseus."

It was strange not dropping Ellie and Cal off to work on Thursday morning. The tradition had somehow seeped into his days and the morning felt off-kilter. The house, exponentially quieter.

Percy checked Josie's list of to dos and headed into the backyard.

The lawn mower was gone.

All Abby's quality gardening machinery and tools, gone.

He tucked his hands under his armpits and stared into the hollow pit. How lovely of his family to make clearing out easy. Really, he should send thank-you cards.

He dragged himself to Crystal's, and she led him to her tool shed.

"Do you have a hose?" he asked.

She pushed shovels and buckets aside and pulled out a long green hose. "Watering the garden?"

"Or maybe washing it and seeing if the dirt comes out."

Crystal pinned him with parental eyes. "Percy."

He flashed her a sheepish smile. "What I mean is thank you. For this. I . . . thanks."

He methodically got to work mowing the grass and trimming the edges. Next, he slipped on gardening gloves for weeding. Two hours, and he was pulling out weeds like a pro. Three hours, and he was swearing like a sailor.

What was the backyard but one grand adventure?

He dug his hand shovel under a mass of roots, and the metal blade clunked against something hard. Ripping away the weed, heart doing a hop, skip, and a jump, he burrowed his fingers into the earth and pulled out an old rectangular cookie tin.

On the lid was a faded picture of a snow-laced barn, pines, and a family of moose. Percy's throat constricted on a laugh.

He pried open the tin, and rusted tubes of Aunt Abby's watercolors stared back at him. He'd buried them one weekend he'd visited. Her favorites. He must have been ten.

"And she still loved me," he said under his breath. Might have to question her judgement.

He carried the tin inside and set it on the table.

Dirt, grass, and melancholy stuck to every inch of him.

Under the punishing pressure of his new showerhead, he managed to clean off the first two.

The tin glinted in the sunlight coming through the bay window, winking at him. "How can I say no, when you leer at me so?"

He gingerly cleaned it, scrubbed off rust stains on the bottom, and stacked Abby's loose recipes inside. Maple nut chocolate clusters. Buttery flatbread. Bundt cake. Tater tot pie casserole. His fingers stilled on a recipe for dog treats, and he set that one aside.

He placed the tin on the counter next to the oven, then busied himself jotting down a list of groceries he needed. Boneless chicken. Eggs. Stock. Flour. Rice. Salt.

When he returned from the supermarket, he set out the ingredients. His aunt would get a kick out of him using her recipe to gnome his neighbor.

He stared at her loopy handwriting vainly waiting for the words to stop blurring.

"Homemade chicken and wild rice dog treats. This one's for you, Mr. Roosevelt."

"For his dog, I hope," came Cal's dry voice, startling Percy.

He dropped the flour package and it burst at his feet, clouding half the kitchen in a fine white mist. He knelt and scooped handfuls into the ugly orange baking bowl that no one had deemed good enough to pilfer.

Sneakers appeared at the kitchen entrance, and Cal leaned against the brick archway and looked down at him. Percy hoped the flour dusted him enough to hide any shimmer in his eyes.

High time Percy got his spare key back from the Glovers. "Oh, it's you. Again."

Cal's gaze narrowed onto his face and he crouched before him. "Are you cr—"

"What are you doing here?" Percy hurriedly interrupted, heart thumping.

Cal's gaze bounced all over Percy as if adding and subtracting and not finding the result he'd expected. He rubbed his thighs and pushed to his feet. "Crystal mentioned you working in the garden, and that made me think I should mow our lawn." He ran a hand through his hair. "You didn't get to your front. I could do it too."

"Are you offering to help me?"

"I just can't stand looking at your mess of a yard."

Percy hugged his bowl and stood, slicking on a smile. "You'll block my beloved view of the neighbors."

"I'll be extra quick."

Not too quick. Cal was still working when the dog treats were baked and cooling. When Percy was wrapping a bow around the cardboard carton, the lawnmower motor cut out.

He tucked the gift under his arm and slipped out the front door, wildly scanning the yard.

Cal stood near the mailbox, forearm wiping the sweat from his brow, other hand holding a phone to his ear. A warm laugh bubbled out of him and he leaned against the lawnmower handlebar. His T-shirt clung to the small of his sweat-drenched back.

"Sounds like you drank too many sangrias. What time is it in Barcelona, anyway?"

Percy stilled at the edge of the porch. Cal's ex was on the other end of the line.

Percy set the box of treats on the porch and re-laced his boots.

"You'll have to tell me all about that when you get back . . . Seventh of July? Got it. Bring pictures." Another laugh, this one sounding a little more strung out. "No, I'm not with anyone.

Might be a while, you know. What about you? . . . Hey, it doesn't have to be a forever thing. I know what we had was . . . yeah." Cal's shoulders bowed, and he shrugged. "You're allowed to be curious, flirt, experiment. . . . Have fun, okay? See you soon."

He hung up, then stared at his phone for a long time.

Almost as long as Percy spent rubbing a sudden twist in his chest.

Before the production got awkward, Percy seized the box of treats and kicked past Cal with the barest glance.

Cal called out to him but Percy kept his eyes on Mr. Roosevelt's house. "I'm packing up. See you at dinner."

∽

AT THE GLOVERS', PERCY FINISHED WASHING THE DISHES AND let the water gurgle out of the sink.

Marg picked up the last plate and dried it, eying Cal scooping leftovers into containers.

"Cal, could you date the leftovers in the fridge?"

"I could try," Cal said, picking up a Sharpie from a box on the counter, "but I have the feeling we'd be better off as friends."

No matter Percy's mood, Cal's dryness had a way of reaching into him and snatching a laugh. He snorted as he snapped out of pink rubber gloves. "Were you that blunt with Jenny? God, I wish she'd slapped you."

She might have still been on his mind. Just a little.

"Don't worry, Perseus. Your words do a stellar job leaving a mark all on their own."

Marg shook a white dishtowel between them. "Okay, boys. Call a truce."

Percy pinched the dishtowel and slung it over the oven handle. "That's not how this game ends, Marg."

She groaned. "Dare I ask?"

"Best not."

"It would be so much easier if you kissed and made up."

Percy shook his head, barking out a laugh. He didn't want to be Cal's curious plaything.

Tempting as it might be.

Cal rubbed his neck, a slight blush staining his cheeks. He honed his attention in on Hannah climbing over the couch, trying to cover Ellie's eyes.

"Time for bath and bed," he said and snapped out of the kitchen toward her. One Amargasaurus later, Percy found himself on the couch cushioned by two female Glovers. One laughing at the TV, the other wincing like her son did as she touched her back.

He clapped his hands once together. "You need a back rub."

He spent a half-hour working knots out of Marg's neck, shoulders, and lower back.

"I have to pay you for this," she murmured on a sigh. "You can't keep helping me out."

"As long as I'm eating here, I'll keep doing it."

"You can eat here forever."

Percy laughed and worked slow circles around her right hip. In the background, Ellie slunk off to her room. Hannah squealed, and a stern Cal flashed past the door chasing her.

Marg let out a groan, and her muscles shifted under Percy's hands like she was about to get up.

Percy slipped his hand up to her shoulder and squeezed. "Let Cal take care of it. Relax."

"He's doing a lot now."

"Trust me, he wants to. Now tell me about your day."

"Work's work. Had a checkup today, though. I was surprised at how many others in the waiting room were close to my age. One woman said it was her first pregnancy. I felt sorry for her."

"Why? Is this one much different from your others?"

"Sort of. I mean, I'm lucky I don't get sick like some women do. All my babies have pretty much been by the textbook. Ellie's was the easiest, followed by Hannah's. I had Cal at eighteen, and though I was fitter back then, I was also half my current size and Cal, well, he was a big baby." Marg set a gentle hand on the curve of her belly. "Surprise baby seems to be taking the cake, to be honest. There is an ache for every one of my forty years."

Marg continued telling Percy pregnancy stories until Percy was done. Then, with a relaxed yawn, she decided it was time for her to enjoy a warm bath. If he was still around when she was done, they'd watch a mystery.

Alone in the great room, Percy sprawled out on the couch and flicked on the TV. Nothing interesting was on, and he pulled out his phone to check his messages. Instead, he found himself swiping to Cal's picture: Scar dripping through his eyebrow, bottom lip ludicrously full, mussed hair.

Percy shook his head and channeled a Serna-style mutter.

An embarrassingly long time passed before he locked his phone and rubbed the hard end of his phone against his forehead.

Why was he thinking of sneaking down to Cal's room where he'd disappeared after putting Hannah to bed? Why was he making up excuses to return the gym mat he'd used to massage Marg?

Socks scuffed along the hall and down the stairs as Percy dragged the mat to Cal's room. He sauntered through Cal's open door without a second thought, then froze halfway to the bed.

Steam billowed from the ajar bathroom door and water pounded against the wall. The sudden knowledge that Cal was showering sent naked lust surging through him. Had Cal left the door open on purpose?

Percy abandoned the mat and promptly marched his ass back across the road.

He could do this. He and Cal would be non-nemeses. He

refused to act on lust, even if Cal ramped up his interest tenfold and blatantly stripped in front of him. "Nope, not falling for it."

He climbed into bed and logged into the Sherlock Gnomes forum. Before he knew it, he was typing Gnome Chomsky a message.

To Gnome Chomsky:
Rendezvous Friday, midnight. The playground.

A loud ding told him Gnomber9 had come online. He sank back into the pillows and opened a private chat with Ellie.

Gnomber9: What are you doing on here so late?

Gnomad: I could ask the same of you.

Gnomber9: Couldn't sleep.

Gnomad: Your mom choose a gruesome mystery? Here's a tip I heard from a certain someone. Log into Hannah's Netflix account and watch *Dora the Explorer*.

Gnomber9: Actually, *Dinosaur Train* is more my thing.

Gnomad: You Glovers have an unhealthy obsession with extinct beasts.

Gnomber9: It's true.

Gnomad: Is Cal still up?

Gnomber9: Yes.

Gnomad: Tell him to log into this Sherlock Gnomes account. I sent him a direct message.

Gnomber9: Who did you send the message to?

Gnomad: Good try. I'm not giving his gnome identity away.

～

WHAT WAS THAT HORRIBLE SOUND?

Percy shoved a pillow over his face, but it didn't stop the sick buzzing. "Fine."

He rolled out of bed and slumped to the front door.

Dark slacks. Leather shoes. Cashmere pullover rolled up at the arms. "Is this payback for the other day, Callaghan? You know you have one of my keys, right?"

"I know. Just mixing things up."

A yawn rippled out of Percy, and he satisfied an itch under his left nipple.

Cal's attention shifted to his chest. "It's ten to eight."

Percy leaped into action, racing back to his room. "Why didn't you wake me earlier?" He was supposed to massage Dorothy, this morning.

Why had he missed his alarm? Sure, he'd tossed and turned all night—and indulged in two jerkoffs too many—but this wasn't his style.

Cal hovered in Percy's bedroom doorway, eyes following Percy as he shoved into a pair of jeans, a clean T-shirt, socks, and lightweight jacket. Shoes on and Mentos slipped into his pocket, he was still nowhere near ready to go. "Can you grab me a muesli bar and bottle of water?"

"I can . . ."

Percy hefted his massage table and snagged his keys. "Would you?"

Smirking, Cal backed down the hall. "Hair looks great, by the way."

His hair would have to do. He couldn't be late for Dorothy's first massage.

He shoved his table into the Jeep and jumped into the driver's seat. Cal sat in the passenger seat holding out a muesli bar and yogurt drink. He'd even peeled down the wrapper and removed the lid. A bottle of water sat squeezed between Cal's thighs.

Percy ate as he drove, gaze straying to the water bottle at every red light.

Cal gripped the bottle with one hand and twisted the cap. A satisfying chi sounded, and sparkling water dribbled over the rim. "Thirsty?"

"Parched."

"Drink up." Cal handed him the bottle, and Percy clutched the warm, hard plastic.

"Peachy," he murmured. Peachiness all around.

"Let me see," Cal said, grabbing the bottle again. His fingers slid between Percy's as he took control of it. A small gasp trickled over Percy's lip. "Doesn't taste peachy to me."

Percy focused on the road. Not the guy sipping his water.

The bottle landed back in his hand. Percy muttered pointed words to whichever deity thought this would be funny, wrapped his lips around the opening, and tipped its contents down his throat. He finished the small bottle in three greedy gulps.

"Parched was an understatement," Cal said.

"You have no idea."

Cal took the empty bottle. "I can refill it before your massage session."

Percy squeezed the steering wheel. "Can or will?"

"Touché. What are your plans tonight? This weekend?"

Oh, Cal.

"Don't know," Percy said. "I'm keen to do something for the *environment* though." Percy gnawed his bottom lip. "Want to check out another prospective house with me?"

A deep, displeased hum. "Not particularly."

"Okay—"

"I'll be there. Someone's got to make sure you don't get murdered."

Percy winked at him. "Bit of a hero complex in you after all."

J urassic Park studies
    noun / ju . ras . sic /park/ stu . dies

DEFINITION OF JURASSIC PARK STUDIES
  : Cal's paleontology masters
  : Cal's passion
  : What Percy needs Cal to get back to.

Chapter Eight

Through thick midnight shadows, Percy slunk to the cul-de-sac playground. Warm breezes made the trees shiver, and crickets and katydids croaked. He sat on the swing and pulled out a roll of Mentos from his leather jacket.

He sucked on an orange-flavored candy and scoured the street for any sign of movement. No distant figure of Cal, only Mr. Roosevelt walking Rooster around the playground.

Rooster barked, and Mr. Roosevelt tugged him to heel and crossed over to the swings. "What are you doing out here?"

"I'm up to no good." Percy innocently smiled at his neighbor. At least as much as he could muster considering he'd once thrown up right where Mr. Roosevelt was standing.

Percy looked past him to the street.

Where was Cal? Why hadn't he shown up? He'd seen him gazing out his living room window as Percy left for the park. He'd thought—hoped—Cal was watching for him and would follow shortly behind. Maybe even catch up on his way here.

"Maybe you got your wires crossed?" Mr. Roosevelt said.

Percy's hands froze around the swing chains. He stared at Mr.

Roosevelt, who taught social studies, history, and—"Philosophy. You're Gnome Chomsky?"

"Nice to meet you, Gnomad." He crouched down and scratched his dog under the chin. "I was surprised by your message but gathered there must have been some mistake."

Wasn't this wonderful? He'd convinced himself Cal was Gnome Chomsky. Told Cal as much. How he must be laughing! "Some mistake, all right."

He hurriedly dragged his hands off the swing and stood. "Excuse me. I have a man to catch."

Mr. Roosevelt tipped his chin. "Good luck."

∽

CAL ANSWERED ON THE FIRST RING.

"You're not Gnome Chomsky," Percy said, striding through the dark, quiet cul-de-sac. Other than light at the Glovers', the neighbors' windows were dark.

Percy willed Cal to the window so he might see the amusement twitching his lips and brow.

Cal remained out of sight. He spoke low and soft, probably for the sake of his sleeping mom and sisters, and it thrummed into Percy's ear. "I told you I was no Gnome Chomsky."

Which gnome are you, then? The only tricky gnome identities left were Gnome More Wood, which didn't sound like Cal's humor, and I Don't Gnome, which was sounding more like the truth.

He supposed since he'd guessed Gnome Chomsky incorrectly, he might've made other errors. Tomorrow he'd have to scour the list with a fine-tooth comb.

Percy tripped up the Glovers' porch and caught himself against the door, his hand almost pressing the doorbell. He righted himself and whispered into the phone, "Let me in, Callaghan. Unless you want me to huff and puff."

Seconds later, Cal stood before him in jeans and the blue hoody Ellie had stolen from him for their *Lord of the Rings* evening. "As much as I'd love you huffing and puffing, just come in."

Cal glanced at the phone still held to Percy's ear. Dropping his arm, Percy shoved the phone into his jacket next to his Mentos.

Hands sinking into his deep hoody pocket, Cal stepped backward, encouraging Percy to step inside.

After kicking off his shoes, he smuggled himself to the basement and Cal's room. He dove onto the pillows piled at the head of the bed. Just as soft as he'd imagined them.

"By all means," Cal drawled, "make yourself at home."

Percy shuffled himself so he sat on one side of the bed, propped up by Cal-scented pillows. He took the side Cal hadn't been sleeping on when Percy had woken him a few days ago.

Cal moved tentatively toward the bed like he wasn't quite sure about his role. He slid onto the other side of the bed, closest to the bathroom, and swung his legs up onto the mattress. "What brings you here?"

"Missed you, of course."

"Careful, Perseus. One of these days I might start believing you."

Percy looked away from Cal's expression of fake annoyance and stared at Cal's bare feet. The long neck of his big toes, the prominent veins along the arches, and the little mole on the right foot under the outer ankle bone. "I was bored. Thought we should take advantage of your day off tomorrow and do some Netflix binge-watching."

Cal shuffled to the end of the bed and reached for his laptop sitting on his bookshelf next to a Triceratops figurine. "Got a show in mind?"

"How about *Elementary*?"

Cal set the laptop on the bed between them and turned it on. "You could use some brushing up on your detective skills."

Percy nudged Cal's ass with his foot, provoking a chuckle. "I'll figure out which gnome you are."

Cal's fingers paused on the keyboard. "What if I just tell you?"

"Don't you dare. I'll figure it out. I might get creative, but I won't cheat."

Cal stared hard at the screen awaiting his password. "It's only fair to tell you that I know yours."

"I assumed you figured that out at Crystal's the day you rescued me."

"I knew before that."

Percy laughed. "Of course. I still want to figure out yours on my own."

"Better start watching then. Pronto."

Cal put on the show and lay back on the bed, head propped up with a triangular pillow. Percy shuffled down onto his side. It was an awkward angle to watch the screen, but a comfortable one to watch Cal. Who kept shifting during the first episode, hand unconsciously rubbing his hip. Percy tucked his hands between his thighs to stop from reaching out and massaging him.

Midway through the second episode, Cal's lips pinched in pain. He tugged free the pillow under Percy, sending him flopping back against the mattress. "Smooth, Callaghan. If you wanted me on my back, you could've asked."

Cal's laugh turned into a groan.

Percy pushed himself up onto his knees and wriggled his fingers. "Lose the flannel and lie on your stomach."

Cal gave him a weary look, and Percy sent him a scathing one in return.

"What are you worried about, Callaghan? I'm a professional."

He was so not a professional.

Not judging by the way his dick responded to Cal stripping out of his T-shirt, revealing a toned stomach and dusting of chest hair.

Cal rolled off the bed, turning his back to Percy as he stripped his pants. A tight pair of Calvin Klein's made a rather unwelcome hello, and Percy quickly adjusted himself.

He couldn't change his mind without raising suspicion now.

Taking a tumble and feigning a sprain, on the other hand, was not out of the question.

Percy started chanting the anatomical names of the muscles he'd be working on Cal's back. If he thought about each individually, maybe he wouldn't think about the whole package. Cal's whole package. Cal's package . . .

He gritted his teeth and squeezed his thighs extra hard. It was physical attraction. One would have to be a robot not to respond to all that lazily shifting, corded nakedness.

Or a much more professional masseuse.

Thank God the only lights were the dim one in the hall and the one from Cal's computer.

Cal slithered toward the foot of the bed, propped his head on his arms, and slipped his feet under his pillows. His gaze darted curiously toward Percy before he focused extra hard on their show.

Percy cleared his throat. "Where can I find some lotion?"

"Three guesses," Cal quipped. His muscles tensed, and Percy rang out a laugh, playfully swatting the back of Cal's thigh.

"I'll manage with one guess."

Percy reached over Cal to the bedside table. The drawer opened smoothly, revealing a Kindle, a notebook and leaky ink pen, a tube of coconut oil, some water-based lube, and a few condoms.

He set his hand on the inside of Cal's knee, feeling the responding twitch. "Gently part your legs?"

"Are all your demands going to be this . . . visual?" Cal asked.

Percy snorted. "Because you'd just love that."

"About as much as you would."

Unfortunately. "Part a bit more, I need to slip between your thighs."

"Seriously?"

"There is no way I can say that without it sounding lewd."

"How about a simple 'spread your legs?'"

Percy grinned. "Are you trying to fuck with me, Callaghan? Because it sure sounds like it."

Vibrations rumbled the mattress as Cal laughed.

Cal spread his legs and Percy settled himself between them, running his fingers up the backs of Cal's thighs. *Semitendinosus muscle.* He tucked the waistband of Cal's Calvins down to his mid *gluteus maximus* and poured some coconut oil onto his hands.

With the tips of his fingers, Percy grazed Cal's lower back. Tension coiled beneath his fingers, and Percy paused. "Try to relax. I'll be gentle."

Cal released his breath, and Percy stroked his skin, starting at the small of his back, working down to the hips before tenderly exploring all of Cal's back. His fingers dragged up and down the long muscle of his back, over his shoulder blades, down his upper arms.

Sheets muffled Cal's words. "Don't you want to prod my lower back and be done with it?"

"I want you to enjoy the massage. Warm into it before I get to the prodding. Does this feel okay?"

"Okay? This feels amazing."

A cocky grin tugged Percy's lips. "Sorry, I could barely hear you. Did you just say I am amazing?"

"I said your massage is amazing."

"I'll take it."

Percy smiled and continued touching Cal until he gave in to Percy's ministrations, sighing when Percy lavished attention to the knots in his neck and shoulders. He eased down Cal's back, his soft touch becoming firmer, more focused.

He swept his hand over the slick top of Cal's right glute, eliciting a pinched groan.

"I know it hurts," Percy soothed, "but it'll get better after a few strokes. I promise."

"It's tender."

"Do you want me to stop?"

"No, I—I like it."

Percy lathered his hands and Cal's lower back with coconut oil, then pressed his palm to Cal's lower back and lightly pushed from the tailbone toward his heart. Cal groaned, and Percy hesitated before stroking up again. He needed to increase the pressure, but he wanted Cal to be ready for it.

Cal read his lingering fingers and said, "You don't have to go too easy on me. I can take it."

Percy stroked upward, stronger this time before pulling back and sliding up again. He settled into a slow and steady rhythm.

"God, that feels good," Cal murmured, eyes fluttering shut.

Percy worked his thumbs over Cal's glutes. He pressed deep in the lowest part of Cal's back and splayed his fingers toward his sides. Over and over, he rubbed up the center of Cal's back. Every time, Percy increased the pressure.

"Deeper," Cal murmured.

Percy gladly complied.

"Feels better now, doesn't it?" Percy said.

"So, so much."

With one hand, Percy reached for Cal's tube of coconut oil. His hand slipped over the oily length of it. He swiped his thumb over the lid. And again.

Cal voice rumbled under him. "You could do this to me forever."

Percy wanted to. He reached for more oil. "We could continue in this position or move you on your side and change the angle."

He'd barely uncapped the tube, when Cal twisted suddenly. Percy collapsed against Cal's half-naked ass, oil squirting all over his hand and Cal's hip.

Cal shuddered at the oily explosion.

Percy slowly extracted himself off him. "Stay right there, I'll clean us up." he found a washcloth in the adjoining bathroom. After cleaning Cal up, he resumed a lazy massage to warm the muscles down.

When he was done, Percy stretched on the bed next to him.

"I'm going to need you to do that again," Cal said.

Percy smirked. "That good, was it?"

"Better than I ever expected." Cal shifted his head to the side so he was looking at Percy. Cal's eyes looked sated like he was close to falling asleep.

Guess this was time to call it a night. He rolled toward the edge of the bed, but Cal clamped his waist, fingers pressing against Percy's stomach. "Not running off already, are you? This episode just started."

Percy had completely phased *Elementary* out, but he loved the warmth of Cal's hand.

"Just the one."

They propped themselves with pillows at the head of the bed, and Cal draped a throw blanket over their legs. "This is the best episode," Cal said.

"Wait till you get to the other seasons. It'll blow your mind."

A soft smile twitched at Cal's lips. "Can't wait to watch your favorites."

Percy bit his lip and stared toward the computer screen. One episode became two, and then Percy began drifting off. Cal moved on the bed beside him, then another blanket feathered over his waist. Cocooned in comfort, his breathing slowed.

A couple of hours later, Percy woke with a start. Cal was asleep beside him, their noses barely three inches apart. A warm leg pressed between his knees, and fingertips curled around the waist of his boxer briefs.

Percy delicately disentangled himself.

Cal stirred.

"I should go," Percy whispered, not sure how much Cal registered in his sleep.

Cal murmured, "Stay, please?"

Percy stared at Cal's resting face, at his heavy bottom lip. Light breaths breezed over Percy's neck. They sure were not nemeses anymore.

And I can handle that. I really can.

～

PERCY SHIFTED ONTO HIS SIDE, MORNING WOOD STRAINING against his boxers. He'd kicked off his jeans in the night?

He tensed a moment, then laughed softly. He never thought he'd wake up in Cal's bed in barely more than his underwear.

His muffled laugh had Cal facing him. Cal was a sight in the morning. Hair sticking up on one side, dried drool framing his mouth, and eyes exceptionally bright. "Morning, beautiful."

Cal rolled onto his elbow toward his side of the bed. Percy held himself rigid as Cal stretched over him. If he poked his tongue out, he would be licking Cal below his ear, in that tender part of his throat.

Cal drew back holding a twin bell analog clock and poised it for Percy to see. "You mean afternoon."

A warm smile stretched across Cal's face, making his eyes glitter. Percy's breath snagged. This was an entirely unfair temptation at the ungodly hour of one o'clock in the afternoon.

Percy pressed the heels of his hands against Cal's chest and pushed him back. He scooted into a sitting position, blankets pooling over his lap, where it counted. Crisis averted.

He rested his head against the wall, then snapped upright again. "Shit. I'm meant to be showing off Aunt Abby's at one."

He scrambled out of bed and struggled into his tight jeans. Glancing over his shoulder, he caught Cal lying on his side, arm propping his chin, watching him. The look wasn't quite as mathematical as Percy was used to, and his fingers fumbled with the button. Twice.

"You're quite the pro at putting on pants, Perseus." Cal's tone tried to be flat, but Percy heard it catch with humor.

"I'm a pro at taking them off too." Percy winked. "Now, get up. You're checking this guy out with me."

All long limbs, Cal lazily rolled out of bed. "I don't need to be there to know I won't like him."

Percy found his shoes and tugged them on. "By the way, I have another house viewing later. The nicest I've seen, so far. Only a short drive from here too. If you know . . ."

Cal whipped his head in Percy's direction. "If you know, what?"

"If I got more massage clients this side of town." Percy swallowed a laugh at the blatant hope creasing the edges of Cal's eyes. "Get dressed and help me lay on the charm."

"Like you need my help with that."

~

TURNED OUT PERCY HURRIED HOME FOR NO REASON. THE GUY was a no-show. A quick email check revealed that he'd already found a place.

Frustrated, Percy sent Cal away when he came knocking, telling him he needed time alone to search for more options. He regretted it the moment Cal nodded and turned his back.

Regretted it more when it was just him in the empty heart of his aunt's house.

Every creak of the floorboards and groan of door hinges amplified as he shuffled into his room.

He busied himself creating more advertisements, then checked out some Chatvica posts. Don'tDeludeYourself had beat him to a bunch of posts with his no-bullshit approach. He logged into the Sherlock Gnomes forum, happy to see Gnomber9 online.

Gnomad: What are you up to today?

Gnomber9: Helping the family decide where to put Mom's baby when he arrives. What about you?

Gnomad: Kicking myself.

Gnomber9: Fun pastime, that.

Gnomad: *snort*

Gnomber9: Why are you kicking yourself?

Gnomad: I turned away Cal.

Gnomber9: And that's bad because . . . ?

Gnomad: We have this thing where I look at him and he distracts me from thinking too much about Aunt Abby.

Gnomber9: Why don't you call him?

Gnomad: Because that would be sensible, El. No, I

think I'm going to bake some muffins for Sherlock Gnomes.

Gnomber9: Up to you, Percy.

After chatting with Ellie, Percy made good on his idea to bake muffins. Opening Aunt Abby's baking book had a hundred memories slamming into him, and he painfully followed her scrawling instructions.

He turned on the oven and greased two scratched-up muffin trays. He stared at the ingredients spread out before him, reread Abby's recipe, then took a five-minute break at the bay window.

He pulled out his phone and brought up Cal's picture, using it like Cal had suggested to siphon off some of the sadness. He liked the picture, but the life-size Cal was infinitely more distracting.

He stashed the trays in the bottom cupboard next to the oven and dialed his number.

"Callaghan," he said, the moment Cal picked up. "I'm short a couple of muffin trays. You got some you could bring me?"

Cal was quiet a moment, then he cleared his throat. "Need rescuing again, Perseus?"

"I could've sworn it was your favorite pastime."

When Cal arrived at the door, Percy grabbed a fistful of his shirt and yanked him into the kitchen. He took the trays Cal was carrying and winked at him. "Just what was missing."

Cal peered at Abby's recipe book. "Are you making carrot muffins?"

"Yes."

"Will they have cream cheese icing?"

They would now. "Uh huh."

Percy spooned batter into the trays, popped them into the oven, and turned back to Cal who was leafing through Abby's baking book.

"The recipe for her famous eggnog," Cal said, side eying him.

"Also found in the dictionary under Fun."

"The one word I don't know the meaning of."

"Ought to change that, some time."

They grinned at each other. Then commenced An Awkward Moment, where Percy didn't know what to do with himself. He looked at his striped socks and then at the lit oven.

Cal backed toward the archway. "I, ah, I should go."

Percy swallowed a lump the size of Mr. Feist's fist. "Please stay?"

Cal straightened. He cooled off his surprise, whipping out that dry cadence of his. "One condition."

"What's that?"

"I get to lick the bowl."

"You can lick anything you want, Callaghan." Percy picked up the bowl and winked. "There's the spoon too."

F riend
      noun / friend

DEFINITION OF FRIEND
   : having affection for and attachment to another
   : what Perseus is to Callaghan; and Callaghan is to Perseus—if they ever let themselves admit it
   : see also environmentalist

EXAMPLE OF FRIEND IN A SENTENCE
   "So, are you two friends?"
   Cal looked at Percy. "How about you take this one?"

Chapter Nine

Crystal was his last massage client of the day.

He set up his table in her living room, then prepared them both a glass of water while Crystal got comfortable.

Two minutes later he returned. Crystal lay on the table, back free, her phone on speaker resting on the floor. "Social butterflies are my Leos next week, fluttering from one gathering to the next. And I finally get to meet my son's boyfriend."

"You've met Jamie before!" Theo said. "There were a crazy number of inappropriate questions involved. And cumin pods."

"I met him as your friend last time. This time will be different. Oh, he'll have more charming to do, even more questions to answer."

Theo groaned. "Mom, I'm begging you."

"I can't wait to see you all."

Percy cleared his throat, holding up two options for Crystal to choose from: lavender or vanilla. She lifted her head and pointed to vanilla, then dived right back into her conversation.

Percy shook his head and started on the problem areas of Crystal's shoulders.

"What is the plan for the Fourth?" Theo asked.

Percy answered that one. It gave him the opportunity to tell Theo he would be there after all. Tradition, and all that. Nothing to do with his new venture into environmentalism. "The Glovers are hosting the barbecue this year."

"Percy? What on earth are you doing with my mother?"

"He's rubbing me down. He's very good at it. Massage is such a great way to relax. But no doubt you're getting enough of that with Jamie."

"If this is heading where I think it is, I'm hanging up now."

"Hush. Physical intimacy is a beautiful thing, and—" Theo started whistling, and Percy swallowed a laugh as Crystal lectured her son on the importance of giving and receiving. At some point, Theo shrieked, and the line died.

Crystal sighed. "I didn't think I had raised a prude."

Percy moved onto Crystal's other shoulder. "I'm sure it's less about being prudish and more about being horrified at hearing such details from his mother. How're your shoulders feeling?"

"You may have a point there. My shoulders are probably good enough that I should say yes to Champey. She asked me to play tennis with her, and I've put off answering because it's been years since I've played. I don't even own a racket anymore."

Percy slowed his touch. Champey used to play every week with his aunt. They'd always come back to Abby's place where Percy would hustle up afternoon tea.

"Tell me how it's going with your house?" Crystal asked. "Mr. Feist thought you were selling, but he must be mistaken. You are far too close to the cul-de-sac to run away."

Percy's tongue clucked against the roof of his mouth. He should tell her he was leaving; should tell her how hard it was to see Abby in every one of the neighbors and not have her here.

Or he could change the subject. "Tell me about Virgos?"

"Do you want to know all about Virgo, Percy? Or just Cal?"

Percy groaned. "I'm that obvious?"

"I was born in 1969."

"I want to be a little more . . . neighborly. You know, lessen the eye narrowing."

"Oh, honey. That boy has had you doing verbal cartwheels since you first got here. I think you and I and the entire cul-de-sac know that you want to be a little more than neighborly."

She wasn't wrong. The first day he'd met Cal, he hadn't fallen off his bike because he was clumsy. He'd fallen off because of the sharp double-take he'd done to see the shirtless guy mowing the lawns across the street, sweat sheening over his cut torso, looking like something out of his nightly fantasies. He'd been punched in the gut with instant physical attraction. And when said fantasy helped him up, those blue eyes made Percy weak at the knees.

Hating Cal had become a necessity to stop Percy from falling for a straight guy.

And now look at him.

"Well, in any case," Crystal continued, "no other sign knows what Scorpio needs better than Virgo. And no other sign can rock Virgo's emotions better than Scorpio. Scorpio loves how Virgo analyzes every nuance of things—every nuance of them. You both deeply respect each other's love of communication and could easily spend all your time together talking. There is a sense of attachment you both have from the moment you met, although any relationship is a slow moving one. Virgo's rational view on romance fascinates Scorpio, and often Scorpio has to make the first move when moving a relationship up to the next level."

"Slow moving?" Percy asked.

"You know the story of the tortoise and the hare? That tortoise is Virgo."

"All about being slow?"

"All about winning the race."

Percy finished massaging Crystal's shoulders and lifted the towel up her back.

"We are just hanging out." He wasn't about to get emotionally close and end up heartbroken. No way. Been there, done that. "That's all it can be."

Crystal shook with laughter. "If you want to be stubborn about it, Percy."

He did. He had to.

∞

"Please? Pretty Please?" Hannah bounced on the balls of her feet, tugging at the hem of Cal's T-shirt.

After finishing an early dinner at the Glovers', Percy slouched on the recliner in the living room, strangely satisfied as he watched Hannah demanding Cal's attention. He understood the desire to tug at his clothes and ask him to play.

Cal eyed the free seat next to Percy longingly, but every attempt to get there was thwarted by sisterly shenanigans.

Percy thought about helping him out, but . . . free entertainment?

"Your tent can't fit me," Cal said.

"But it fits Ellie and me."

"Then Ellie can tent with you."

Hannah threw her head back face pinching into a laughing whine. "But you have to."

Ellie, doodling in a notebook, reached over and tapped his knee with the spine. Percy pivoted toward her and winked. "Yeah?"

"Maybe Cal can borrow your aunt's tent?"

Hannah shimmied up Cal's thigh, gripping his neck like her life depended on him saying yes. Cal hooked an arm under her and helped her up.

A tender flare of memories overcame him. The time his aunt had tried to persuade him to go camping with her, and him never relenting. Not like Cal seemed about to do.

He pasted on a smile. "Looks like he's going to need something to sleep in." He caught Cal's amused eye. "Give in to her demands, Callaghan. You've a bad back to think about."

Cal set her down again and whispered loudly in her ear. "Convince Perseus to join us, and I'll tent with you in the back yard."

"What?" Percy shook his head vigorously. "I like a bed thank you very much."

Hannah jumped on him, plaits flicking him under his chin. "Pretty please, Percy?"

"Say that ten times real fast."

He'd meant it as a joke, but Hannah started saying it over and over, face lighting up.

What else was he supposed to say? He couldn't let her down. Cal smirked knowingly as he finally flopped into the free seat.

"This makes you all far too happy," Percy grumbled.

Ellie laughed. "We should tent in your yard, Percy. It's bigger." She used her marker to doodle on the base of her jeans. "Hannah and I can share one tent, and you and Cal the other."

All Glover eyes were hot on him, and he sweated under the hope leaking out of them. Percy felt Cal reading how tense he was, how his heart rate spiked.

He scratched the arm of the couch, foot jiggling.

Hannah clapped her hands on his face and forced it into a nod. "There's one problem with that," he said with a rather high-pitched laugh. "My yard is haunted."

Hannah threw herself off his lap. "Cal! Tell Percy what we do to ghosts."

She ran out of the room, yelling for their napping mom to find her flashlight.

Cal leaned forward and slid his hand over Percy's, fingertips slipping between his fingers and lingering for three heart-stopping seconds. "We like to kick their butt. We'll be your best ghost-busting team ever."

∼

IN THE WARM NIGHT AIR OF AUNT ABBY'S BACKYARD, surrounded by a chorus of cicadas, Percy and Cal pitched their tents.

Actually, Cal pitched the tent while Percy hauled Hannah's blankets and toys that she wanted with her for the night.

One step onto the back porch and her green plastic flashlight stopped working. "That's what happens if you keep turning it off and on," Ellie said.

Hannah's bottom lip wobbled. "But we need it against the ghosts."

Percy steered her into her tent and sat her on the sleeping bag next to her sister and teddies. "Play with your things. I'll fix this."

He couldn't fix it.

Changing the batteries did nothing. Hunting for another flashlight, he scavenged through the boxes of his aunt's belongings in the attic. Nothing there, either.

A bit of a pickle, then. He traipsed back to the yard, banging the end of Hannah's flashlight against his thigh as if it might miraculously turn on. He passed Ellie and Hannah's tent next to the washing line and made for the back fence. Against the wrought-iron picnic table, he leaned and watched Cal under a canopy of magnolias hammering a stake into the soft ground.

"Hannah's flashlight is busted."

"They're a dime a dozen at Target."

Percy tucked the flashlight under his arm and felt for his keys. "I'll be back in twenty then."

Cal lifted a brow. "I didn't mean for you to get another one."

"It's that or tears. I don't do tears."

"Things might be easier if you did."

Percy paused, clenching the plastic flashlight. Cal set down the hammer and crossed to him. "If you insist on making the trip to Target, bring back some snacks." He fished out a debit card from his pocket. "Use this, the PIN is—"

Percy clamped a hand over Cal's mouth, and a surprised burst of breath warmed his palm. "You're going to tell me your PIN?"

Cal hummed, and the tickle shot right to Percy's groin. Whip-fast, he pulled back his hand.

"I'll tell you if you let me."

"Giving your PIN away is careless."

Cal slanted an exasperated look at him. "When am I ever careless?" He proceeded to tell him his PIN.

"I could take off with all your money now."

"I wouldn't care about the money."

Percy clutched the card so hard the sides cut into his skin. He sounded breathless when he spoke. "What do you want to eat?"

"Anything you like."

∼

Percy brought back chocolate, Pringles, and roasted nuts.

He barely ate any of it though, preferring to suck on his Mentos while watching the Glovers interact. When it was dark, Cal led Hannah around the garden waving their flashlights, singing, and stamping their feet. Hannah laughed and laughed, even when it was clear she was forcing it.

Twenty minutes later, she'd fallen asleep on Percy's lap. He cradled her into her tent and whispered to Ellie as she slipped into her sleeping bag and felt for her headphones. "It's cool of you camping out for your sister. Is there anything you want to do tomorrow?"

Wishing he'd never asked, Percy trekked across the yard into the second tent. The flap was open and he ducked inside with a groan. "Soccer. She wants me to kick the ball around with her."

Cal tied his flashlight to the tent ceiling. Weak light showcased their blankets and pillows.

"Why would she want that?" Cal asked. "She was there the last time."

Percy threw his hands up and accidentally hit the top of the tent, dislodging Cal's flashlight. Their tent drowned in darkness. "Exactly."

Laughter and blankets shifted around his feet as Cal patted the floor for the flashlight. Percy slipped out of his flip-flops and crouched to help him. Cal was a featureless form on all fours, blacker than the rest of the tent. Soft blankets Percy'd taken from his bed contrasted with patches of cool nylon flooring.

He glimpsed a flashlight-shaped outline and reached to snag it. At the same time, Cal lurched toward something at Percy's side. Cal's face slapped against Percy's groin, right on the seam of his briefs. Cal made a surprised sound that leaked warmth through Percy's cotton khakis.

Percy's traitorous cock swelled.

With a tight laugh, he palmed Cal's head and pushed him—though Cal was already retreating.

"I prefer to bump uglies in the light, Callaghan."

"There'll be no bumping uglies between us, Perseus."

"I found the flashlight. What were you lunging for?" Percy switched it on and Cal handed over a Mentos roll. "Oh." They must have fallen out of his pocket.

Not wanting to draw attention to the rather visible bulge in his shorts, Percy tossed them onto his pillow and chased after them, drawing the blankets over himself. The light swung wildly with his movements. "Goodnight!"

Cal pinched the flashlight from him and laid it between their pillows. It shed minimal light at the low angle, and Cal twisted it so the beam fell more to his side. "Will the light bother you?"

There was barely any at all. "It's fine."

With their bodies less than a foot apart and Percy's cock

uncomfortably tight in his briefs, it was hard to concentrate on anything but what ifs.

What if he threw caution to the wind and bruised Cal's stupidly beautiful lips with kisses? What if Cal returned them, hands shaking with need as he ripped off Percy's clothes. What if Cal tossed his blanket aside to reveal a hard, throbbing cock begging for attention? What if he said this wasn't just curiosity for him?

Percy squeezed himself under the covers. He had to stop these thoughts from spiraling somewhere unhealthy. He shut his eyes and silently named all the muscles of the body, tossing and turning as his cock refused to calm down.

Frustrated, he rolled onto his side and glared at Cal. This was all his fault. And look at him, just lying there on his side, reading a book!

Percy snapped Cal's book closed, and then regretted it. The thick book of paleontology looked like a textbook. Was Cal warming up to the idea of continuing his studies?

A softer tendril wrapped around his chest, gently squeezing. The blood drained from his cock and traveled where it was better used: his head.

He looked from the cover to Cal's waiting expression.

"Tell me about your master's thesis," Percy said.

Cal reopened his book. He must have been squinting to read under the shitty light. "Why?"

"I can't sleep."

"You're a right charmer, you are. My thesis looks at dinosaur coloration. I chose it because I'm curious to know if it played a role in their mating rituals."

Percy scrambled into a sitting position, fluffed his pillow into his lap, and leaned his elbows on it. "Rituals? Tell me everything."

Cal's laugh hit Percy's forearm in boisterous bursts. His eyes swept up to meet his, and he began describing scrape marks left in sandstone and how the irregular groupings might be clues ancient theropods left behind that supported one possible scientific theory of dinosaur foreplay.

". . . might be a similar ritual to modern birds. There's still so much to discover, but some ancient scratch marks suggest they might have been an energetic bunch that competed for a mate."

"They didn't jump each other?"

"It's possible they danced. Courted. Ruffled their feathers."

"Do you know a lot about this?"

Cal hesitated, looking down at his book with a frown and then up again, catching Percy's eyes. "Maybe I do."

"Dinosaurs procreated for millions of years, they were obviously doing something right."

"I like to think so." Cal held Percy's gaze until Percy was sufficiently robbed of breath.

Percy grabbed the flashlight and got to his feet.

"What are you doing?" Cal asked.

Percy tied the light to the poles directly over Cal's side of the tent, casting better light over him and his book. "Keep reading. All night if you have to."

&

Percy spat out a stray leaf and picked up the dirt-caked ball that had slammed into his mouth. "Which of you kicked it?"

Ellie pointed at Cal and backed away.

Cal shook his head. "Really, El? After all I've done for you?"

Ellie's bright, bubbly giggle was almost worth this degradation. Almost. He lined up his body toward Cal and kicked the ball out of his hands—

Five feet to the left of Cal's flushed face.

Cal jogged to the ball, scooped it up, and shoved it into Ellie's hand. "Quick, to the hatchback."

Percy chased them back to the car. Catching up to Cal, he

whisked him around and they were suddenly eye-to-eye. Gravity plastered Percy against Cal's chest. Percy groaned into the crook of Cal's neck. "Your neck is disturbingly tasty."

Cal's chest flexed beneath his fingertips as he shifted and set him upright. "It's my bodywash."

Thanks for yet another shower-related image, Cal.

"You missed your opportunity to say that it is just you. No wonder you're still single."

"Do those lines work for you, Perseus? Do you like a man who's too big for his britches?"

"Well . . ."

Cal snorted and opened the passenger door for Percy. "I prefer a more modest approach around the one I like. Now, shall we eat out? My treat."

At Ellie's request, they went to a pop-up tapas bar. The makeshift restaurant utilized an old courtyard at the back of a co-working space.

It was packed, but Ellie scored them a corner table under a canopy of wisteria. Pockets of evening light filtered through the purple blossoms. Percy leaned back in his seat and watched the way it softly shifted over them.

Cal seemed mesmerized with the light playing over his side of the table as well.

Ellie didn't stop talking throughout the entire meal about food fusions and how they might want to try a tapas night at home. "Maybe when Dad gets back."

She went quiet and tipped her head until her hair curtained her face. Cal shuffled over on their shared bench and hooked an arm around her neck. "We'll see him on Saturday."

She shrugged. "Yeah."

Percy folded a napkin into a swan—the only origami he knew —and gave it to her. "I still have vanilla ice cream in the freezer if you want to hang out with me when we get back."

That earned him a peek from behind her hair. "Promised Mom to help set up the crib when I got home."

"Where will the baby sleep?"

"With Mom at first, then he will move in with Hannah. But if Cal moved out again, we'd each get our own room."

Cal ruffled her hair. "You don't care that Hannah and the baby will have to share, you just want the basement."

"It's not the basement I want, it's the en-suite bathroom." She batted her eyelashes at Cal. "Pretty please?" At least her mood had picked up.

"I need to be close to help out when the baby comes."

"So live with Percy. He has space, and it's just over the road."

Percy straightened.

Cal dropped his arm from Ellie, and pulled his wallet from his pocket. "I would if that were an option, but Percy's leaving." He tucked cash into the bill folder and stood. "So that's that."

"Besides, we'd be at each other's throats within the first hour," Percy added, standing up too until he and Cal were in familiar territory. Literally and figuratively in each other's faces.

Cal bared his teeth into a smile and stared squarely into Percy's eyes. "I'm sure we'd slay each other with words."

Percy cupped his hands around his mouth and stage-whispered, "Something you haven't managed yet."

"Trust me, I'm working on it."

Ellie rolled her eyes as she made toward the exit. "Seriously, get a room."

Percy tossed out a laugh as he followed her. "Not one of mine."

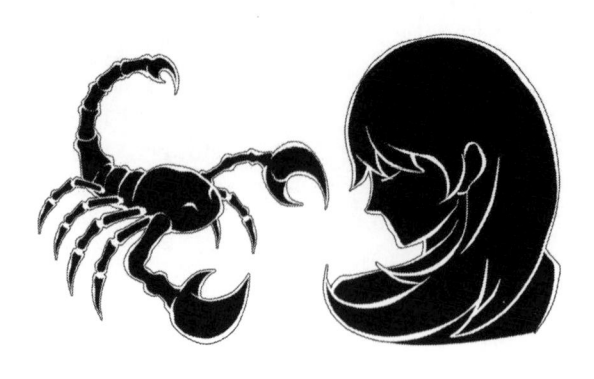

Fun
noun / fun

DEFINITION OF FUN
: drinking eggnog in excess
: what Callaghan doesn't know the meaning of according to Perseus

EXAMPLE OF FUN IN A SENTENCE
"Come on, I'm just having a little fun."
"Three glasses, Perseus?"
"Fine, a lot of fun."

Chapter Ten

Percy's next house viewing was early Friday evening after he'd finished giving Dorothy a massage. He and Cal had driven into the city together, so Cal had to check out the place with him. It was on their way home, after all.

"Looks like a bachelor pad," Cal said under his breath after the lovely introduction by a barely dressed Chad. Chad showed them the great room, then kicked back on his leather couch the minute his phone rang. With a casual flick of his wrist, he gestured Percy and Cal to look around.

Percy tugged Cal toward the master bedroom for a peek. Floor-to-ceiling blackout curtains, plaid bedding, sleek floating shelves, and not a book in sight. Clean and tidy, but too gray and cold.

They should probably cut their wonderful guided tour short and hit the road again.

"What is that?" Cal tugged leather straps that hung from steel rods in the ceiling.

Or maybe they could stay a little longer. "That's a swing."

"This is hardly a child's room."

Percy clasped Cal's shoulders and whispered in his ear, "Not that kind of swing."

Cal's voice came out scratchy. "How do you know?"

"Maybe because I'm not a virgin?"

Cal leaned out of his touch toward the swing. "Neither am I—and I still wouldn't have any clue how to strap that thing . . . on? Around? In?"

"Wonderful. Now those images are stuck in my mind."

"Mine too. That's an ugly sight." Cal left the room and Percy trailed behind, amused.

"You like your sex vanilla, Callaghan?"

"Well . . . French vanilla."

Percy stopped, staring a hole through the back of Cal's head. Had he heard him right?

Cal didn't seem to realize the grenade he'd tossed. He poked his head into the next room and shook his head. "Good lord, a heart-shaped bath? That might take some getting used to."

French vanilla?

Cal twisted around, concern creasing his brow. "Are you okay?"

Percy's whole stomach somersaulted. "Peachy."

Cal stepped up to him, hooked a finger under his chin, and tilted his head. "You look hot."

"Hot?"

"Feverish."

Percy licked his lips. "I'm fine, I just . . ." He bowed his head, focusing on drawing out his Mentos. He pinched at a candy but it didn't budge out of the packet. "I just realized . . . I don't think this place is for me." The last part poured out.

Cal lifted an eyebrow, staring at him quizzically. "I knew before we stepped in here this was not the place for you. At what point did you realize?"

Stupid candy, pop free! Pop—

A strawberry Mentos hit him on the nose. He caught it as it

ricocheted off his chest. "I guess I should have realized it sooner."

"Jesus, Perseus, it was glaringly obvious. Couldn't you tell from looking at the details online?" Cal turned his hand palm up for a candy. Percy mustered a laugh as he gave him the strawberry.

"The first impressions looked different."

"How many pictures were there?"

"A lot?"

Cal shook his head. "And you pride yourself on knowing things before anyone else, Mr. Detective. You should have known."

Maybe he wasn't so intuitive after all?

Or maybe deep down he suspected it but didn't want to admit it? Because that . . . complicated things.

Cal continued, "It would have been easier to call and ask more questions."

"I'm not good at calling. I'm afraid of saying the wrong thing and embarrassing myself."

"Better a bit of embarrassment than getting your hopes up."

Percy withdrew a candy for himself with practiced ease. "Don't worry, I'm good with disappointment." He sucked on the candy. "Besides, I'm not disappointed we came here today."

A gentle lift of his eyebrow. "Why not?"

Percy winked at Cal, jerking a thumb toward the bedroom. Cal's pink cheeks said he was thinking of the swing. "I don't know. I suppose some of the tour has been enlightening?"

"Know what? I think it's time we head home."

"Yeah, I want to whisk Ellie away after dinner. Then I've got online research to do."

"If you're house hunting, you need to look for a warmer place full of color and sunshine. Something without sex-swing bolts in the ceiling."

"Oh, I wouldn't turn down a warm, sunshine-filled place if it happened to have steel in the walls. I don't mind a few accents."

Cal's eyes sparked as he shook his head, lips twitching into a grin. "Let's get a move on."

~

After dinner at the Glovers', Percy dragged a semi-protesting Ellie to the local ice cream parlor: black-and-white tiled floors, sparkly red booths, and mint-green walls studded with old-timer advertisements. Percy breathed in the sweet chill in the air as he steered Ellie into a corner booth.

"Sit here, I've got this."

She looked skeptically at him as she sidled onto the bench, and Percy held himself back from an embarrassed laugh. "Um, okay," she said. "Thanks?"

Percy ordered at the counter with instructions to wait a couple of minutes before bringing their ice creams over. He returned to their booth. "It'll be ready soon."

He sat across from her, resting his forearms on the table. Percy thumbed a tear in the menu, making a soft clicking sound.

"You're fidgeting," Ellie said. "What's up?"

He dropped the menu and splayed his hand against it as though it could stop his procrastination. His nerves lurched. "Are you . . ."

"Am I . . . ?"

If he did this, there was no fooling himself he'd made a mistake or he'd misunderstood. "Are you looking forward to seeing your dad tomorrow?"

She tilted her head in a remarkably similar way to her brother, as though she could read the bullshit sweating out of him. "Yes," she said. "You sure that's what you wanted to ask?"

He raked a hand through his hair and looked at her squarely. "No, it wasn't."

"Try again, Percy."

She definitely took after her brother. "Do you play soccer?"

She squinted at him. "Yeah?"

"What number are you?"

"Why?"

"I'm piecing together some loose ends."

"I like playing number 9."

Shoulders sinking, he picked up the menu again. "Oh. Nine? Really?"

Ellie leaned over the table. "Yeah, it was Cal's number when he played. I wear his old shirt all the time for good luck. Nine's my favorite number."

His pent-up anxiety melted in a giddy whoosh as he sank against the plastic cushioned seat.

"You're acting strange tonight. Like a puppy from the pound who can't believe his luck."

"I couldn't have said it any better myself."

"I know you've figured out who Gnomber9 is."

Percy slid the menu to the side of the table. "I first thought it was you."

"That's because it was me, until it wasn't. I saw you watching me after work and, to be on the safe side, I made Cal swap gnome names with me."

"Aren't you a sneakster?"

"Aren't you an eavesdropper?"

"Yes, and on that note, you're going to have to tell me more about this Matt."

"Matt?" Ellie said, too innocently.

"The cute Asian-American that flirted with you after work."

It was her turn to fiddle with the menu, cheeks blushing. "What do you want to know?"

"Have you told him you like him yet?"

"Ha! No."

"Are you going to?"

"I haven't decided yet. That's a lie. I decided if he leans in halfway, I'll lean in the rest."

"Have I told you how awesome you are, El?"

She gnawed her bottom lip. "Cal thought the swap was a grand opportunity to fool you. For like a whole day. He's been grumpy about it since. I think he wants you to know."

Percy settled back against the bench. Probably didn't help that he'd been telling Cal not to tell him.

Ellie's eyes widened as the server set down two large sundaes in front of them.

"S'mores sundae," Percy said, digging his spoon into the flambéed marshmallows. "Homemade hot fudge, graham crackers, and stuffed with extra chocolate."

"This is ice cream."

"Right? Cal has no taste."

"Yeah," she said with a smirk, "look who he chooses to spend all his time with."

Percy pointed the spoon at her. "Hey, you spend time with all this too."

"I do enjoy our afternoons playing soccer."

"We'll keep doing them, okay? Even if it makes me want to throw an actual hissy-fit."

She laughed. "You'll get better. Jenny was—actually not quite as pathetic—but she improved too."

"Jenny?" he spluttered, before collecting himself.

Mischief glinted in Ellie's eyes. "Yeah, Jenny. She's popping around next week when she gets back from Spain. She loves Cal."

Percy clutched his spoon, feeling its edges stamp into his skin. "What are you up to?"

"Nothing. I'm saying Cal and Jenny will stay friends forever. I like her." She shoveled a spoonful of fudge and ice cream into her mouth. "Might like you more right now, though."

Appetite waning, Percy batted the marshmallow into the

fudge with his spoon. "If your brother asks, can you tell him I bought you vanilla ice cream?"

"How about telling him the truth?"

Yeah, because he loved making himself vulnerable and giving up control. He should call Cal and bare his whole heart. "It's just . . . I want to have a little fun first."

"Vanilla is fun?"

"More than I ever could have thought."

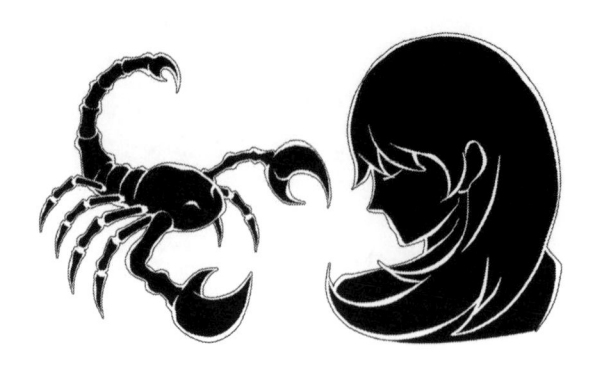

P eachy
   adjective / peach . y

DEFINITION OF **PEACHY**
   : not fine at all
   : a bad situation that seems impossible to get out of or solve
   : bordering on calamitous
   : God help him

EXAMPLE OF **PEACHY** IN A SENTENCE
   "It's insanely hot in here," Cal said.
   "That tends to happen when I walk in the room."
   Cal gripped his T-shirt and started pulling it over his head.
   Peachy. Now one of them was half-naked and the other half-mast.

Chapter Eleven

Gnomad: I enjoyed our moment together earlier.

Gnomber9: The trip to the ice cream parlor?

Gnomad: The ice cream was also good.

It was strange hearing Cal's voice as he read the replies. Strange yet fitting. He'd gone over every chat they'd had since the beginning, and it was embarrassing that he hadn't heard Cal sooner.

Gnomad: I have a question.

Gnomber9: When don't you?

Gnomad: You said it's fun hanging out with me.

Gnomber9: This is true.

Percy bit a small smile.

Gnomad: You also said it's fun with Jenny. That she'll be around forever.

Gnomber9: She probably will. What are you getting at, Percy?

Gnomad: Do you think I'll be around as long?

It took Gnomber9 a long time to answer, and Percy rubbed his fingers over the sheets as he waited.

Gnomber9: I don't know I can answer that but . . . color me all shades of curious.

Curious.
Just the "yes" or "I hope so" he'd wanted to hear!

Gnomad: Too much fun to keep up with, am I?

Gnomber9: Probably.

Gnomad: You all packed to see your dad?

Gnomber9: Can I ever ask you questions?

Gnomad: What kind of questions?

Gnomber9: BFF ones, what else?

Gnomad: Color me afraid.

Gnomber9: Why, think I'm going to ask you to tell me something embarrassing?

No, just that he'd answer embarrassingly honestly.

Gnomad: It took me until I was twelve to tie my shoelaces.

Gnomber9: That is late.

Gnomad: I still wish more shoes had Velcro straps.

Gnomber9 threw two more lighthearted questions at him and Percy answered. He was just getting into it when he saw it was past midnight. Cal had to leave the house at 5:30 in the morning.

Gnomad: Three last things: Get some sleep. Have a good trip. You think your mom would like me to hang out with her and Hannah while you're gone?

∽

THE NEXT DAY, CAL AND ELLIE FLEW OFF TO SEE THEIR DAD too early for Percy to wish them off. He felt off, and he was unreasonably anxious to check if Gnomber9 was online.

After three massage sessions, Percy ate a lonely dinner at the Glovers' with Marg and Hannah.

Noting the exhaustion in Marg's posture, he offered to take Hannah to bed.

"Are you sure?" Marg asked, holding up her head, elbows braced on the table.

"How hard can it be?"

A soft laugh. "Famous last words."

Turned out Marg was right. Getting Hannah into bed wasn't challenging so much as getting her to stay there.

Twice he'd almost made it to the living room when she scampered out of bed and giggled after him. It was cute. At first. After the third time, it tired him out.

He was running out of dinosaurs to mimic while carting her back to her room.

"Time to stay in bed now, Hannah."

She pulled up her blankets over her nose and blinked puppy-dog eyes at him. "What about my night time story?" Her muffled words became clearer when she sat up. "Cal always reads to me before bed."

"Well, I'm not to be outdone by Cal, so . . ." Percy fingered through the stack of books on her bookshelf, smirking at *Dinosaurs Say Goodnight*. "Of course," he murmured, plucking that one.

Hannah attentively listened as he read the story, and promised she would go to sleep. Little liar. The moment he sat on the couch next to Marg, Hannah peeked around the doorframe. He gave a tired laugh as he once more hefted Hannah to her room. A Percytaur this time. The quickest, smartest, best-looking dinosaur of all.

How did Marg and Cal do this every night? "Why won't you stay in here, huh?" he asked, tucking the sheets around her again.

Hannah twisted onto her side and pouted. "Cal always says goodnight."

"Should we call him?" Percy's belly rolled as he suggested it.

"Yes!"

Percy dialed Cal's number, sinking to his knees next to the bed. On loudspeaker, it rang and rang, but Cal didn't pick up. Percy pouted with Hannah. "I guess he's busy talking to your daddy."

"I miss him."

"I hope your dad decides to come back."

"I miss Cal."

Percy's chest tightened. He stroked her bangs out of her eyes. "Want to know a secret? So do I."

"Why is that a secret?"

"Because I don't want Cal to know."

"Why not?"

"His smug smile for one."

"What's wrong with his smile?"

"It does bad things to my knees. If he flashes that smile too much, I might fall."

"Falling over makes me cry."

"Yes, me too. Especially when no one's around to help you up off the ground again."

"You must have bad knees if you can't push yourself up."

Percy snorted. "I do."

"You need stronger ones. Dinosaur strong. Ask Cal how. He knows everything about dinosaurs."

Behind him, air stirred. Marg stood in the doorway clasping a glass of water and a fat book. She smiled, her eyes glittering with kindness. She had heard.

Thank his lucky stars the dim room hid the heat slamming into his cheeks. "Seriously, you're a wonder-mom to put this Rascalinosaur to bed."

Hannah giggled.

"On nights like these, this particular favorite never fails to put her to sleep." Marg drummed her fingers over the book's hard cover and strolled into the room. "How about I take over?"

He gave a humored laugh. "Please. If I don't put her to sleep, I'll never hear the end of it."

"Cal would understand."

"I, however, would not." He beckoned for the book. "Get back to the couch. We can pop on a mystery as soon as I'm done."

"Okay, Percy. I'll be there when you're ready." She left the room, and Percy looked down at the book she had slipped into his hands.

An illustrated dictionary. "Should've guessed."

Hannah fell asleep two pages into the C section. Percy snuck to the living room and watched an episode of *Sherlock* with Marg.

She twisted and turned on the couch beside him, unable to find a comfortable position.

"Looks like you need a massage," Percy said. "I'll grab the mat from Cal's room."

"Would you do me a favor and take Cal's laundry with you?"

Percy picked up the pile of folded clothes and brought them downstairs. Half the clothes were folded T-shirts, and almost all of them were nerdy.

He smiled and stepped into the turquoise room, breathing in Cal's moisturizing scent. He jumped when his phone buzzed. Setting the laundry on the corner of Cal's bed, he pulled the phone out of his pocket. Callaghan.

A hot bubble of laughter formed in his chest and he had to sit to answer. "How many dinosaur T-shirts do you own?"

Cal hummed. "I take it you've been in my room."

"In your room. As in, right this second."

"What are you doing in there?"

"Deciding how much I should like you."

"In that case, don't look too deep in the closet."

Percy flung open that closet and dug through Cal's hanging shirts expecting to see a filthy stash of porn. Nothing. "You're right. I don't like the sight at all."

A dry laugh. "Why did you call?"

"Hannah wanted to say goodnight."

"Of course." Did he sound disappointed? "I would've called her, but things here . . ." Cal's low voice was gravelly and raw.

Percy frowned. *Are you holding up okay?* "I thought maybe I should crash at your place. You know, in case Hannah wakes up during the night. I could let your mom sleep in and take Hannah to day care in the morning."

"My home is your home."

Percy drenched his voice with cheekiness. "And your bed will be my bed."

A short, sharp laugh. "Your lifelong dream come true."

"Oh, Callaghan. How did you know?"

The tension that had reared earlier dissipated. "How was it getting Hannah to sleep?"

"Piece of cake. She went out like a light. Easy peasy."

"That hard, was it?"

Percy huffed, pinching the phone between his shoulder and ear as he put Cal's clean clothes in the closet. "We read from calamity to cavalry in the dictionary."

"Started with cal words, did you? Should I read into that?"

"Uh huh, of course. Hannah had nothing to do with that decision." She really hadn't. With a nervous laugh, he knelt at the side of the bed and drew out the gym mat from underneath. "As lovely as it has been chatting, I've got to get back to your mom. Talk tomorrow!"

"Can't wait," Cal signed off with exaggerated dryness.

Percy lugged the mat to Marg. *Can't wait either, Cal.*

~

Gnomad: How are you holding up?

Gnomber9: Grandad is far more understanding than I expected. Always smiling for us grandkids and telling us to give Dad time. But I'm afraid he's not going to change his mind and come home.

Gnomad: I'm so sorry. Is there anything I can do for you?

Gnomber9: Talking helps.

Gnomad: Tell me more about your grandad. I met him once. I remember him always giving inspirational advice.

Gnomber9: He's the same. Shouts things like "Be brave enough to live your dreams!"

Gnomad: Actions speak louder than words!

Gnomber9: If it's both terrifying and amazing, pursue it!

Gnomad: Sounds like this other Glover man I know.

Gnomber9: Wonderful?

Gnomad: Wordy.

~

THE NEXT NIGHT, AFTER GETTING HANNAH TO SLEEP, PERCY fell back on the couch with Marg. He pinched the pressure points either side of his nose, and stared at the ceiling. "Shall we watch something?"

Marg patted his knee. "It's not easy putting her to bed. You're doing a fantastic job."

"She likes when Cal calls."

"She's not the only one." She waited a beat, smiling cheekily. "I love it when he wishes me goodnight. My boy turned out better than I could ever have wished for."

"How hard is it not having their dad around?"

She smoothed Mr. Glover's shirt over her belly. "Hard. Sad. Lonely."

She said it with a smile that Percy knew far too intimately. He wrapped his arms around his knees. "Why do they all leave?"

"Oh, sweetheart, come here." Percy let himself rest against her, sighing at her fingers stroking his hair. "It's hard now, but the sadness won't last forever. Having good friends and good support helps."

"Maybe."

"Maybe? Definitely." She tugged his hair playfully. "We might have had some bad luck, but luck changes. Now, what about your cousin? Have you two made up yet?"

"Frank? Ha. No."

"I understand he hurt you, but Cal seems to think he was hurting. Grieving just like—"

Percy stiffened, and Marg squeezed him gently.

"I'm used to people dropping out of my life," he said. "Really, it's fine."

"Aunt Abby liked Frank though, didn't she? Maybe talking would help you move on."

"Cal thinks Frank is sorry?"

"He thinks you should try not running away. That you should talk. Now, on the fifth Hannah and I are scheduled to fly down to Pittsburgh. I'm debating buying another ticket for Ellie to come with me."

"She'll have basically have just gotten back."

"Cal needs time off from the kids."

"Ellie is a lovely girl. I'm happy to drop her to and from work if she stays."

"Would you? Because Cal needs a few days to relax and have some fun."

Percy gave a soft laugh. "Consider Ellie taken care of. As for Cal, I'm not sure he'd know where to start having fun."

"You'll help him."

He held his breath. It must have been an obvious gulp of air because Marg shook her head, smiling.

Fun. With Cal. Probably meant hitting the Museum of Natural History.

Percy's lips tugged into a grin. "Marg?" he said, head warmed by her shoulder.

"Yes?"

"Cal needs to get back to his masters."

She murmured her agreement, and then gasped.

Percy jerked back, hoping his clingy weight hadn't hurt her. "Are you okay? What's hurting?"

Marg took his hand and placed it against her belly. A tiny jab punched his palm. "He's moving."

Oh. "That's weird. And amazing."

Another bump along the pads of his fingers. He looked at Marg's elated face and back at the bump stretching the checkered flannel. He whispered conspiratorially to the baby. "You have no idea what a big, beautiful family you'll be born into."

"Yes," Marg said. "It is a nice one, isn't it?"

∽

Gnomber9: Is it just me, or are the days dragging?

Gnomad: It's just you. Now hit me.

Gnomber9: What's your biggest pet peeve?

Gnomad: When people cut lines. There are social rules, you know.

Gnomber9: Is it the little things or the grand gestures that count the most?

Gnomad: Little things, like someone making a coffee for you after a hard day. Or someone dusting dandruff off your shoulders and making sure you think it's a hug. Or sharing their favorite food because they know you like it too.

Gnomber9: Or offering lifts when you're stranded.

Gnomad: Or offering lifts when you're not.

Gnomad: Grand gestures have their place too though. Next!

Gnomber9: What was the last book you read from cover to cover?

Gnomad: Aunt Abby's cookbook.

Gnomber9: Do you like people talking about the memories they have with her?

Gnomad: I have mixed feelings.

Gnomad: Have you ever wanted something not good for you? Like a gooey dessert that will give you a heart attack if you eat it?

Gnomber9: Vanilla is always a safer option. What feelings?

Gnomad: Not answering.

Gnomber9: Fine. What's your favorite thing about yourself?

Gnomad: My hands, they can take people's pain away. One more.

Gnomber9: Do you still fantasize clubbing Cal around the ears?

Gnomad: I fantasize a lot.

∽

Gnomad: I got gnomed again today!

Gnomber9: House coming along nicely, then?

Gnomad: How'd you know it was house related?

Gnomber9: Lucky guess.

Gnomad: Gnome More Wood fixed the broken pillars on the porch frames.

Gnomber9: Can't wait to see it.

Gnomad: Can't wait to see you.

Gnomber9: Soccer when I get back or something?

Gnomad: Or something.

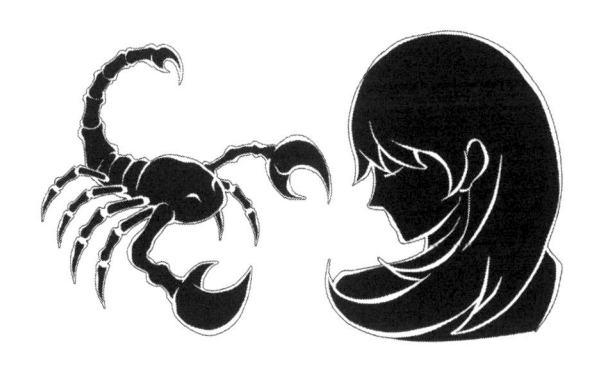

R ascalinosaur
noun / ras . cal . li. no. saur

DEFINITION OF RASCALINOSAUR
: a sweet little girl who doesn't stay in bed
: term of endearment Percy finds fits perfect for Hannah Glover

EXAMPLE OF RASCALINOSAUR IN A SENTENCE
"What do Rascalinosaurs look like?" Hannah asked.
"Like minxes. The size of a small pony."
"I want one of those for my birthday."
"A pony?"
"A Rascalinosaur!"

Chapter Twelve

Morning arrived quickly and with it, Mrs. Yoshida, a mid-fifties Japanese-American businesswoman looking to buy. She'd called an hour earlier, asking if she could check out the property with a building inspector.

Percy let her in, handing over the disclosure statement. Forty minutes later, Mrs. Yoshida was beaming at him over a cup of tea. "I'm interested, Mr. Freedman. How quickly could you vacate the property?"

Tomorrow quivered on the tip of his tongue, but the joke wouldn't fall. His stomach churned Darjeeling and milk, and he clutched his mug like a blanket. "I'm flexible."

"I will review the paperwork. I have a couple of other places to check out, but if I buy, I'd want to move in immediately."

∽

Percy didn't know how he'd ended up at Frank's. A rundown place with asphalt shingles, a detached garage, and a grassy front lawn swamped with puddles.

He climbed out of the car and picked his way around the

puddles. He shook his head. Somewhere a village was missing its idiot.

What if Cal was right? What if it *was* grief? If they could work things out?

The moment the door opened, Percy was met by his cousin's glare. Frank folded his thick arms, his A-frame stance blocking Percy from feeling welcome. "What do you want?"

Well, this was a promising start.

"I wanted to chat."

Frank squinted. "About selling Aunt Abby's?"

Show me that not everyone I let myself care about leaves.

Prove that we can be the cousins we used to be. The cousins who snarked and bitched—but did it together.

"I don't want us to have any hard feelings about our inheritance."

"It's not really about the house," Frank said.

Percy shoved his hands into his pockets. "So why were you one, rifling through her things, and two, so angry on the phone?"

Frank hesitated, glancing toward the chain-link fence. "Ever heard of sentimental value?"

He was surprised Frank had. "There was not much left, I know. There are recipes. I could give you some."

"How long before you sell?"

"There is someone interested. If she takes it, she wants to move in quickly."

His eyes shut, and lips thinned. "Leave."

"If you didn't want to make amends," Percy asked, "why did you call me?"

"To tell you to pick up the box of shit you left here."

Right. Percy plastered on a grin. "Guess I can take it off your hands now."

"You never answered, so I threw it out with the trash."

"You're a real stand-up guy."

Frank stepped back inside his house. "Piss off."

With a whoosh of cigarette and stale-booze air, the door slammed in his face.

Percy scuffed his way back to his Jeep, laughing until his eyes stung.

Just the rainbows and sunshine he thought the visit would be.

~

AFTER THE CHARMING ENCOUNTER WITH HIS COUSIN, PERCY busied himself baking, then frustrated himself with some DIY projects, then moved on to gnoming.

First, he designed Champey some pens with quotes from her stories and sent them to her.

Then he pottered around the Feist's gardens, digging up weeds and adding nutritious soil to the agapanthus.

Half the time, their cat Gingerbread wove between his feet, demanding attention.

Percy petted her, then watched her scale the gutter and slunk over the half-piping above the Feist's garage. She rolled herself into the small space, paws skyward, and Percy whipped out his phone and recorded.

All the fun without the fur.

To reach a better angle, Percy climbed the sycamore tree that overhung the garage. He'd just wriggled himself over a protruding branch when a voice whipped through the leaves from below. "Never stop surprising, do you?"

Percy jerked his head toward Cal, his whole body taut, every inch quivering like he was a freshly restrung guitar being plucked. It took master effort to steady his reply. "Back already?"

"Happy to see me, I see."

"Happy is not the word. You look . . ."

Cal's eyebrow quirked as he waited for Percy to finish.

"Tired."

A light laugh seeped out of him, and he looked out toward

the cul-de-sac with a shrug. "I'm fine. Just in need of distraction."

Well, didn't Cal get what he wished for.

Gingerbread took an interest in the sunlight playing off his hair. She reached over the gutter with her paw, swiping at his head. Sensing the air shift above him, Cal froze.

Percy struggled to still the phone, gut clenching on his first real laugh of the day as the cat pounced onto Cal's shoulder.

Cal jumped like a hyena on the run. Gingerbread tumbled off him and scuttled under the porch.

"What the . . .?" He furiously dusted his shoulder, sneezing twice.

Percy barked out a laugh that had Cal glaring up at him. "All elegance, that was—" He lost his balance and tipped sideways over the branch. He grappled at the tree limbs but crashed to the driveway close to Cal's feet.

He groaned and twisted onto his butt, dusting the soil off his knees.

Percy grabbed his phone, then winced as he accepted Cal's hand. When he was on his feet, Cal spoke, voice dripping in that fake disdain Percy had sorely missed. "When you quote me, choose your moment."

Percy tightened his hold on Cal to lessen the weight on his foot. "I'll make a note."

Cal's eyes roamed him for injury. "Are you okay?"

"Might have tweaked my foot a bit. It's nothing."

Sympathy warred with amusement, and Cal slipped an arm around his waist.

A hit of terribly appealing lotion had Percy almost sticking his nose in Cal's armpit.

In a remarkable display of sanity, he braced his hand on Cal's shoulder, fingers resting on the bare skin of his neck under the erratic ticking of his pulse. "Come on, then. Get me home."

~

Inside Aunt Abby's, Cal steered him to the couch. "Prop your foot on the coffee table. I'll bring something from the freezer."

Percy sat and pried off his shoes. One ankle looked more swollen than the other.

Cal returned toting a bag of frozen peas. Percy reached out for it, but Cal set it on the coffee table next to his foot and knelt. A jolt skipped through him as Cal's thumb and index finger cupped the curve of his leg as he dragged his hand over Percy's blond hairs.

"Looks tender," he murmured, wrapping his fingers above his puffed ankle. He eased the frozen bag under his heel and calf, mushing its contents to support the arch from heel to ankle.

Cold relief numbed his ankle. Percy wished he might use the peas against the not-so-sudden swelling somewhere else.

"While you're waiting on me hand and foot"—Percy winked at a mildly amused Cal who was picking himself off the floor—"Mind setting up some *Elementary* for me? And maybe bring me one of those delicious cream cheese iced muffins I made this morning?"

"You baked for . . . you baked?"

"Your trays were winking at me, and I had a bad taste in my mouth to get rid of."

Five minutes later, the big screen flared to life with another mystery episode. "This one has a fun end," Cal said, heading out the door to the living room. "I think you'll enjoy it."

"Wait, where are you going? What about my muffin?"

"It's coming. Don't worry, you haven't seen the last of this ugly mug."

Percy watched the screen, smiling a bit. "It's quite a mug, all right."

Cal hoofed it out of his house and returned fifteen minutes

later toting a paper bag. He glanced hello at Percy and whisked himself into the kitchen. The sounds of cupboards opening and shutting and kitchen utensils clattering piqued Percy's attention. The defrosting peas flopped to the floor as he stood up. He gingerly put his weight on his sore foot and hobbled to the kitchen.

Spread before a concentrated Cal were milk, eggs, sugar, rum, and tiny spice containers.

Percy leaned against the brick arch and watched as Cal crouched, searching cupboard after cupboard. When he opened the one next to the oven, Percy froze. A flutter of butterflies took his chest hostage.

Cal's frame tightened and stilled, and his Adam's apple jutted in a slow swallow as he stared at Aunt Abby's muffin-tray stash. Tapping the trays absently, his gaze flicked up to the counter where the Glover trays sat full of fresh muffins.

His chest expanded on an inhale and he slowly released it, his expression flicking through emotions, too fast for Percy to read. Cal's lips finally settled into a gentle line.

Ignoring his clammy palms and the sweat pearling at the nape of his neck, he pushed off the brick arch. "Find what you're looking for?"

Cal looked back into the cupboard, pulled out a saucepan, and tapped the cupboard shut. "Yes. I think I did." He peeked at him with a soft expression as he set the saucepan on the stove. "Go sit down, you'll make your foot worse."

"It'll be fine," Percy said, face pinching as pain shot through his ankle.

"Do you need me to sweep you there again?"

Percy folded his arms. "With what broom?"

Cal turned off the stove and twisted around. Before Percy could register what was happening, Cal swept him off his feet, heaving him into his arms. Butterflies in Percy's chest scattered to all his extremities. Percy threw his arms around Cal's neck.

Pressing close to Cal's warm chest, he said, "Callaghan Glover, you are crazy. You'll make your back ten times worse."

"Guess I'll need ten more massages then."

Cal's gaze filled with playfulness that Percy hadn't seen on him before. Cal's arms strained around him, and his breath puttered with effort and a short laugh.

Cal deposited him back on the couch, their eyes connecting for a breathless instant. "I want you to stay right here."

Percy clenched his hands against the fabric seat to stop himself from balling Cal's T-shirt and holding him there. "But you're in the kitchen and I'm all alone out here."

"I'll join you soon. We'll binge on *Elementary* and drink eggnog."

That sounded perfect. "Fine."

Fifteen minutes and two blue mugs of tea later, Cal joined him on the couch with a plate of two carrot muffins. He sat close, but not close enough. "Eggnog needs an hour to cool, then put it in the freezer for bit."

Percy eyed the muffins. One had a finger-stripe through the icing. "Couldn't wait, huh?"

"I'm usually big on waiting. Today, not so much." Cal swiped another fingertip of icing and swirled his tongue around it. He smacked his lips and withdrew his finger with a pop.

Percy refused to be jealous of a muffin.

Icing, on the other hand . . .

"I'm serious about those massages," Cal said.

"Fifty dollars an hour." Percy held out his hand, palm up.

Cal placed a muffin there.

When Cal's phone rang, he leaped off the couch to answer. "Mom, you all right? . . . Okay. Be there in a second." He hung up. "I've got to help get Hannah ready for bed, and Dad wants to Skype call. I'll be back soon."

Soon turned out to be three hours later. Percy had given up spying out the bay window and shuffled to bed with his laptop.

He turned on his bedside lamp, stripped to his boxers, and climbed under the covers. His phone chimed.

Callaghan: I'm coming now.

Perseus: I'm in bed.

Callaghan: I'll let myself in.

Percy heard the front door opening. He shimmied upright, pulling his knees to his chest when Cal paraded in with a pitcher of eggnog and two glasses. He halted, drinking in Percy's state of undress, before continuing.

He squeezed past Percy's boxes, set the eggnog on the bedside table, and swung into the bed, shoving his bare feet under the blankets. "You should put your clothes in the closet."

"Hannah get to bed okay?" Percy asked.

Cal frowned and poured them drinks. "Mom's a little tired. I told her to get to bed and leave Hannah and the washing to me."

"What dinosaur were you tonight?"

"Maiasaura."

Their first glass of eggnog went down easily with a side of *Elementary*. Same with their second. At the third, the internet crapped out.

Percy clinked his glass against Cal's. "Guess this is where we pour our hearts out, and you tell me all about your tragic life."

Cal snorted. "Yes, this is where I tell you how much I wish Dad would have come home with me."

Percy was warmly drunk, but not so much so that he couldn't read past Cal's sarcastic façade. "Yeah, and I respond by telling you that I'm sorry it's so hard keeping everything together. That you're doing a good job with your mom and sisters. I might finish by offsetting the pain climbing up your chest."

Cal sipped and swallowed hard. "I tell you to offset it by sharing something vulnerable about you."

"Of course. Seeing me cry would be the ultimate offset. You'd forget about everything else."

"I would."

Percy hesitated with his lips poised on the glass, then tipped it up and polished off the last of it. "Then I lay it all out there and tell you how I wake to creaking wood and jump out of bed just to double check Aunt Abby's not still here. How she was the only one in my family to show me what love is; how every time I walk through this house alone, a little piece of my heart crumbles. Maybe I'm not meant to have a family that lasts, not meant to know what it's like to belong. Home is this shaky idea close to a myth. When I think it might exist, I'm left falling through its mirage."

Cal set down his glass on the side table and rolled onto his knees, facing him. His voice softened. "I assure you it exists."

Hope and frustration twisted in Percy's belly. "And I laugh and say it's a nice thought, but remains to be seen."

Cal tipped up Percy's chin with his finger and drilled him with that analyzing gaze. "I insist you look harder."

"I insist we change the topic."

"I urge you not to."

"Well," Percy said, turning onto his knees and pressing firm fingers against Cal's chest. "I make it happen anyway."

Cal's eyebrow quirked upward. "By pushing me out of your house?"

Percy wrenched his hands from Cal's shirt and dropped them to Cal's knees, then he leaned forward and kissed Cal.

Their lips brushed with a zing of electricity. Cal's mouth parted, accepting Percy's soft kiss. One of Cal's hands braced against his hip. Percy waited for fingers to push him back, and whimpered into the kiss when they didn't.

Stubble prickled his jaw and Percy wanted more of it. He

lifted one hand off Cal's leg and dragged it up his back to the base of his head, where he squeezed lightly, crushing Cal against his naked chest. The brush of cotton against his nipples sent a slam of desire to his rapidly hardening cock, and Percy swiped his tongue into their kiss, reveling when Cal's joined in. Each slide of their tongues sent goosebumps over his entire body.

Cal tasted of eggnog, lemon icing, and a thousand dormant verbal grenades.

Cal thumbed Percy's side and ran it over his shoulder until fingers raked through his hair. Percy moaned, and Cal pulled back, cheeks flushed, lips raw. Not a smile in sight, just that shrewd analyzing gaze.

Immediately, panic seized Percy's chest. What had he done? Sure, he sensed Cal's interest in the kiss. But this wouldn't last. They'd have a fling, and then it would be over. It'd be Josh all over again.

Percy smacked his lips together and saved the moment as best he could—with the shrug of his shoulders and a light laugh. "That was to shut you up."

Cal's swiped his tongue over his bottom lip. "That was a lot of shutting up."

"Which you actively involved yourself in."

"I was curious what peace and quiet would feel like between us."

Percy laughed as the frozen wheel on the screen finally flickered and the next episode queued up. He whacked Cal on his bicep and nodded at the TV screen. "Shh. The internet is back on. Settle down and watch with me."

But as the next three episodes played, all he concentrated on was the incredible chemistry of their kiss and the stomach-clenching confirmation of the word: curious.

Noun / semi . co . lon

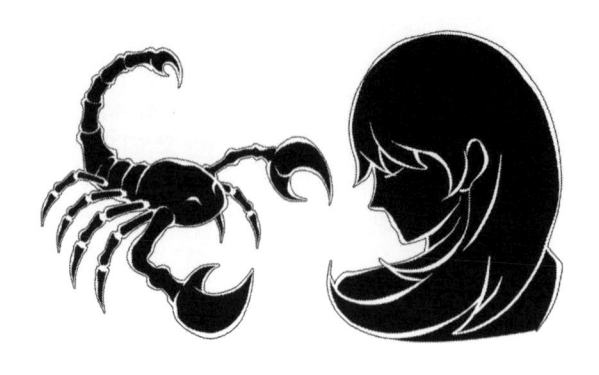

DEFINITION OF SEMICOLON
  : a powerful grammatical tool that, used appropriately, turns Cal on.

Chapter Thirteen

Sleep teased Percy senseless, making him relive the kiss until he was so spent he didn't think he could come for a week.

Which proved untrue the moment he stepped into his morning shower.

He was starving by the time he'd dressed and dragged himself into the kitchen.

He grabbed a couple of muffins and made his way to the bay window. What was the ruckus outside?

Car doors shut and laughter rang out in the dewy morning. Crystal, mouth running a mile a minute, yanked a handsome man into her arms right there on the sidewalk.

Theo led his sister Leone toward their house. Was that Jamie?

Jamie said something to Crystal that made Theo raise a middle finger over his head, grinning.

Percy smiled stiffly, throat stinging when he swallowed.

He pushed away from the window and slouched back to his room. In a wedge of sunlight, Cal's keys glittered on the bedside table. Percy snatched them up and cuddled back into bed. His stomach flipped and flopped until he couldn't handle it anymore. He grabbed his laptop.

He checked to see if Gnomber9 was online, but the forum was quiet. Keeping that tab open, Percy commented on his own Chatvica post.

> **GayDude: I might have crossed a line. By that, I mean I kissed him. I'm not going to lie, it felt different from any kiss I've had before. More familiar. Like he coaxed me into warm, reciprocating arms, and I could trust him. His arms were safe.**
>
> **Then panic slammed into me because it shouldn't have felt that good. The grief that hit me . . . damn. It'd barely finished, and I was already frustrated and sad knowing I wouldn't get it back.**
>
> **Don't get me wrong. He was into the kiss, and he's curious about being with a guy, but this already has an end date stamped onto it. I feel like I'm tight-rope walking a live wire. One part of me thinks I should continue like nothing happened and make sure not to cross any more lines because I like what we have and don't want to ruin it. But why not enjoy what we could have if he wants to?**
>
> **If he's nice to me and he's curious, maybe he is interested in something real? Help me get rid of this destructive flare of hope.**

He'd barely returned from the bathroom when four new comments came in. Percy wasn't sure he had the stomach to read them.

He played with Cal's keys as he scrolled through the unread comments.

> **Don'tDeludeYourself: So much for you being rational. Look, like we earlier established, a guy can be**

friendly. A guy can also be friendly and curious. This doesn't mean he is gay or bi or loves you or ever will.

Go there at your own risk.

SomeLikeItFun: @Don'tDeludeYourself: Who squeezed all the happy juice out of you? (I'm guessing he was straight?)

@GayDude: I'm team Have Some Fun. Live in the moment. A slice of pie is better than no pie at all.

Don'tDeludeYourself: @SomeLikeItFun: Not that it is any of your business, but no one squeezed anything out of me.

@GayDude: I'm only trying to save you from heartbreak.

SomeLikeItFun: And no one squeezed anything out of me. Sounds like you'd be better off if someone had. ;-)

Percy laughed, grateful for the distraction. He was about to reply when the Sherlock Gnomes page notified him of a gnome entering the chat room.

Immediately, he switched tabs. Gnomber9. Of course. Who else had ever been on the site? Grinning like an idiot, he punched out a message.

Gnomad: I've been staring at Cal's three keys all morning. The blue one's for the hatchback. Yellow's for your house. The green one is still bugging me.

Gnomber9: What an exciting morning you are having!

Gnomad: It's certainly something.

Gnomber9: A good something?

Percy swallowed a nervous lump in his throat. Cal was fishing.

Gnomad: That remains to be seen. How did Cal get in the house without his keys?

Gnomber9: Maybe the same way you sneak in?

Gnomad: I do like sneaking in.

Gnomber9: Ha! It probably makes sense if you get your own key.

Gnomad: Think I could get away with bugging you guys more than I already do?

Gnomber9: I think you could get away with anything.

Dammit, Cal.

To prevent himself from running across the road and pouncing on him, Percy steered the conversation in another direction.

Gnomad: What have you been up to this morning?

Gnomber9: Playing with Hannah and generally daydreaming.

Daydreaming? Kill him now.

The doorbell rang. All too fortunately, since he probably would have asked Cal more about these daydreams...

Gnomad: Crap, I gotta let this guy check out my place. Later!

It was strange to open the front door and not see Cal. Instead, a young man in an ill-fitting suit blocked the daylight sporting a salesman's smile.

"Vincent, right?"

Vincent's smile brightened, and Percy double-checked he wasn't toting a bible under his arm. "That's me. Thanks for seeing me on a federal holiday. It's the only time I had off."

"No problem. We're not firing up the barbecue for another few hours."

First, there'd be a round of Zombie Apocalypse and the traditional cul-de-sac crisis. It happened to one neighbor every year. Last summer, Champey had locked herself out and needed Cal to hoist Ellie onto his shoulders to climb through a window. The year before that, Crystal had flown out of her house, chased by a serial-killer ferret that she'd regretfully promised to look after.

The year before that, Mr. Feist's cat had thrown up over the potato salad.

Bets were probably already laid as to who would cause drama this year.

Percy had his money on Theo and Jamie.

Over Vincent's shoulder, Percy glimpsed Cal coming down his path trying to dislodge Hannah from around his leg.

Maybe it'd be Cal this year?

"Come in, come in." Percy left the front door open and jerked his head for Vincent to follow. The man cautiously entered with a haughty lift of his chin.

In the living room, his gaze swept over the furniture, landing on the view of the bright houses outside the bay window. "What's the community like here?"

"The neighbors are a tight-knit group. Very inclusive and

accepting. If you need anything, they're there for you. They can be a bit nosey, but it's well meaning." To be fair, he might be one of the nosier ones. Who didn't like a bit of gossip? "Trusting too. We look after each other's pets and properties. If someone's house needs painting, we work out a weekend to get it done together."

"Sounds intimate," Vincent said stiffly.

Percy shoved his hands in the back of his jeans. "I guess we're all kind of close."

"Good Christian folk, then?"

"Not all Christian," Percy said as Cal strolled into the room, all fresh clothes and bed-tousled hair, eyes skipping over Vincent to land on Percy. "But quite wonderful."

Cal raised that eyebrow of his as Vincent pivoted toward him. "Wonderful?"

"We were talking about the neighbors," Vincent said.

Cal's lips curved, brighter than Percy had seen before, his eyes twinkling. "Some more wonderful than others."

Percy's stomach threatened to drop out through his feet, but he forced out a laugh and tugged Cal into the hall by the elbow, beckoning a frowning Vincent to follow. Percy leaned into Cal, keeping his voice low. "Did it squawk a lot?"

"Did what squawk?"

"The canary when you ate it."

"Sounds like it's still squawking."

Percy choked on something that might have been a laugh or the start of him begging to be eaten.

Bypassing Aunt Abby's empty bedroom to show off the bathroom and laundry room, he forced himself to keep it together. Vincent had grown quiet and held himself rigidly.

Now Vincent was peering around Percy's bedroom, and Percy lingered in the doorway. Cal leaned against the doorframe and folded his arms, side-eyeing Percy. "You missed your aunt's room."

"I thought maybe you could show him."

Cal twisted to face him, looking as though he'd say something earnest and pitying. Percy's stomach churned, crushing all those sweet butterflies. He didn't want to discuss this right now. He focused on Vincent. "I'm happy to leave any furniture if you want it."

Vincent's lips pinched. "I could never sleep on that bed."

Cal uncoiled from his slouch. "That bed?"

"I . . . prefer my own."

A slither of unease prickled Percy's neck. Cal cocked his head, assessing Vincent. "I don't like what I think you're implying."

Vincent's gaze swung between them. "I don't like what I'm seeing in front of me. The house is fine, but I won't take any furniture that has been exposed to your lifestyle."

Oh, this just got real peachy.

Cal waltzed into the room between him and Vincent, rubbing the light stubble covering his chin.

"You seem to like judging by appearance, so allow me to do the same. You look like a little boy playing dress up in his daddy's suit, like a guy who doesn't think for himself but spits out anything anyone's ever taught you about the world. Let me tell you something, our lifestyle is simply being good people and good neighbors. Anyone would be lucky to be a part of that."

Vincent pursed his lips, glancing between them. "I think it's time I left."

"I think it's time you did."

"If it's unclear," Vincent's gaze flashed to Percy, "I'm not interested in buying from a gay twink."

Cal's laugh was sharp, empty. "We're long past interested in selling to a homophobic prick."

Vincent shoved past Percy into the hall. "Do you let him do all your talking?"

"I probably should," Percy answered, waving good bye with his middle finger. "He's better at it."

Once Vincent slammed the front door behind him, Cal rolled his eyes. "That went well."

Percy dropped onto his bed and scrubbed his hands over his face. His obviously gay face. He needed a tattoo. Something to mellow out the twink in him. "God, I hate how I look."

"Yeah, such a chore to have flawless skin, thick shiny hair, and people swinging their heads to get a second look at you."

Percy stopped scrubbing and peeked between his fingers at Cal, who stood at the foot of his bed, staring in the direction Vincent had left. "Nobody does that."

"Everyone does that." Cal pivoted sharply and walked toward the boxes teeming with Percy's clothes. "You still haven't unpacked."

"Maybe I'll sell the house next week."

"At the luck you've been having, you'll be here forever. Wouldn't hurt to put your clothes away."

With Cal suggesting it, it was vaguely tempting. In fact, with Cal in the house, Aunt Abby's absence didn't feel so heavy. "I suppose you have to prepare for the afternoon."

"I have to haul out the grill and make a last-minute run to the store for ketchup."

"You're driving there? I'm out of milk."

Cal kicked off his shoes and reclined on the bed, facing Percy. "If you want to save gas, we can take your Jeep."

Percy picked up the keys Cal left behind and rolled on his side, jingling them. "I am all about environmentalism."

Cal plucked the keys from him, grimacing. "You know I lied about the hatchback."

"I also know why you lied." Cal needed him.

"I don't usually make a habit of lying."

"You probably shouldn't, you're not very good."

He was better at his Gnomber9 facade, although that was not

technically a lie considering the game rules and Percy's insistence Cal keep his identity anonymous. Still, they were both using their gnome names to secretly be . . . more honest, ironically.

"What would you be doing if I wasn't here?" Cal asked.

"Looking at house listings, answering Chatvica posts, spying on Theo's new man. Maybe even plotting how to gnome the last two neighbors." El and you.

"More trysts in attics?"

"And up sycamore trees."

"What types of Chatvica posts do you answer?"

"Guys with questions about their sexuality, mostly." Percy waited for Cal's reaction. Hoped for a hard swallow or a nervous tic, maybe even a mention of their kiss last night, but Cal nodded easily. He repositioned the pillows at his back and cozied into them.

"What do you think of my bed?" Percy grazed the comforter, bumping Cal's splayed fingers. A frustratingly delicious shock worked havoc in his body.

"The mattress is harder than I'm used to," Cal said, bumping Percy's hand back, "but it's comfortable. My sheets fit nice too."

Percy cleared his throat, lifting his gaze away from Cal's lips. "Since I can't get rid of you, how about we check out some houses?"

He rolled toward his side table where his laptop sat. The warmth of Cal's hand and the following squeeze on his shoulder stopped Percy. He turned around at Cal's gentle urging.

Cal was staring at him intently, his gaze stroking Percy's face. Was he going to kiss him? Temptation caught in his throat.

"What're we going to do with Abby's room?" Cal's words were kind, firm, and totally disappointing.

"What more needs to be done? I got rid of her bed."

"What about painting the room? Refurnishing it?"

"How about we watch *Elementary*?"

Cal leaned in, a soft sigh feathering Percy's cheek. "You need to embrace the hurt. Maybe then you can move on to acceptance."

"Callaghan," Percy said, lips aching with a smile, "I don't want to stay here."

"Do you ever want to hook someone's gaze, stare them deep in the eyes, and whisper . . . *liar?*"

Percy grappled for a comeback to keep the emotional distance.

Cal waited, then sighed. "I could help you with her room."

Percy's stupid voice cracked. "Why are you pushing this?"

"Because you have no one else to push you."

His words punched Percy's gut. He scrambled off the bed, backing up against his cupboard doors. "Stop."

"Stop, what?"

"This. Everything. You're trying to keep me here because you can't make your dad come home."

Cal pushed off the bed and stood in front of him. The unnerving look on his face was too soft, too caring, too forgiving. "We are not fake nemeses anymore, Percy."

Another punch to his gut. One that sent butterflies into a sudden flurry down his legs, up his arms, all through his chest. Percy. He'd called him Percy.

Cal was breaching the line they only crossed in the Sherlock Gnomes forum. "We don't get points for pretending to hurt each other."

It was Percy's turn to apologize and say something equally meaningful and genuine. But all that tumbled out of his mouth was, "What do we get points for?"

Cal huffed out a laugh. "Three guesses."

P ercitaur
    noun / per . ci . taur

DEFINITION OF **PERCITAUR**
    : a specific group of made-up Dinosauria
    : the quickest, smartest, best-looking dinosaurs of them all, according to Percy.
    : Perseus Freedman's dinosaur namesake

EXAMPLE OF **PERCITAUR** IN A SENTENCE
Percitaurs were a charmingly feisty lot. Especially when in the vicinity of Callosauruses.

Chapter Fourteen

Percy dumped his clothes on the bed and stared at the three-foot gap to the closet. After all that strenuous staring, he stormed to the kitchen and made himself a cup of tea.

In one of the mugs Cal had bought him.

Great. He couldn't even drink tea without thinking of Cal.

He supposed it was his turn for candidness, but he wasn't sure he'd be any good at it. Good fences made good neighbors, and if nothing else, he and Cal had always been superior neighbors.

He drained the last dredge of peppermint tea, and impatiently grabbed his phone when it started ringing in his pocket. Not Cal.

Mrs. Yoshida.

He answered with a hello that knotted his stomach.

"Hello, Mr. Freedman. I've reviewed the paperwork, and I have an offer for you . . ."

Ten minutes later, with the promise to think about it, he hung up. She wanted his place for ten grand less than he had advertised.

Not a bad offer.

He should sleep on it a few nights, though.

Just to make sure . . . he couldn't get more.

A banging sounded at the door, accompanied by Theo and Leone's voices.

Percy slipped into his sneakers and shoved necessities into his cargo-shorts pockets. The moment he stepped outside, Theo whipped him into a hug. Leone followed, using her hands to sweep the top of his head and down to his shoulders. "Have you shrunk, Percy? I could've sworn you were taller."

Percy playfully scowled at his own reflection in her sunglasses, which he had to look up into because he was a good two inches shorter than the Wallace twins. "That better not be possible."

Theo patted the familiar canvas bag that bulged at his side. In it were the Zombie Apocalypse foghorn and colored sashes. "How ready are you?"

"Born ready."

They shoulder-bumped each other, and Percy scooped an arm around Leone as they jogged toward the center of the cul-de-sac, where the other neighbors had gathered. Twenty-two in all. Most wore T-shirts, shorts, sneakers, and an overabundance of sunscreen.

Last year, Cal's dad ran through the program of the day. This year, twenty-two years his junior, Cal stood on the hood of his hatchback, motioning everyone to gather in. He wore a casual pair of charcoal chinos and a tight-fitting T-rex T-shirt with the phrase "*Good luck reaching* a compromise."

His mom shifted at his feet with Hannah hooked to her hip. Her baby belly peeked out from her "We're hoping for a dinosaur" shirt that Cal must have given her.

Cal bent over and hitched Hannah into his arms.

Percy growled—Cal's back!

Cal delegated barbecue chores between the Feists, Sernas, and Wallaces, stated which backyards the neighbors were welcome to mingle through, humorously cautioned them to drink wisely, and motivated the younger kids to take a special role in cleaning up.

Marg said something to Cal and he nodded, searching the crowd. "Hannah tipped the kiddie pool and soaked our backyard. We need another backyard for hosting the barbecue."

Something about the way Cal skipped over Percy bugged him. Did he think Percy was so caught up in his own pathetic miseries that he'd bail instead of lend a hand?

"You can use my yard."

Cal finally focused on him with a flicker in his eye. "Are you sure?"

"I wouldn't have offered, otherwise."

A small smile accompanied the shake of Cal's head. "Thank you." He gestured toward Theo. "Now our first game."

Theo didn't bother with a tiresome climb onto the car. He lounged against it with a lazy smile over the crowd to his boyfriend, who had snuck up on Leone's other side.

"We know the rules to Zombie Apocalypse, right?"

Most people murmured yes. Theo looked like he was going to dive right into separating them into teams.

"No," came Jamie's deep voice. "Could you explain it? In detail?"

Theo laughed. "You're smart, I'm sure you'll figure it out. Everyone grab a sash."

"It wouldn't be too difficult to explain, would it? Teaching is easy after all."

Something was going on between the two of them. Whatever it was, Theo scowled as he spoke. "Fine. There are three teams," he said. "The Survivors, the Zombies, and the Cul-de-sac-ers. You either run, chase, or protect—in that order—and when all survivors are either home or zombified, the game's over." He pulled out a bundle of the sashes and passed them around.

"I give you a B-, Theo," Jamie called out, a humored laugh ringing through his posture.

"B-?" Theo straightened. "No way. I demand a do over."

Leone giggled. "You'll have to be a lot clearer if you want an A."

Theo glared and then reddened when Cal leaned over and said something in his ear. Percy wasn't jealous of that ear at all. He was squinting because of the sun reflecting off Cal's hair.

Theo sank back against the car, crossing his ankle. "The goal of the game is for the Survivors to get back "home"— Percy's front porch—without being tagged by a zombie. Survivors have a two-minute head start to find hiding places before the Zombies hunt them. Another minute after that, the Cul-de-sac-ers can run out and try to protect and guide the survivors back home."

Theo beckoned for a few sashes and held them up, looking through one of the loops directly at Jamie. "Red side of the sashes is for Zombies. Green side, Survivors. Survivors turn their sashes if tagged. The blue sashes are for the Cul-de-sac-ers—that is, the helpers. They can't be turned."

Theo pressed the vibrant blue sash against Cal's stomach, making him a Cul-de-sac-er. He balled another red sash and tossed it to Jamie. Mr. Feist handed Percy the two last sashes, one blue, one red/green. Leone asked to be a helper and paired up with her mother.

After slipping the blue sash on Leone, Percy shrugged into the red sash.

Cal, watching him, leaned over and spoke in Theo's ear.

Theo lifted his voice. "There are too many Zombies. Percy, make yours a survivor. Jamie, don't even think about it. Since you seem to be on the hunt, today you can chase. Not that it'll work out for you"—he shook his sash, green side up—"I'm getting home untouched."

Percy snickered. "Does that really count as a win?"

Jamie folded his arms. "Trust me, he didn't even think about it the way half of us heard it."

"Also," Theo continued, hitching two thumbs behind him,

"all front and back yards this end of the cul-de-sac are in bounds. Outside only."

"Not my yard," Mr. Serna muttered, until Josie elbowed him in the ribs. "Fine. Not my backyard."

Ten minutes later, they were in the thick of the game. Two foghorns had sounded, releasing the Zombies and the Cul-de-sac-ers.

Percy hid behind a shed in Mr. Feist's backyard near a scraggly vegetable patch. Leaning against exposed wood and hot, corrugated iron, he peered over the chest-high brick fence at Theo not three feet away, crouching behind the base of a chestnut tree.

Theo's gaze snagged on him and he nicked his head.

"I still can't believe you have a boyfriend," Percy blurted. "He's hot too, by the way."

Theo's eyes glazed dreamily. "And kind, thoughtful, and infuriatingly right."

"How did it happen? Were you curious about being with a guy, and it developed from there?"

Percy released his breath with disappointment when Theo shook his head. "We were friends. Best friends. Then best friends with benefits. Then I got my head out of my ass and figured out how much I loved him."

Percy scanned the side of the house where a Zombie might appear and put him out of what was threatening to be a jealous funk. "You're lucky."

"Cal will figure it out eventually."

Percy's head whipped around.

Theo smirked. "Come on, you two have been flirting for years."

"Flirting? We've been nemesizing."

"Is that even a word?"

"I don't know. I'd have to ask Cal."

"He could barely take his eyes off you in the street. That is a man who likes what he sees."

A man who is curious about what he sees. Who might like to kiss, touch, experiment—but like everyone else in his life, would eventually leave.

A sobering thought that should keep him from crossing any more lines.

Shrieks resonated in the distance, followed by laughter and garbled zombie yelling. Percy and Theo quieted as footsteps crunched over the gravel at the side of Theo's house. Jamie meandered around the corner, scanning the yard with determination.

Percy ducked, rocking on his feet. Should he make a run for it? Or wait for the Cul-de-sac-ers to help him home?

Movement came from next door. Percy peeked over the fence to find Theo sneaking around the tree in the opposite direction Jamie approached.

He might have gotten away with it too if he hadn't snapped a twig. Theo yelped and dove toward freedom, but Jamie was three easy lopes away from tackling him against the tree trunk. The Zombie went in for a hard kiss and Theo melted into it.

Jamie pulled back an inch, an arrogant smile on his face. "It worked out fine after all."

"Stop that eye twinkle."

"Maybe you wanted me to grab you like this."

Theo scowled, skating his fingers down Jamie's chest to his crotch. "You think you're irresistible. But I'm pretty sure I can go longer without grabbing." He gave a light squeeze to emphasize his point.

"Careful, Theo. If you're trying to out-stubborn me, well, as your mother is constantly reminding me, I am an Aries."

"Aries holds no cards to Leo."

Jamie cupped Theo's jaw and kissed him. "I love you, Theo, but you're going to regret this."

They looked at each other with fire and purpose, and Percy wasn't sure who he'd place his money on.

Sliding his thumb down Theo's sash, Jamie prepared to twist it from green to red. "Any last words, survivor?"

"Did I get a better grade for my second explanation?"

A laugh bloomed out of Jamie. "Of course."

"Of course I did?"

"Of course those would be your last words."

"Well, if you give me more words, I might also tell you I never said teaching was easy." Theo leaned in and pressed their lips close. "I said you made it look easy."

Percy itched to run off, but Josie—a freshly turned zombie—was pacing Mr. Feist's yard, close to sniffing him out. Where was the help?

Almost as soon as he thought it, help entered the yard in a tall, ridiculously handsome package, the blue sash making his eyes far too intense to be real. A prince from a fairytale.

Well, Zombify him now.

"Your knight in shining armor," Cal said dryly the moment his gaze latched onto him.

He paused in the middle of the yard, head swinging from Josie batting through sheets on the washing line—who Cal had clearly calculated in his plan—to Jamie and Theo—who Cal clearly had not.

Percy pushed off the dry vegetable patch and dusted his hands over his thighs. "I'm not liking my chances. Where are the rest of the Cul-de-sac-ers?"

Theo stroked his red sash and eyed Percy with an evil grin.

Time to run.

He dashed down the side of the house, Cal sticking so close behind him that his panting breath fanned over his neck.

Jamie and Theo thwarted their escape at Mr. Feist's gate, barely looking out of breath.

Cal yanked Percy back from their outstretched hands. With Josie closing in from the other side, they were cornered.

"Guess there's no winning for me," Percy said.

Cal's breath stuttered against his neck. "I'll fight to get you home."

"You seem to be a few dictionaries short for a fight."

"I have all the words I need."

"Now would be a good time to throw a few, Merriam."

Cal projected his voice, stilling Theo and Jamie's approach at the drooping agapanthus. "Ellie is behind my hatchback all alone and vulnerable. Go get her."

Percy tried to whirl around, but Cal clutched him under the arms and drew him up against Cal's firm chest. "Did you just give up your sister for me? That seems a bit callous. Oh, wait . . ."

Cal's breath hit the top of his ear, and it was quite remarkable Percy didn't squirm them both into the hammock hanging on the porch behind them. "Not the way to win points, Percy."

Percy again. Gravity chased through his chest and out the soles of his feet.

Cal's lips grazed the shell of his ear. "Besides, three Cul-de-sac-ers are sneaking toward her."

Forget it. Squirming didn't cross any lines he couldn't handle.

"It's a trick," Theo said, motioning for pregnant Josie to hurry and close in on them.

Percy scowled at Theo and his doting Jamie. "Yep, we're done for."

"Don't give up. I'll get you there yet." Cal hoisted Percy off his feet, spun him around, and tossed him into the hammock. Before Percy could squeal in indignation, Cal climbed on top of him, stretching his length over Percy, cocooning him in Cul-de-sac safety.

Theo grumbled at that development, and Jamie whispered something about waiting them out.

Wisps of fresh air seeped past Cal's shoulder into their bright-yellow hammock nest. Cal held himself up on his elbows either side of Percy's head, their stomachs, groins, and legs snug together as they swung.

Percy raised an eyebrow. "What now?"

"We wait for the Cul-de-sac-ers to surround us. Then we herd you back where you belong."

"And in the meantime?"

Cal's gaze lingered on Percy's mouth. "Why don't you tell me?"

Percy weaseled a hand into his pocket between them and drew out the Mentos. Cal hissed in surprise, pressing his groin against Percy's rapidly hardening cock as he shifted. And . . . Percy wasn't the only one responding to these tight quarters.

He knew better than to point that out to his usually-straight-and-likely-curious ex-nemesis. "Mentos?"

Cal's gaze didn't leave his. "No."

Percy popped out a candy and slipped it into his mouth. He probably shouldn't have trailed his finger slowly over his lip, but Cal's protective weight on him made rational thinking extremely hard.

Cal's lips tipped up as he watched Percy chew and swallow hard. "I bought you milk."

"Milk. Mugs. What comes next?"

"Nothing else with M. God forbid I gift in alliterations."

The hammock rocked with the snort of Percy's laughter, and Cal soaked it up with a grin. Slowly, the swaying stopped. The air pillowed between them, hot and faintly scented with vanilla and lotion. Cal continued to look at him, that kink in his brow asking too damn much.

Percy pressed his thumb against it. "You called me Percy."

Leaning in, Cal whispered, "That is your name."

"Why didn't you look at me when you asked about using another backyard?"

Cal frowned. "You sound annoyed."

"You sound surprised."

"I didn't want you to feel pressured. Not like the last time when we camped in your yard."

"That turned out"—an important step toward environmentalism—"all right in the end."

"I still thought you should decide for yourself this time."

A tender lump formed in Percy's throat, and temptation owned him. He skated his fingers down Cal's jaw, the slightest stubble jolting him with electricity. "Thank you, Cal."

Cal sucked in a breath as his shortened name rolled off Percy's tongue. His eyes glittered with joy, amusement, and possibly relief.

Percy lifted his head toward Cal's parting lips, their bodies tight with delicious friction.

Shrill voices halted them, and sweaty hands were hauling them out of the hammock.

A few blinks later, a tight group of blue-sashed neighbors surrounded him—and then Crystal and Leone, the Sernas, Mr. Roosevelt, and Cal were buffering his walk.

Before he knew it, he was back on his porch. Safe. Home.

Just as Cal had promised.

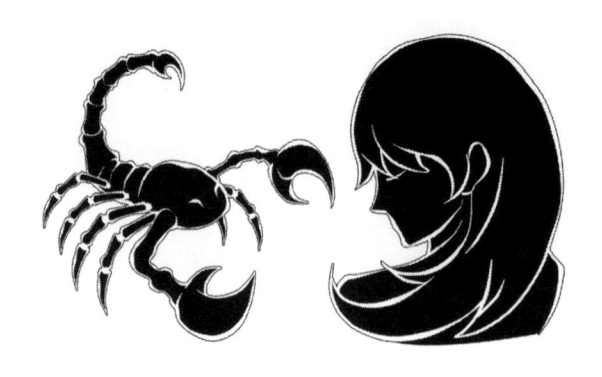

E nvironmentalist
noun / en . vi . ron . men . tal . ist

DEFINITION OF **ENVIRONMENTALIST**
: the word used by Percy and Cal to mean friend
: one concerned about the environment/friendship, who advocates for its continual growth and improvement
: see also friend

Chapter Fifteen

Percy bounded into his backyard cradling half the onion rolls he'd made. The other half was still baking. Sausages and steaks sizzled, and a handful of neighbors were already enjoying the barbecue.

The Sernas were sitting on the bench in the shade. Mr. Serna was eyeing his sausage skeptically while Josie happily licked ketchup off her fingers. Mr. Roosevelt was chatting with Marg, Rooster yapping at his heels for more scraps. The Wallace family and Jamie were playing poker at Abby's wrought-iron picnic table. Hannah and Ellie were plucking daisies right where Cal and Percy had pitched their tent.

Cal was grilling in the middle of Percy's yard.

Percy dropped his rolls off at the salad table and made his way over. Cal twisted a lamb kebab skewer with his tongs without taking his eyes off the meat.

"Looking good there, Cal."

Cal jerked his head up, eyebrow lifting, smile enough to knock the breath out of him. He glanced toward the meat. "What, this?"

"Yeah, it all looks delicious"—Percy lightly bumped his side

—"and smells amazing." Cal side-eyed him, lips quivering on a repressed laugh. Percy leaned in and whispered in Cal's ear, "Do I get points for that?"

The laugh ran out and Cal slung an arm around his neck. "Possibly. Now, how careful do I have to be offering you meat?"

Josie shuffled up to the grill with paper plates for her and Champey, who'd just joined them. She motioned for two sausages, eyes hopping between them. "Are you two friends finally?"

Cal's gaze flashed to his, full of certainty. Percy liked it. A lot.

"We're not nemeses anymore," Cal said.

"We're environmentalists."

"And weird asses," Ellie said, coming up behind Josie and demanding another grilled chicken breast. She handed over her plate just as the Feists entered the backyard.

Mr. Feist blocked the sun as he hulked over. "Percy, a man is knocking on your front door, insisting you open up."

Percy groaned. Was Frank back? He pointed to the large knife next to Cal's spatula. "Do you need that?"

"Want me to go with you?" Cal asked.

"Nah," Percy said over his shoulder as he bounded to the back door. "I've got this."

"If it is your cousin," Cal called after him, "maybe try talking?"

∽

IT WASN'T HIS COUSIN. PERCY WISHED HE'D BROUGHT THAT knife inside after all.

In floral-print shorts and a turquoise shirt that only his ex could pull off and still look masculine, Josh stood at the door.

"I forgot you threatened to show up," Percy said, opening the door.

Josh slid his sunglasses onto his head. Angry red marks either side of his nose gave his otherwise handsome face a pinched look. Percy focused on that.

"Percy," Josh said, flashing straight white teeth. "Here I thought you were refusing to let me in."

"I haven't let you in yet."

"Just as snide as ever, I see."

"You don't have to see for long. You're quite welcome to go."

Josh lifted Percy's blue leather jacket off his arm. "Thought you might like it back."

Percy hugged the jacket against his chest. It was his favorite. "How long are you in the city?"

"Just to drop that off."

He came in for that? Maybe Percy was a touch harsh. "You're heading home now?"

Josh grimaced and peered over his shoulder. "I thought you might want to catch up, but it's clear you want me gone."

Percy clutched Josh's arm as he turned to leave. Damn Cal and his advice. "We're having a barbecue. Come eat before you leave."

∽

Cal stopped turning meat the moment Percy and Josh crossed the lawn. Most neighbors recognized his ex, and politely waved or murmured hello.

Percy led Josh to the bench the Sernas had been sitting on. Their conversation was all small talk, and stilted at that. Josh sighed and shook his head. "You didn't have to run back here as soon as your work contract ended."

"Why would I want to stay down there?"

"I don't know. For Joe and Danny, maybe?"

A raw laugh worked up his throat. "They were your friends."

"They liked you too."

"It's not the same. They would have eventually distanced themselves."

"So you cut them off first? How far is that kind of attitude going to get you in life, Percy?"

"Why do you care?"

Josh angled himself toward him and rested a palm on Percy's knee. "We were together two years. We weren't right for each other, and if you're honest, you know that too. But we should have stayed friends."

"You left me for someone else. And you said some pretty ugly things at the end there."

"For as long as I've been with you, you've been obsessing about your aunt's neighbor." Josh smiled and shook his head. "And you let the air out my tires."

"Obsessing! I . . ." His outrage faltered. "I suppose there is that."

A shadow fell over them. Cal stood holding two paper plates, coolly eyeing Josh and the hand on Percy's knee. He passed Percy a plate piled with a lamb kebab, sausages, Crystal's famous potato salad, and a roll. "You haven't eaten anything. Thought you'd like the last kebab." Cal gestured for Josh to vacate the bench. "Grab yourself a plate if you want anything."

When Josh took the hint and left, Cal plunked down on the bench a good two inches closer than Josh had been sitting. The heat radiating off Cal tickled his side.

Cal parted a roll with his thumb and slid a sausage in it. "Josh is back, then?"

The words sounded short and blunt, and sure packed a surprising punch.

"Why Cal, dare I say you sound a little . . . flustered."

Cal paused, roll at his mouth. "I'm not flustered."

"Pity. Flustered is a good look on you."

Josh returned with a beer. He studied them, lips pinched in mild amusement. "I'll stand."

Cal's stiff smile didn't reach his eyes. He set down his roll. "I wanted a moment to thank Percy for all the help he's given me with the family. Embarrassing himself at soccer for Ellie, pretending to camp out with Hannah, massaging Mom's bad back." Cal looked him in the eye. "You're going to make a great dad someday."

Josh snorted beer out of his nose. A very unattractive look that Percy gratefully witnessed. "Napkins are next to the coolers."

Josh followed his directions across the yard. Percy leaned back on the bench, spreading his legs so the outside of his thigh touched Cal's. "What are you trying to do? Convince him to take me back?"

"You know that's not what I'm doing."

Maybe. "Why are you pimping me so hard?"

"He should know what he's missing out on."

"Oh, Cal," Percy said, sliding half the lamb and mushrooms off the skewer and setting the remainder on Cal's plate. "I hate to break it to you, but this burning resentment you have toward my ex? It's making you very, very flustered."

Cal stared at the half kebab on his plate. "Josh needs to open his eyes."

Percy sighed, set his plate on his lap, and looked over at Cal scowling across the yard. "One last question before I reluctantly save Josh from those laser beams. Is nemesizing a word?"

Cal picked up the skewer off his plate and played with it, expression softening. He opened his mouth to say something, when a shrill cry interrupted him. Cards flew into the air as Crystal leaped from the picnic table, pointing toward the house. "Smoke!"

Percy shot up, knocking over his paper plate. "The rolls! I've got it," he called back into the yard as he darted inside to an alarming wall of smoke.

He covered his mouth and nose with his shirt and blinked back the sting in his eyes as he raced for the kitchen.

A small fire roared from the pan on the stove. He must have left the gas on after sautéing the onions, and he'd tossed a couple of overcooked rolls into the pan to throw away once they'd cooled.

A fine cook he made today.

Flustered and a little frightened, he grabbed Aunt Abby's apron and dunked it in the sink of dishwater. Tap water sprayed wide, and the fire hissed. He jumped and threw the apron onto the pan, praying it smothered the flames.

It didn't. Angry flames ate through the apron and ripped along its strings to the counter next to the stove. To Aunt Abby's cookbook he'd been using.

A cry ripped out of him as he watched its pages shrivel to ashes.

There was still the tin of recipes. He leaped toward it, but strong arms yanked him back. He fought Cal's hold. "I'll kill you if you don't let me go."

"You won't be able to if you're already dead." Cal dragged him back. "Promise me you'll stay here."

"When have I ever promised that?"

Cal tightened his hold against Percy's chest. "Please." Then he let him go, picked up the fire extinguisher he'd dropped to grab him, and released the pin.

White foam exploded from the nozzle, dousing the stovetop and stopping the fire. Percy coughed and sank back against the sink. He hugged his chest as his body trembled.

Cal turned everything off, and whisked around. "Come, we'll close the door to the living room and open the windows in the rest of the house."

Percy gave him a shaky nod and coughed again.

Cal's steady arm clutched him around the waist and steered him out of the room. Percy fumbled as he opened the front door.

He kept his head down, unable to look at Cal, and they moved through the house to let air in. In his room, Percy made quick work of unlatching the lock and opening the window. Still, he caught Cal pause at the sight of his clothes heaped on his bed, empty boxes framing one side of the bed, an empty closet on the other.

"Are you okay?" Cal asked.

"Oh, yeah. Peachy."

Cal sighed. "I'm sorry about her recipes, but her house is still here."

Percy blinked back the sting in his eyes. The smoke sure had done a number on him.

He ducked out of the room to Aunt Abby's room. The door handle bit coolly against his palm, but it was not enough to counteract the heat of Cal coming up behind him.

He made quick work of twisting and entering. The smell of smoke was barely detectable in her room, which still smelled faintly of perfume. He hauled in a deep breath. A fire. He'd started an actual fire.

He was all good luck and cleverness, wasn't he?

He opened a window, and gentle breezes washed into the house. Outside, Champey and Roosevelt had joined the neighbors settling back into their afternoon enjoying dessert. Laughter trickled into the room, possibly at Percy's expense. He had been the one to cause drama this year.

He turned and met Cal's studious blue eyes.

Percy slowly dropped his gaze, tracing Cal's features: cinnamon-colored locks, freshly shaved cheeks, muscular arms and chest trapped beneath his dorky T-shirt. He looked gorgeous. Even more than that, Cal was genuine and dependable. Cal had saved his house. Deep gratitude filled Percy. Gratitude he could never admit to Cal's face. Because if he did, Cal might win more than a game of words. He might win something that would kill Percy if it were rejected.

"An extinguisher. Good thinking."

"I always have one next to the grill." Cal leaned against the wall, over the light patches where pictures used to hang. He folded his arms. "You asked me outside if nemesizing is a word."

"And is it?" Percy held his breath. His veins thrummed with an urgent need to touch, caress, kiss.

"No, not anymore. Maybe it never has been."

Clenching his fists at his sides, he forced himself to move out of the room. When he reached the door, Cal whispered his name, and his self-control hitched a ride on the thousands of butterflies out of his belly.

Curiosity be damned.

He shut the door and whirled back around.

Cal swallowed, Adam's apple jutting. He didn't move when Percy stepped up to him. Close. Closer.

"Admit you were flustered outside." Percy barely managed to keep the pleading out of his voice.

He wanted to grab Cal by the shirt and kiss him. God, he wanted to kiss him so damn hard. Explore his lips and dip the tip of his tongue over Cal's parted bottom lip. But first, give him flustered. Give him that.

Cal's limbs trembled, and his blue eyes shuttered closed. "I wasn't . . ."

Percy hauled in a halting breath and rocked back.

Cal's eyes pinged open. His arms shot out and he pulled Percy forward. Their lips were so close his skin tingled. "I wasn't flustered, Percy—"

Theo and Josh burst into the room, door banging against the wall. Cal startled and shoved Percy back.

"There you are," Theo said.

"We thought you might need our help," Josh added, eyes pinging between the two of them.

Percy felt the heat of Cal's hands where he had pushed him. Inside, he gave a sore laugh. If he secretly hoped this to be anything more than a few nights' fun, that little shove sure proved otherwise.

"Don't worry," Percy said, striding toward them, Cal a short distance behind. "We can look after ourselves."

Theo looped an arm around Percy and ruffled his hair. "Guess what? Your Josh and my Jamie went to the same high school."

"We were in different years," Josh said at the same time Cal murmured, "He's not his anymore."

"Small world, right?" Theo said as they headed outside into the warm afternoon. "Since Josh lives only a few miles from Leone's boyfriend, she's going to bum a ride to surprise him a day early."

"I suppose that means you'll be leaving soon?" Cal asked Josh in a burst of sprightliness. "Pack some cake to take with you."

At the word cake, Theo shot across to the yard, leaving Cal, Percy, and his ex in an awkward triangle in the shade of the back porch.

Josh caught Percy's eye and gave him a look.

Percy shrugged. "I guess this is it, Josh. Good bye."

Josh stepped back, tipping his head to him and Cal. "Good luck."

"Good riddance," Cal chimed the moment Josh was out of earshot.

"Really, Cal?"

"I don't like him. Never have."

"He's not so bad. I thought you'd like him. He's extremely smart."

Cal's face drained of fluster, and insecurity flickered at the corner of his eye. He rubbed his neck. "Not so smart if he left you."

With those gut-dropping words, Cal turned to the dessert table. Percy leaned on the railing to catch himself from melting into a puddle.

"What are you so dreamily smiling at?" Ellie asked as she and her mom approached.

Marg followed Percy's gaze, and her lips lifted knowingly. "I think he's eyeing up dessert."

That threw Percy into a hearty laugh.

"Go get some then," Ellie said.

"Even if it's unhealthy for me?"

Marg's smile dissipated, while Ellie rolled her eyes and said, "Unhealthy but delicious. Come on, Mom, you have to pack."

Marg let her daughter lead her away, but glanced back at Percy. "Hannah and I won't be back until next week. Make sure to look after yourselves until then."

Ellie snorted, her words audible but trailing off as they rounded the side of the house. "If I didn't have to work, I'd binge on ice cream and never leave the bed."

Percy glided over the lawn, the soft afternoon light warming his back. Cal sat with Crystal at the picnic table, halving a custard tart.

". . . been hurt too many times before. Scorpio hates vulnerability."

Percy stooped behind Mr. Feist and continued listening to Crystal talking about Scorpio. Had Cal asked about the sign? Or was this meddlesome advice?

"What do they love?" Cal asked.

"Good sense of humor. Scorpios thrive on telling you what they want without explicitly telling you." Cal huffed out amused laughter. "They often cloak themselves in sarcastic comments— much like Virgo that way. They want to be with someone who gives as good as they get."

Percy peered around Mr. Feist's thick bicep. Cal prodded his plastic fork into the custard tart with a mesmerized smile. "Do they ever drop that cloak and say what they mean?"

"Yes."

"When?"

A large hand landed on the top of his head, and Percy

unglued himself from Mr. Feist's side with a sheepish grin. "Tight guns you have there. Ever thought about regular massage?"

"Percy!" Cal said, seeing him now their neighbor had shifted. "Sit here."

Percy crammed next to him on the bench as Cal took his first bite of tart. His face pinched as he swallowed. "Don't eat it, Crystal. It's truly terrible." He shoveled more custard on his fork and offered it to Percy. "Try it."

"All chivalry you are." Percy parted his lips anyway, and Cal's expression lifted in surprise.

Cal drew the fork away. "Look, I was thinking. . ."

Crystal hopped out of her seat, gathered their plates, and left the table. All subtlety.

"What insanely smart thing were you thinking, Cal?"

That earned him a wry glance. "Your house is too smoky. Tonight, you're sleeping with me."

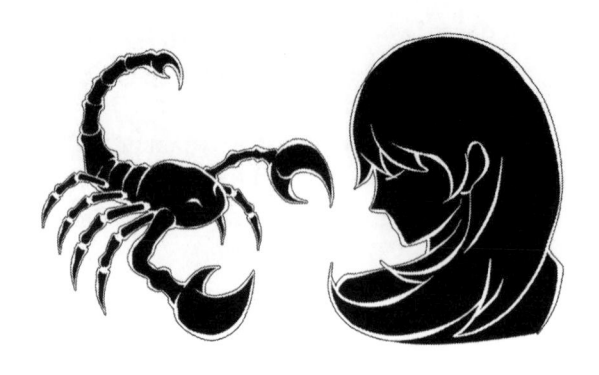

Nemesis
noun / nem . e . sis

Definition of NEMESIS

: Perseus throwing verbal grenades at Callaghan to get a rise out of him.

: Callaghan throwing verbal grenades at Perseus to get a rise out of him.

: A supposed enemy

: A frenemy

plural **NEMESES**

: two guys flirting

Chapter Sixteen

They didn't do much sleeping.

There was a lot of tossing and turning, and Cal's almost naked body sweating under the sheets.

Unfortunately, not the fun, sexy kind Percy would have liked.

He rolled onto his side and steadied a thrashing Cal with a hand against his shoulder blade, noting with alarm how Cal's skin burned under his palm. He pushed himself into a sitting position, switched the bedside light on dim, and turned Cal onto his back. "Cal, are you okay?"

Cal moaned, eyelids stuttering open. "Percy?"

He sounded confused. Surprised and confused.

Percy swept Cal's damp hair back and checked his temperature. "What's hurting?"

Cal sharply twisted onto his side, curling his legs toward his chest. "Everything."

His breathing grew labored, and Percy scrambled nearer. He shoved the blanket off Cal's legs and dug into the pressure points four finger-widths under each knee to help with dizziness and pain.

"Are your muscles aching? Is it a headache?"

Cal stilled under him for a single moment before he lurched out of Percy's grip, stumbling off the bed and into the bathroom.

Percy winced when he heard Cal vomit, then swear, then vomit again.

Food poisoning. Peachy.

Percy slipped off the bed and into the open bathroom. Poor Cal was plastered over the toilet.

The floor was not a pretty sight either. Percy stepped past it and laid a comforting hand on Cal's heaving back, sympathy tightening his chest. "Get it all out, Cal. This will pass. Might pass like a bitch, but it'll pass."

More vomit. "You don't have to be in here," Cal said between bouts.

"I know."

Percy rubbed large circles over his back. When Cal shakily sat back on his haunches, Percy grabbed a hot washcloth for him.

Vomit from the floor had splattered over Cal's legs, and Percy turned on the shower. "Shower while I clean up the floor. Then we'll get you back to bed."

"Teeth," Cal murmured, staggering to the sink and grabbing his toothbrush.

Percy left him brushing his teeth while he hunted down a bucket, scrubbing brush, disinfectant, toilet cleaner, and rubber gloves.

Cal spat out mouthwash into the sink and lurched ungracefully toward the cleaning gear. Percy stopped him. "As much I like the idea of you on your hands and knees, I'd prefer you in the shower."

Cal managed a weak laugh. He touched his stomach with a furrowed brow. With another groan, he wedged his boxers down over a dark patch of pubic hair and cock that clung to his thigh. He bent to push the sweat-drenched material over his knees, and the curve of Cal's ass spiked Percy's heart rate.

Percy lunged for the cleaning supplies as Cal schlepped into the hot water, and scrubbed vigorously until the bathroom reeked of lemon. In case of another mishap, he left the gear in the corner of the bathroom.

Plastic squealed, and a frightening thump echoed from the shower.

"Cal?"

A groan.

Percy flung open the misted shower door to find Cal on the floor, back against the wall, water spraying over his soapy knees and feet. He looked up pathetically, and Percy couldn't watch.

"Let's rinse you off and get you out of here."

He stepped in toward Cal and pulled the showerhead off its stand. Water sprayed over his torso and the briefs he had decided to leave on. It smelled like Cal had poured half the bottle of bodywash over him, pleasant but almost overwhelming.

Percy crouched to wash the suds off Cal's legs, crotch, and chest. He set the showerhead back and slickened Cal's wet hair back.

Cal stared at him, expression pinched with nausea, words sighed. "This is not how I imagined our first time in the shower."

"Not how I imagined it either." Percy offered a cheeky smile that earned him a pained laugh. "Come on. Time to get up." Percy hooked Cal under the armpits and heaved him to his feet. "Remind me to thank Mr. Feist for making me work on my arm strength."

Cal's foot slid over the slippery floor, and their wet chests smacked together. "Remind me to curse him for making those custard tarts."

Cal tried to carry most of his own weight, but his limbs were shaky. Percy planted himself at his side, dried him off, and steered him to bed.

Cal flopped onto the mattress and crawled under the sheets without fresh underwear. Percy kept his wet ones on as he raced to the kitchen to make tea and grab water. When he returned with the liquids, he found Cal passed out, mouth parted, lightly snoring toward the ceiling.

Percy set the steaming cup and bottle on his bedside and pulled the blanket over Cal's chest. All his strong angles slackened to make him look vulnerable.

Percy got rid of his briefs, tossing them with Cal's into the laundry basket before helping himself to a fresh pair of boxers.

Back in bed, he grabbed his phone and searched online for recovery tips.

Percy palmed Cal's forehead and checked his temperature. Warm, but it seemed to be going down. He shifted his hand under the edge of the blanket to Cal's heart and checked its rhythm.

Cal stirred, one eyebrow weakly lifting.

"Making sure your heart's not skipping any beats."

"If it is," Cal murmured, "it's got nothing to do with food poisoning."

Percy gave a shaky laugh. "Is that you or the fever talking?"

The only response was Cal's snores.

∼

THREE MORE TIMES, CAL ENDED UP OVER THE TOILET.

The third time, Marg and Hannah were already awake getting ready for their flight. Marg helped Percy change Cal's fevered sheets, looking about ready to cancel their flight to help her son. Percy encouraged her to go. Cal needed to rest, and Percy would make sure that happened.

While Cal slept, Percy drove Ellie to work.

Matt was waiting for her outside the diner. As soon as he saw her, he lowered his headphones, a shit-eating grin lighting up his face. Of course, Percy watched.

With a bounce in her step, her hair pulled back, and fresh confidence clinging to her, Ellie walked inside with him.

Percy returned to the cul-de-sac with a grin rooted on his face. He grabbed his laptop and fresh clothes from his house and headed back to Cal's bedroom.

"I'm feeling better," Cal said from the bed, tentatively prodding his stomach.

Percy swiveled onto the bed, picked up Cal's wrist, and massaged the pressure point that worked great against nausea.

Cal sighed into the touch, head sinking into his pillow. "It's almost worth being sick for this."

Percy side-eyed him, shaking his head. "Yes, because getting sick is the only way I'd do this for you."

Cal stretched his legs, toes pointing, hips lifting. "I'm so glad you didn't eat that tart."

The corner of the blanket covering his groin slipped, revealing Cal's thick cock, half-hard from sleep.

Percy's tongue clucked against the roof of his dry mouth. "After last night, you'd think I'd be put off by dessert altogether."

"You're not?"

"Not even a little."

"I am. Maybe not all dessert, but I don't think I'll ever eat a tart again."

Percy gave a shallow smile. "Once you're over this, you might change your mind."

Cal stared at him, searching his face. Then he focused on Percy's vice-like clamp on his wrist.

Percy let go and swung off the bed.

Cal gave a resigned sigh. "Leaving?"

"Not yet." He pulled a book of dinosaur facts from Cal's shelves and flung himself onto the bed. "We're going to have some fun first."

Cal modestly rearranged the blanket over his hips as he turned onto his side. "Start already."

Percy cracked open the book to a random page and read aloud. "'Dinosaurs often consumed rocks that helped grind food in their stomach.'"

Cal groaned. "I don't think I can handle any talk on food or digestion."

"I'll skip T-rex's Stegosaurus-filled menu then."

Cal's groan sounded pained. "Percy, T-rexes didn't eat Stegosauruses."

"I didn't take T-rexes for discerning carnivores."

Cal rubbed his stomach. "Don't make me laugh, it hurts."

Percy scanned the book looking for what T-rexes ate.

"Stegosaurus was a Jurassic dinosaur."

"If that was meant to clarify things, Cal, you're doing a fantastic job."

Cal gently kicked Percy's leg, toe nudging the side of his foot. Percy pushed back until their feet were fighting to dominate each other. Percy lifted his leg and threw it over Cal's, pinning his to the mattress. The contact of their skin seared heat through Percy.

Cal pinched the book from him and cleared his throat. "Stegosaurus was extinct for eighty million years before the first T-rex. We are closer to being on the T-rex menu than a Stegosaurus."

"Seriously?"

"No, I studied dinosaurs to make facts up. Yes, seriously."

"Fine. Since we're being all serious . . . when will you get back to your Jurassic Park studies?"

"Paleontology masters."

"Callaghan."

"As soon as everything has settled."

～

PERCY RESCHEDULED HIS CLIENTS TO THE FOLLOWING WEEK,

and he and Cal spent the day lounging in bed and watching *Elementary*. Cal napped after a wave of nausea gripped him.

He watched him while he slept, trying to think how he could gnome him and Ellie. Nothing seemed good enough.

Percy picked up Ellie from work and took her out for a pancake dinner. Back at the Glovers', he made Cal eat dry toast, then left him playing on his laptop while he watched TV with Ellie.

Later, when Ellie disappeared to take a call in her room, Percy opened his laptop at the dining table and peeked into the Sherlock Gnomes forum.

Seeing Gnomber9 online didn't cause his insides to hum louder than the Glover fridge at all.

He wriggled his fingers and smirked . . .

Gnomad: Hit me.

Gnomber9: What are you doing?

Gnomad: Sitting all alone in the great room.

Gnomber9: What is the one thing you can't start your day without?

Gnomad: A five-minute stint at the window spying on the neighbors.

Gnomber9: What would you like for your birthday?

Gnomad: Binoculars.

Gnomber9: Percy, Percy, Percy.

They spent another half-hour chatting online. Percy's foot

tapped against the floor, part of him itching for the next question, part of him ready to jam himself next to Cal in bed.

Gnomber9: Have I told you how much I like getting to be the inquisitor?

Gnomad: Yes.

Gnomad: There's a sick boy I need to get back to, so one more answer before I sign off.

Gnomber9: Something's been burning in my brain . . .

Gnomad: Ask.

Gnomber9: Can you hula-hoop?

∽

TWO DAYS AND ALMOST TWO SEASONS OF *ELEMENTARY* LATER, Cal was healthy again.

Percy dropped Ellie off at work not at all bummed when she reminded him Jenny was back in town. Back in town and supposed to be visiting later.

He shoved the thought back and cooked a big breakfast in celebration of Cal eating normally.

His favorite Glover entered the great room after a quick shower. Water dripped from his hair onto a blue T-rex T-shirt. Numbers and the words "*Good luck reaching* the 1" floated above the short-armed-dinosaur print.

Percy stopped pushing bacon around the sizzling pan to admire the view.

Rain-speckled light coming in from the bay window slid over his body. "I think we should get out of the house today."

"Charming weather for it." Percy opened the carton of eggs on the counter next to him and picked out two. "How do you like your eggs?"

"In eggnog."

Percy's lips turned up and stayed up all throughout breakfast. When they were done, Cal did the dishes, and there was, without a doubt, a suspicious glint in his eye.

"What are you thinking about?" Percy asked.

"Get your keys. I'll show you."

～

Rain pattered on the umbrella he and Cal were sharing, and Percy gazed up at the bulky building from the bottom of the entrance steps.

Cal set a nudging hand on the small of Percy's back, leaning in as if to impart the answer to his whole heart and everything. "This is a library."

Percy combed his bangs to the side with his middle finger. "I know what a library is."

At the top of the steps, Cal opened the door and beckoned Percy out of the rain. "To a tour you'll never forget."

The tour held Percy's attention. Cal had numerous facts up his sleeve, from the history to the politics of libraries. Better than that, he had to whisper. Libraries were quiet places.

Every inch of skin on the right side of his face tingled—the scalp where Cal's breath shifted his hair, the shell of his ear where the heat of Cal's breath pooled, the jaw where Cal's occasional laugh drifted.

At the kids' section, Percy reluctantly withdrew from Cal's side and crouched at a low shelf filled with picture books. "As much as I love dinosaurs and the dictionary, Hannah needs something new. A book on diggers, perhaps. You'll lend me your library card, right?"

"No."

Didn't sound like Cal was kidding. A tone Percy was still getting acquainted with. Fingers gripping Digging Deep, he looked up at Cal pulling an envelope out of his pocket. He held it toward him.

"Proof of your address for you to get a card of your own."

Cal must have snatched the postmarked envelope from his mailbox. "Proof of address?"

"So they know where to send the fines."

"Familiar with that, are you?"

"I am full of vices."

Percy smiled, but it was a wavering one. "I don't have photo ID on me." A lie and they both knew it. What he needed to say was that he'd already found someone interested in buying Aunt Abby's. He'd be out as soon as next week.

Cal closed his eyes, and Percy noted the brief resignation and disappointment. A sharp sting clinched his chest and he shot to his feet grabbing the envelope as Cal pulled it away.

Their eyes met, and Percy heard himself lying. He would tell him the truth. He would. When Mrs. Yoshida had signed the contract. Anything might go wrong before that. "With my luck, I should probably hang onto this."

It was as though Cal was festooned with tea lights and they all illuminated at once. "In that case, I wish you all such luck in the world."

"Now who's the charmer," Percy said.

Cal ignored that, whisking him away from the children's section.

Percy stuffed the envelope into his pocket as they cruised the aisles. Cal seemed to be searching for something. Maybe it was the dictionary section. Or where they kept the books on extinct beasts. "What's your favorite word, Cal?"

A sideways glance.

Percy shrugged. "Seems an appropriate library-related question. What is it?"

"Depends on my mood."

Oh, really? "What mood are you in right now?"

A flush crept up Cal's neck, and he tightened his hold on Percy's wrist. "Facetious is an interesting word."

"Using inappropriate humor in serious situations?"

"It has all the vowels in alphabetical order."

"Interesting but not your current favorite."

Cal stopped at the end of an aisle, releasing Percy to point. "Oh, look."

"Good try."

Cal pointed again with genuine amusement. "Really. I think you should look."

When Percy folded his arms, refusing the bait, Cal sighed and steered Percy in front of him. Warmth from Cal's front plastered his back, and Percy sucked in a sharp breath. A cursive sign hung above a large alcove off the main room: Restricted Section.

"You're kidding me."

Cal propelled them into the alcove. The shelves were stacked with large atlases and dictionaries from the Middle Ages. There was a rack of periodicals and a locked shelf containing manuscripts. "These books are for inside library use only."

"Did you know about this little library joke?"

"I'm as surprised as you are."

Percy narrowed his eyes at Cal. "This wasn't what you were dragging me around for?"

Cal's throat jutted with a swallow.

"Cal?"

"It's quiet here."

It was. Quiet, and cozy, and currently very private. Deep-red carpet covered the floor, and light ricocheted off curved lamps sitting atop each shelf. Cal shuffled a step back toward the dictionaries, his gaze slipping to Percy's lips and then fleetingly to his crotch.

A river of desire flowed through Percy at the clear arousal sparking Cal's eye. He stepped closer. "It is deserted."

"Yes." Cal's tongue darted over his bottom lip. Percy splayed his hands over Cal's chest and backed him against the dictionary shelf. He dropped his voice to a whisper. "What's your favorite word?"

Cal trembled under his touch, breath hitching against Percy's cheek. "It's a small one."

"It doesn't matter how small it is, it's how you use it."

From knee to chest, Percy pressed himself against Cal, breathless at how hard they both were, how eagerly Cal slipped his arms around his waist. One of Cal's hands slipped to the curve of his ass, delicate, tentative.

"Kiss," Cal said, voice croaky. "It's kiss—"

Their lips touched with a shock of static that made Percy's cock pulse in his jeans. Cal hesitantly swept his tongue over the seam of Percy's mouth, eliciting a rather slutty groan.

Cal's eyes fluttered shut and he rolled his palm over Percy's ass as he deepened their kiss. Their tongues twisted and teeth bumped, and Percy nibbled that beautiful swollen bottom lip.

With shaky pants, Percy pulled back. Their gazes met, and Percy read Cal's precisely. Aroused, curious, and slightly apprehensive—but not enough to stop him.

Cal pulled Percy against him, chasing light kisses with deeper ones. Cal cupped his face, thumbs sweeping over his cheekbones. Despite alarm bells warning him this would only be a fling, Percy melted into each kiss.

He leaned hard against Cal, knee pushing between Cal's legs until he straddled his thigh. Cal's hand drifted through his hair, swept down the back of his neck, and rested on the small of his back.

Percy's T-shirt rode up under Cal's roaming fingers. The touch of his skin made Percy shiver.

Cal slowed their kiss and drew back, lips ravished, cheeks flushed.

"Definitely used that word well," Percy said. "I wonder how we'll use my other favorites."

Cal's body rocked nervously against Percy as he laughed. "Shall we find out?"

Nemesizing

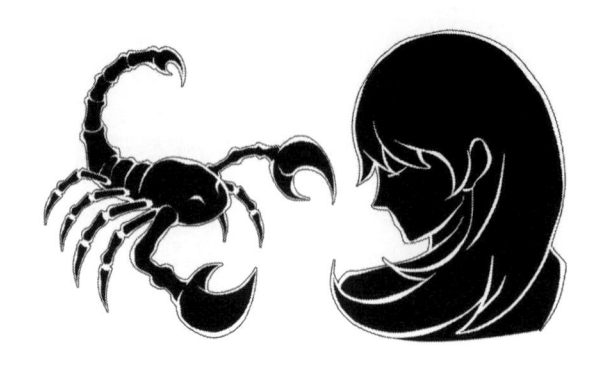

THE WORD YOU ARE TRYING TO LOOK UP DOES NOT EXIST IN the second edition of the percalinary.
Alternative spelling suggestion below:

NEMESIS

Chapter Seventeen

Back in Cal's room, they began their investigation.

Piece by piece, Percy stripped them out of their clothes until they wore nothing but their briefs.

The room was warm, the air still heavy from their days cooped up in bed. It smelled like Cal's bodywash and traces of sweat. Percy had turned on both bedside lamps to brighten the basement room before pushing Cal against his bookshelves, picking up where they'd left off in the library.

They stood there almost naked, Cal biting his bottom lip and looking delightfully ragged. Percy tucked himself against Cal's chest, savoring the drumming of their hearts as he brushed their lips together.

He found Cal's hands and set his thumbs into the waistband of Percy's briefs, steering the material down to his upper thigh. Cal sucked in his breath and kissed Percy harder, spinning him around until his back hit the cool wood, jostling a model dinosaur onto his shoulder.

Cal caught it with his chin, then tossed it onto the bed behind him.

"Not how I expected you to treat your T-rex collectible, Cal."

"It was two dollars from Target. But I'd have chucked it the same if it were two hundred."

A smile ghosted over Percy's lips. He rubbed his cock over the impressive bulge in Cal's briefs.

Air sifted between them as Cal stepped back, curiosity shimmering when he peeked at Percy's cock. He stared at it for tortuously long, barely blinking.

Then Cal looked up, and his darkening gaze gave him away. He liked what he saw. Liked it, and desired it.

Percy tilted his head and half-heartedly bit back a smug grin.

"You can wipe that off your face, Percy. It ruins the overall package."

"Where would you like me to wipe it?" Percy hitched his fingers into Cal's briefs and tugged them down. "Around your lovely, thick cock?"

Said cock strained toward him, and Percy kicked off his underwear and dropped to his knees, taking Cal's briefs to his ankles. The carpet felt cool and spongey against his lower legs. The engorged head of Cal's cock poked his chin, hot and hard.

"You don't have to do that if you don't want—"

Percy clamped Cal's warm thighs and pushed him to the end of his bed. "There is nothing I don't want to do to you." He curled a hand around the base of Cal's shaft and touched his wet lips to the tip of Cal's cock, right at the slit. "There is also nothing I don't want you to do to me."

Cal fisted the blanket the moment Percy sucked him deep into his mouth.

Percy let out a pleased hum around Cal's hard cock. He tongued the ridges of his head and the bulge of a thick vein running his length. The salty taste of him had Percy gripping his own cock and thumbing his pre-come. Percy worked his mouth over Cal, loving every uncontrolled buck of Cal's hips, his guttural moans, his hands drifting over Percy's shoulders and to the back of his head, resting tentatively, as if he wanted to grip

Percy's hair and slam all the way down his hot throat but didn't dare.

Percy squeezed Cal's hands tighter on his hair and opened deeper for him. Sliding his hands under Cal's flexing ass, he urged him to use him. To go wild. He wanted everything Cal could slam into him.

He wanted Cal to love this.

To want to do it again.

Percy worked Cal with everything he could give him, loving every slide of Cal's cock over his tongue, loving the still gentle yanks on his hair, loving the way Cal's chest seized and caught on a breath as he chased his orgasm.

He clumsily tried to withdraw from Percy's mouth, and Percy growled around his pulsing cock.

A broken grunt escaped Cal as he thrust one last time. His cock pulsed in Percy's mouth, spurts of hot come collecting at the back of his tongue. He swallowed and continued to hold Cal in his mouth until every second of his orgasm had passed. Reluctantly, he released him with the pop of his lips.

Cal trembled, hands rubbing the bedcovers, pupils dilated, cheeks ruddy. Wonder filled his expression, and his lips parted on soundless words. He dropped his gaze to Percy's aching cock.

Cal looked up at him with heart-twisting curiosity and uncertainty. Percy stood and gripped himself. He slowly stroked, winking at Cal. "I can take this to the bathroom if you want . . ."

"Or?" Cal lifted that brow of his.

"Or you could lie back on the bed and watch me take care of myself."

"Can I suggest a third alternative?" Cal said, shuffling onto the bed and lying on his side. He patted the bed next to him.

Percy stretched himself over the cool bedcovers, the stitching deliciously scratching his ribs, hip, and knee. The T-rex prodding his shoulder had to go, though. He stuffed it under the pillow and then fisted his cock, barely holding back from pumping. "What did you have in mind?"

Cal's throat worked with a deep swallow. His hand was already back at his cock, gently pulling it. Percy was impressed at how quickly it responded, swelling to half-mast.

"What did you have in mind?" Percy asked, a wave of lust making him push Cal's back to the bed and roll on top of him. The press of their naked skin together had their breaths hitching.

Cal cupped Percy's face, then swept his hair back. Cradling his neck, Cal kissed him. "I want you inside me."

"That jumped a few levels in intensity."

"Yes, but you know how I like my ice cream," Cal said, watching him, chest heaving under Percy's.

"So we're BFFs now?" Percy's heart hammered.

They stared at one another as the truth shifted between them. Percy knew Cal was Gnomber9, and this time he had continued the charade.

Percy bit his lip, and Cal surged upward, tangling them into a kiss.

Hands roamed his back and hips pistoned, bringing their hard cocks together with delightful friction. "I really want you inside me," Cal said again.

Percy tasted the tipping edges of Cal's lips. "We don't have to do everything at once."

"I've worked myself up for this. So, if you like the idea and want to . . ."

Oh, he wanted to. Badly.

"How about you slide that wonderfully large cock inside me?"

"I'd break you." Said so dryly.

"I'd like to feel you try."

Cal combed Percy's hair. "You'd really let me in you?"

Percy nodded. "I've been dreaming of us between the sheets from the second I first saw you."

"I can't say the same."

Percy shook his head, front bangs flopping over his eye. "Right where it hurts, Cal."

"We were nemeses, Percy."

"Fake ones."

Cal pressed his lips together and glanced to the side. "I meant this has been something I've wanted to try only after spending all this time with you."

Try. That was a sucker of a word.

Percy tamped down a flare of hurt before it ruined the moment. If this was the only time they'd have sex, Percy wanted to make it an afternoon to remember. "I'm glad you trust me enough to try this with me."

A relieved sigh escaped Cal. He reached between them, and Percy bucked into the fist he curled around their cocks. "The things you say turn me on. So. Surprisingly. Much."

"I'll be sure to keep talking then."

Cal jerked them with tantalizing slowness. "I want to feel everything you're willing to give me, and I hope you're willing to give me everything."

Percy whimpered against Cal's neck, thrusting together once more before sliding onto the bed on his side. "Turn on your belly and spread your legs."

"Wait. Just like that? No lead up?" Cal twisted onto his stomach anyway, stretching horizontally across the bed.

Percy laughed, moving between Cal's legs. He opened the bedside drawer and pulled out the coconut oil, lube, and condoms. He uncapped the tube with a flick of his thumb and squeezed it in a line down Cal's back.

Thumbs pressed to the base of Cal's spine, he pushed up through the oil to his neck. He did the motion again, sweeping outward over Cal's shoulders and down his arms. Percy braced himself over Cal. Only his hands touched him—and the tip of his aching cock against the small of his back.

He dipped his head and whispered, nose brushing Cal's ear. "I'm going to hit every one of your buttons." He nibbled from the top of his ear to the lobe. "You can tell me to stop at any moment."

Percy massaged every inch of Cal's body, laying attention on parts of his body infrequently touched: the backs of his elbows, knuckles, knees, and ankle bone.

His cock begged for attention, and Percy lightly dragged the sensitive head over Cal's oiled body as he worked his ministrations. Cal relaxed like putty under him, moaning at his touch. Percy straddled Cal's thigh as he bent his second leg at the knee and massaged his foot.

Cal curled his toes, his leg flexing under Percy's ass and balls. Percy sucked in an impatient breath and set Cal's foot down on the pillow. It shifted, and once more the T-rex toy winked at him.

Percy picked it up, running his fingers over the long length of his tail.

He repositioned himself between Cal's legs. A rumbling laugh had him glancing up from the T-rex in his hands to Cal, who was looking at him over his shoulder. "Planning on something kinky with that T-rex?"

"Many things." He teasingly ran the tip of its tail over the outer crack of Cal's ass, gently parting him.

Cal's eyes darkened, and his ass shifted as he rubbed his cock on the bed. "I'd prefer it was just you this time," he said.

Percy's cock pearled with pre-come. "I want to do something memorable."

Cal dropped his head to the side, voice breathy with exasperation. "Perseus!"

"Fine." Percy jumped off Cal and dashed into the bathroom for a wet cloth. "I just liked the idea that every time you look at one of your dinosaurs, you'd think of me."

"Like I don't already," Cal called after him.

A wave of need far more powerful than lust charged through

Percy, as though falling from a great height. He swiftly wiped his cock free of oil and ran it over Cal's ass. He suited up and generously squeezed lubricant over his pulsing cock and Cal's wriggling ass.

He draped himself over Cal's back, breathing in the heady scent of their sweat. He rocked his hard cock between Cal's slickened cheeks, and the sweet slide against his shaft made him flex his toes against Cal's heels and do it again.

Cal clenched around his shaft with a low hum. "I've never felt so intoxicatingly aroused and nervous. Go slow, okay?"

Percy lightly bit Cal's shoulder. "What, so I shouldn't bring out the swing?"

Cal snorted, making his muscles slide under Percy and bump his hard nipples.

By the textbook, he prepared Cal. He used fingers and lube, lube, and more lube to stretch him. At three fingers, Cal's moan pinched with pain. "This burn better have a pleasurable return rate."

Percy sank one hand under Cal and gave attention to his cock. When he made approving noises, Percy rubbed his finger against his prostate.

Cal's voice pinched with pleasure. "Now we're talking. Do it again."

"The first time, sex can burn a bit," Percy said, ghosting kisses over the swell of his ass cheeks. He rubbed again. "Then it's like a whole new world."

"Let's get a head start there."

Percy glimpsed Cal's soft smile, and it hit him. Cal might hate this. Might wish to stop "trying" anything after this. If this was their one time together, Percy didn't want to miss a single moment. He needed to see every flicker of Cal's reaction.

"Turn around," he said, urging Cal onto his back and hitching one of his legs up. "I want to watch your mouth."

Cal's lips twisted wryly. "You always have."

Percy bent down and kissed him hard. A hot, bruising kiss that made Cal writhe desperately. He squeezed Percy's shaft and cocked his hips, angling himself.

Percy slowed the kiss, helping Cal line the tip of his cock to his lube-slathered hole. "You can change your mind at any second, okay? I'll stop, easy peasy."

"Be that hard, will it?"

Percy bumped their noses together and looked Cal in the eye. "I'll do it."

Cal tilted his chin and swept a soft kiss over Percy's lip.

With that kiss still tingling, Percy pushed the head of his straining cock past Cal's ring. Tight heat suctioned around him, and he shook with the effort not to surge forward. Cal bit his lip and took his cock in hand. "Everything you can give me, Percy," he said.

A hoarse groan slipped out as Percy pushed himself deep inside of Cal, the clenching of his ass around him already drawing him close to orgasm. Everything. God, how much he wanted to give Cal everything.

"Keep touching yourself like that," Percy said with a shallow thrust. He wanted Cal to enjoy this as much as he could.

Percy rocked into Cal, picking up a steady rhythm. Percy's veins sang with every thrust. Goosebumps prickled the small of his back, his toes curled, his scalp tingled. His balls tightened as the mother of all orgasms rapidly snowballed toward desperate release. "Oh fuck, Callaghan!"

"That's what we're doing, Perseus."

The break in Cal's voice as he moaned his name sent Percy over the edge. Cal jerked himself faster, and came seconds into Percy's release, ass pulsing around his cock and taking his orgasm to a surprising new world. It coursed through him, wringing him of every syllable, until he was left speechless, plastered against Cal's come-covered chest, chasing his breath.

His cock began slipping out, and with a sneaky kiss against

Cal's heart, he took care of the condom and cleaned up Cal, who lay on the bed watching him closely, smiling.

He pulled Percy in against his chest, trapping the washcloth between their stomachs. "That lasted a long time," he said.

"That's me. All stallion."

They measured each other as they always did, but this time Cal's nicked eyebrow didn't mock him. Added to the gentle spark in his eye, Cal looked . . . besotted.

Percy walked his fingers up Cal's chest to his chin. "What's your favorite word now?"

"I'm not sure I can choose. Sleep is definitely up there."

"Along with sore, I imagine."

Cal sucked in the tips of three of Percy's fingers and kissed each one. "Surprised too."

Percy lifted both brows.

"You felt better than I imagined."

A grin warmed Percy from the inside out. "You've imagined?"

"With growing frequency."

Percy rolled on top of Cal and looked down at him. "Does that mean you want to do it again?"

Cal's laugh shook under him. "Not immediately."

"Some *Elementary*, then?"

"Speaking of mysteries. Answer me this. When?"

Percy needed nothing else to know what Cal was talking about. When had Percy figured out that he was Gnomber9. "You like your sex French vanilla."

Cal closed his eyes briefly. "It was around then you started answering my questions."

"I really can hula hoop, you know."

A sigh crested over Percy's jaw. "You've an uncanny way of deflecting when things get personal."

"I'm full of vices. Now let's dress and pick up some lunch. What do you fancy—roasted, fried, or boiled duck?"

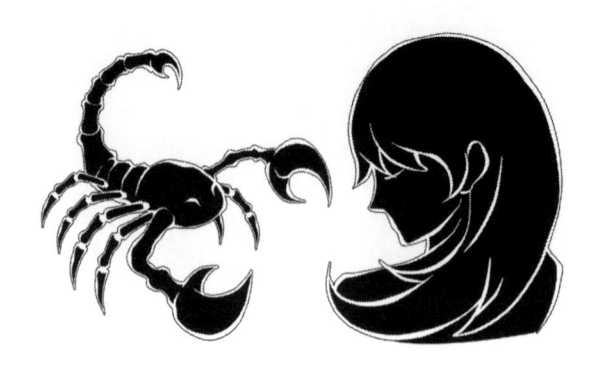

F luster
   transitive verb / flus . ter
  also: flustered

DEFINITION OF FLUSTER
   : the physical manifestation of intolerance toward a rival who has the attention of a loved one
   : turning red with jealousy

EXAMPLE OF FLUSTER IN A SENTENCE
   Watching him go on a date made Percy fluster.

Chapter Eighteen

It all felt very . . . domestic. Comfortable. Eerily safe.

And didn't that put Percy on edge?

His stomach tightened waiting for the other shoe to drop. They ate fried duck and then hung out on the couch, an *Elementary* episode wrapping up on the big screen.

He stared at their empty take-out containers, the half-filled water glasses, and Cal's keys as he fought off the pre-emptive dread souping up his insides.

"What are you thinking about?"

Cal cupped Percy's neck, thumb rubbing the sensitive spot under his ear. Shivers scuttled from the highly charged skin under Cal's fingertips to the tips of his toes in his yellow ankle socks.

"Your green key."

Cal laughed and picked up his keys. "Don't you recognize it?"

"No."

Cal pressed the keys into his hands, then fished in Percy's leather jacket until he returned with another set of keys. "You should know this one, Mr. Detective," Cal said, smirking. "Like I told you, it's the key to my heart."

The moment Cal gave Percy his keys, it clicked. His insides simultaneously lurched toward his feet.

It was the spare key he had given to the Glovers. The key was circular instead of square like his because it had been a copy. It looked so permanent like it was one of Cal's regulars.

He wanted to ask Cal what this meant. Wanted to know Cal was saying what Percy thought he might be saying. He wanted to believe so badly.

The hope was too big though.

Percy jumped to his feet, gripping his keys. "I need to pick up Ellie."

"So early?"

"Might be traffic."

"Going on your own?"

"No, I want you in the passenger seat while I have my little melodramatic meltdown. Yes, alone."

Cal studied him. "Whatever you're angsting about, keep in mind I'm a Virgo." He tentatively leaned in and kissed Percy. "I do like to talk."

∼

Percy also liked to talk. To himself, apparently. Which was exactly what he was doing on the drive to the diner. He was staving off the drama so he wouldn't make a scene picking Ellie up from work.

He held it together well.

The leftover wrappings of some Mentos, his hand-raked hairstyle, and Miley Cyrus blasting from the car stereo could attest to that.

Ellie threw him a funny look when she approached the Jeep.

Percy hooked an elbow out the window and tapped the outside of the door in a wave.

"Having an emo moment, Percy?"

He turned down Miley. "Or two."

"Those days suck."

Matt lingered in the shadows under the neon sign, glancing toward them once, twice, three times.

Percy lifted a brow. "How's your day looking?"

"Pretty good. Might get better. Matt asked if I want to check out this pop-up poetry reading?"

Ahh. "Is that a question, El?"

"What would I have to do to get you to convince Cal to let me go? I'll catch a bus home."

"You'll do no such thing." Disappointment washed over Ellie's face. Percy reached out and gently tugged at a bang that had escaped her knotted-up hair. "I'll convince Cal and pick you up."

"Are you serious?"

"Some of the time."

Percy already had the phone in his hand, texting Cal.

Perseus: Your sister wants to go to a poetry reading with a boy from work. She should go.

Callaghan: What boy?

Perseus: Cute one. Your sister has taste.

Callaghan: She's fourteen.

Perseus: It's poetry. I think we're safe.

Callaghan: Take a photo of him and get his number.

"Cal gives you his blessings," Percy said. "Now stand together so I can get a photo of you lovebirds."

Matt shyly shrugged an arm around Ellie and smiled. Percy took the shot. "Nice photo. Gimme your number, Matt. I'll send it to you."

Photos sent, Percy winked at a nervous Ellie. "Text and I'll pick you up any time."

She bit her lip, glancing at Matt. "Nine? From the café across the road from the library. Also, could you drive us there now?"

"Jump in."

Percy quizzed Matt until he knew everything short of his social security. The boy was eager to jump out of the car when they parked in front of the library. The library that now gave him goosebumps.

He rolled off a shiver and leaned out his window, calling after the lovebirds. "Matt, do anything more than PG and there'll be ass-kicking dominoes with me in the middle."

Ellie grabbed his arm and yanked him across the street.

The café swallowed them out of sight, and Percy sat alone in his car. The library stretched tall, a sea of words about to break over him.

He left the music off and drove back slowly.

Making pacts with the devil had not helped him, so maybe he should give God another try.

Give him a sign this would work out with Cal, and he would totally, no holds barred, stop being sarcastic for an entire week.

Give him a sign, he would totally give up all manner of alcohol, including his favorite eggnog over lent.

Give him a sign that they would be together for many years living happily ever after, and he would consider being candid with his ex-nemesis-and-environmentalist, Callaghan Glover, once and for all.

Back at the cul-de-sac, Percy parked the Jeep and hunkered

down in the front seat watching the evening settle over their houses.

Seriously.

Give him a sign this was real, he might cry.

He nervously slid out of his Jeep toward the streaks of sunset reflecting on the Glovers' windows. Cal's house looked like it was holding its breath, hoping it'd had its last first kiss.

Kind of how he felt going over there.

He smiled at the parted door, a warm coil springing through him as he crossed the porch. Had Cal spent the last couple of hours standing there, waiting for him to return?

Movement shifted down the hallway and Percy glimpsed Cal's flannel pajama bottoms first, followed by the rest of Cal. Percy stopped and admired the toned muscles flexing under his T-shirt, the way Cal swept a hand through his light reddish bangs, the warmth flooding Cal's expression when he caught Percy watching him.

"Cal," Percy said breathlessly.

"Percy."

He was about to spring into Cal's arms when Cal looked over his shoulder and smiled. Percy turned on his heel, expecting to see Marg and Hannah lugging their suitcases back up the path. Instead, Jenny trotted up to the house in strappy heels, flinging out her arms. "Cally, I'm back."

A tidal wave of disappointment slammed into him. This was his sign? *God, you outdid yourself.* "Cally?" he murmured bitterly under his tongue.

Cal slated him a look before passing Percy and curling Jenny into a hug.

"How was Spain?" he asked, stuck against her like a wet leaf on a windshield.

She squeezed him tighter, her vibrant laugh rocking them. "I could just live there."

Sounded like a good plan to him.

Cal finally stepped back. "Come in and I'll make us all a drink. You can tell me everything. You remember Percy?"

Jenny's laughter simmered to a sweet smile. She looked back at Cal, a knowing look passing between them. "How could I forget?"

Percy extended his arm between them before she could lunge at Cal again. "Jennifer, right?"

She shook his hand. "Jenny."

At his side, Cal's stare bored into him, and he refrained from rubbing the prickly spot at his ear.

"Percy." A trace of amusement and irritation touched his voice. "Maybe you could help me make drinks?"

"Oh, I can do that!" Jenny said and bounded past Cal into his house like she belonged there.

Percy scowled after her.

A laugh hit his cheek and then Cal was whispering in his ear, "I know how you feel."

"Flustered?"

Cal shook his head and turned into the house with a sigh. "Not flustered, Percy."

∽

THE RIGHT THING TO DO WOULD BE TO HELP CAL AND JENNY in the kitchen, but watching them laugh from the hallway stirred his stomach into knots.

He stumbled across the road toward his nicely cleaned-up house complete with beautiful porch, edging, and trimmed grass hopping with fireflies.

Frank's car caught his eye, haphazardly parked in front of his Jeep, and he pirouetted for joy. Fun times ahead.

He quickened his pace, beelining inside to the main room. His cousin stood in the kitchen, cupboards flung open, blue mug in his hand.

Percy strung out a laugh that emptied him from heel to heart. "Perfect timing."

Frank jerked dropping the mug. It shattered between them. He looked up, eyes ringed with shadows. "I came after work. You said there were recipes?"

"How did you get in?"

"Jimmied the backdoor lock."

"You're all kinds of handy." Percy picked up the largest part of the mug and rubbed his thumb over it.

"Give me something, and I'll go. You'll never see me again."

"Ah, but I'll see you every time I have a nightmare."

"In that case, I should apologize. Your whole life is a nightmare."

Frank slammed the cupboard doors, and Percy caught his breath. He saw it plain as everyone in the cul-de-sac had seen it: Frank was deeply hurting. Grieving.

The shard of mug dug into his palm where he clutched it. "I'm so sorry, Frank."

Frank's face pinched.

Percy moved to the tin of Aunt Abby's loose recipes. He carefully took out the surviving bundle. "Here they are."

Frank eyed them, swallowing thickly. He plucked them out of Percy's hands, turned his back, and dragged his feet through the porcelain pieces shooting across the floor.

"We don't have to be like this," Percy called after him, noting Frank pause. "We could talk. Try piecing something together. Play hockey or something that doesn't involve a soccer ball."

"No," Frank said, but he said it a little too intently, as though he was forcing himself.

"The door is always open—and if it's not, jimmy it again."

Frank left.

As soon as the front door banged, Percy's chest caught on a hiccup and didn't let go. He cradled the mug shard, vision blurring until he saw it twice. Cal and everyone had been right.

This whole time. They'd seen it.

His phone rang, and Percy answered without looking at the caller. He was convinced that somehow Cal would know because, in times like these, the cavalry was supposed to arrive.

Instead, a female voice cut down the line. "Hello, Mr. Freedman, Mrs. Yoshida. I'm calling regarding the offer I made on your house."

Percy barely managed to nod.

She continued, "I want you to know I have a second house in sight. I'd prefer yours, but if I don't get an answer in the next twenty-four hours, I'll withdraw my offer and go with that."

He gripped his phone long after she'd hung up. Phone in one hand, mug in the other. His heart mid-flip somewhere in between.

He barely heard the front door open.

Cal's voice sliced through the house. "Get the Pringles. We are about to have a real fight."

Cal rounded into the kitchen and halted. He took one sweeping look at Percy and took a large step forward. "Percy?"

Percy lifted his head, eyes prickling. "This whole time . . ."

Cal was right in front of him, pulling both phone and porcelain from his hands and setting them on the counter. "What's going on?"

"I've been fucking stupid." He stretched his lips into something he hoped resembled a smile. His voice wobbled though. "Now it's time we broke up."

The emotion twisting Cal's face ripped the air out of Percy's lungs.

Cal wrapped strong arms around him and held him. Words tickled through Percy's hair above his ear. "Are you okay?"

"I'm Scorpio. Nothing gets past my stinger."

"Clearly." Cal drew back and wiped Percy's damp lashes. "I came over here so mad, and you had to bring the tears."

"I was cutting onions."

"Must have been a lot of onions."

Cal tugged Percy out of the kitchen to the couch and sat him on it.

Percy's eyes blurred as he winked at him. "Going to offer me tea or coffee?"

"How about you talk to me."

"What did you think we were doing? Serenading?"

"Stop it." Cal dropped next to him on the couch, sitting forward. "Be real with me."

He couldn't help it. A dam had broken in him, and his natural defense was to throw walls up. "Where's Jenny?"

"She left, and you know it."

"I didn't make her leave early."

Cal stared at him. "Is this where you want to start? Fine. You stormed over here and refused to join us because you wanted me to choose."

Percy folded his arms. "I did not."

He did. He had wanted another sign. A do-over.

He just hadn't expected Frank.

"I choose *you*, Percy." Cal's voice held a striking punch of exasperation. "I've been choosing you since we first met. Just like you've been doing with me."

Percy floundered, his mouth opening and shutting. He tugged out a half-hearted chuckle. "Are you saying you've always known how much I don't exactly despise you?"

"You're an open book—my open book—and I've been studying you for a long time."

"Stop reading me so well."

Cal didn't laugh. He leaned in and cupped his face, fingers sliding over his jaw. "I can't."

Percy swallowed. "What else do you know about me?"

"You think you're cursed to have everyone you care about up and leave."

The weight of this conversation left Percy naked and

exposed. Not a look he usually went for outside the bedroom. "At least I have a crazy awesome dessert routine for when things don't work out, right?"

Cal shook his head, lips curving down sadly. "I know that when it hurts too much inside, you toss out a joke, a laugh, something spectacularly mundane. Are you trying to convince everyone else you're fine or trying to convince yourself?"

A nervous laugh escaped Percy, and Cal tilted his head, that analyzing gaze working him thoroughly. So thoroughly, Percy looked away.

"Spoiler alert," Cal said, leaning in. "You're not convincing anyone."

"I'll be fine, I'm used to it."

"You don't deserve dessert this time!"

Percy pulled back from Cal's outburst. "What does that mean?"

"The only one who's been saying they'll leave, Percy, is *you*."

"What if you're just curious, if you eventually—"

Fingers stroked him tenderly, Cal's thumb catching on the corner of his lip. "I'm not."

Percy's throat felt raw. "Not?"

"I'm not just curious. It takes me a while to sort out my feelings, some parts developing more slowly. But when I know who I like, I know."

"What do you mean?"

Cal shifted, then flattened his lips and looked right at him. "I only feel sexual attraction after spending a lot of time with someone. Do you understand what I'm saying?"

"We've spent a lot of time together?"

"No. Yes. No, you stubborn man. I'm saying that I waited to explore any tension with you until I thought we were emotionally on the same page."

"But I thought you were just curious. You said as much."

"Did I? Or has grief made you believe that?"

A shiver raced through every inch of his sarcastic soul. "You said you were curious what peace and quiet would be like between us."

"One has not to do with the other."

"You shoved me away when Josh and Theo walked into Abby's room."

"I shoved you. I didn't shove you away. I was so lost in us, they startled me."

"I overheard you with Jenny. You told her she should be curious, flirt, experiment. Have fun. That it doesn't have to be a forever thing."

"We work differently. Jenny felt guilty for wanting a fling, when with me, we worked toward intimacy. I like that, but she's allowed to do it her way. To be curious, experiment, do it for fun."

Percy leaned in curiously. "Are you demisexual, Cal?"

"I think I'm demipansexual. I've been trying to figure out my feelings toward you. I even went on Chatvica and read some posts about it, and demipan seems to describe the way I feel going into relationships."

Percy fumbled in his pocket for a Mentos. Something—anything—to distract him from the hope of this conversation. He patted his pockets and couldn't find them. "You've never been with a guy before, though, so maybe—"

"Stop searching for reasons we would never work."

"But—"

Cal rubbed his neck. "Did you go into this thinking I could be nothing more than a cul-de-sac?"

Percy opened his mouth to defend himself, to stop the hurt flashing over Cal's face, but Cal leaned in and pressed a startlingly soft kiss on his bottom lip. "That was unfair. I'm sorry. You've been hurt too many times, I understand. I do." He dropped his hands and rested his head against the couch. "I fooled myself into thinking you had grown to trust me. But nothing has changed. Has it?"

The question rose at the end like a bubble of hope, and Percy grappled at it. "Of course things have changed! We're not nemeses anymore—"

A hollow laugh puffed out of Cal. "You can't even say what we are."

"Why say it if we both know it?"

"You're killing me." Cal shook his head, then stared at the books scattered over the floor.

"I might have sold the house." The words burst out of Percy.

Cal stilled, then parroted the words back. "You sold the house?"

"A buyer looked while you were visiting your dad."

Cal grew silent. Long seconds passed before he spoke again, and when he did, it was a whisper. "Dad decides to leave for good, and now you?"

"Cal—"

"I'm so angry at you right now."

"I should have told you a buyer was interested, but . . . I couldn't."

Cal sighed. "Could that be because of what is right in front of you?"

Percy's heart leaped into his throat. "What is that?"

"Me with ruffled feathers, Perseus Freedman."

Cal interlaced their fingers and squeezed. "I feel butterflies every time I see you. I constantly want to tease you and draw you into conversation. I'm nervous when we touch, yet I find myself needing to do it more. When you look at me, it makes me feel giddy and absurdly attractive. It's awkward how aroused I get when I look at the photo you put on my phone. I constantly am making excuses to be near you, even if it tortures me when we go house hunting. I was jealous when Josh showed up. My insides lit up like electricity when I saw Aunt Abby's hidden muffin trays, and they did again the moment you took that envelope from me in the library."

Cal kissed the base of Percy's palm at the creases on his wrist. "I am genuinely head over heels for you."

Percy's heart stuttered, tenderness consuming him. "I . . . I don't know what to say."

"I want you to say that you know it."

"Well, I—"

"But don't say it right now when you might speak because you think you have to. Not after I've poured my soul out." Cal reluctantly pushed to his feet. "Take a day or two or three."

"That's a lot of thinking."

Cal pinned him with a look. "Attempt it. I'll send you a link to a listing I saw and ashamedly hid from you this morning. Check it out. Imagine yourself living away from here. When you've done that, when you've thought about what you want, then tell me how you feel."

Percy blinked. Why did he need him to do this?

Reading his mind, Cal softly lifted his eyebrow. "Set them free, right?"

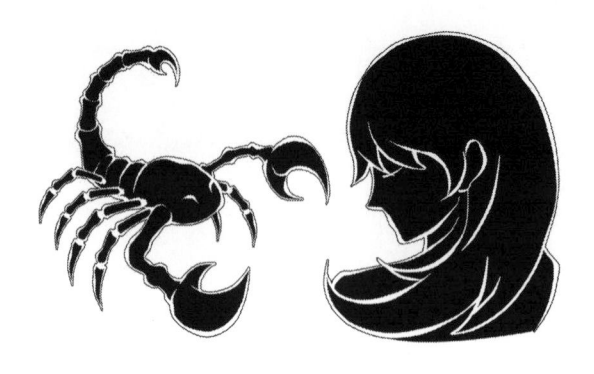

G nomber9
     noun / gnom . ber . nine

DEFINITION OF **GNOMBER9**
    : the creativity that played a big part in Percy's summer
    : the powerful connection the stars had promised would be forged
    : an alias for someone Percy fears losing

Chapter Nineteen

To: percyfreedman, wilhelmroosevelt, callaghanglover, ellieglover, champeyong, kelvinserna, josieserna, nathanfeist, jemmafeist

From: @cul-de-sac

Subject: Dear Neighbors

Thank you all for participating so eagerly in our inaugural Sherlock Gnomes event! All your kind gifts and secret services made bellies flutter and even the grumpiest lips smile (Yes, yours, Mr. Serna!).

Although this event was planned to continue another week, I've decided to wrap up the game. Submit your guesses for all gnome identities as soon as you can. The game officially ends tomorrow at 8:00 p.m. Answers will be posted on the Sherlock Gnomes forum.

Thank you for Sherlock Gnoming!

~

Gnomad: I figured I could just use my phone to message now, but I wanted to say goodbye to Gnomber9.

Gnomad: One other thing I've wanted to write here for a while now . . .

Gnomad: Cal. Cal, Cal, Cal, Cal. Cal.

~

Percy barely slept, haunted the entire night, not by Abby, but Cal's declaration.

He stared at the pile of clothes he'd slept next to and still hadn't put away. He pulled on shorts and a white button-down that he rolled up at the arms. Wrinkled and smelling of smoke, but he didn't care. More pressing was to see the listing Cal had sent him.

After arranging a viewing with the seller, he sank his feet into green canvas sneakers and scuffed his way toward a bowl of muesli. Perched on the sill at the bay window, back pressed to the cool glass, he stared at the living room. A nice, warmly decorated living room thanks to Sherlock Gnomes and his generous neighbors.

Percy dumped his bowl into the sink, grabbed his keys and massage table, and dragged it over to the Glovers' as Marg and Hannah were running out the door.

"Sorry, got to hurry," Marg said. "But I got your welcome home email and it put a smile on my face. Catch you at dinner."

Ellie flew out of the house next, followed closely by a sleep-torn Cal. Clearly, he'd tossed and turned the whole night if his hair and blue inside-out T-shirt was anything to go by.

Ellie threw her hands up for a high-five and Percy automatically accepted. "*I* leaned in halfway, and he leaned in the rest!" She bounced toward the car.

Cal came to an abrupt standstill in front of him as though he didn't think Percy would come over there so soon. As though he believed Percy had restraint or something.

"I have no restraint." Certainly not when it came to Cal. "I know you want me to check out that house and think, and I will, but if you don't give me your keys and let me drive us to work, I'm going to call you out as the worst environmentalist ever." A wedge of morning light made the keys Cal clutched glitter, and Percy leaned into Cal as he pinched them. "Worst environmentalist and worst friend."

Cal's tired eyes transformed with light as he gestured Percy to take the lead. "We can't have that."

Percy lugged his massage table to where Ellie leaned against the backdoor of the hatchback, arms folded, watching them. The twitch of her lips suggested she had a good idea what was going on between them.

Table in the car and Ellie buckling herself in the back, Percy gestured a cautiously stunned Cal to hop in the passenger side.

They were quiet for the first stretch until they were close to Ellie's work. Cal hooked a hand around the handle on the ceiling and said, "So why is it you are driving?"

"Because you look like shit." Percy felt Cal's laser focus on him and caught the shake of his head in the corner of his eye. "Hey, you wanted candid."

Laughter slipped between Cal's lips, and Percy soaked up the warm sound. "You look shit tired, and I kind of want you getting to and from work safely."

"Should I point out you look just as shitty?"

"Don't say that with such a grin, Callaghan."

"Can't help it, Perseus. It makes me unreasonably hopeful."

Percy looked in the rearview mirror at Ellie, who had

hunched forward, gaze swinging between them. He chuckled as he reached over and settled his hand on Cal's leg. His index finger brushed over the hem of Cal's shorts and rubbed the delicate skin of his inner thigh.

Their eyes met. "It's not unreasonable."

"You thought of me all night, then?"

"That is nothing new." Cal's quad stiffened under his palm, and Percy squeezed gently. "Only this time I had to stop myself from sneaking over and pouncing on you. I was trying to respect your wishes."

"You haven't quite respected them," Cal pointed out without admonishment.

"I know it's hard, but you mustn't mistake me for a saint."

Cal's fingers found the back of Percy's head and he gently thumped him. "I still—I need you to be sure . . ."

"Hey, guys?" Ellie said, voice dripping with amusement.

"Hmm?" Percy looked at her smirking in the mirror.

"You did it again."

"Did what?"

Cal knocked his head against the headrest and laughed, but more nervously than before. "We got distracted."

One U-turn and double-park later, Ellie jumped out to work —and Matt.

Percy parked outside the community center, then leaned over the console and kissed Cal like the saint he wasn't even trying to be. Raw lips, their breaths snagging, Percy pulled back. "I need to borrow your car today."

"Like you ever need to ask. Pick me up after work."

"I'll pick you up, all right."

∾

WELL, DO HIM SIDEWAYS.

The Cape Cod house was everything Percy wanted. A

charming starter home with shutter-flanked windows and a symmetrical façade, and a kitchen connected to the dining room through an arched opening like Aunt Abby's.

Every room, down to the painted woodwork, called Percy's name.

There was even a bay window overlooking the well-groomed residential street. Perfect for spying on the neighbors.

"What do you think?"

Percy smiled and looked out onto the one-way street. Warmth washed through him. Try as he might, he could not ignore it. This was as peachy as peachy could get.

Cal would call him all manner of names, idiot among them.

But he'd have to accept it.

"I think I've finally found my place."

∼

AFTER CALLING MRS. YOSHIDA, PERCY SCHLEPPED TO Crystal's for her massage.

He clumsily set up the table in her living room. He wanted to finish this session so he could start moving his things. He had twelve hours.

Crystal strolled into the room with a magazine tucked under her arm. Percy stopped fighting the sheet cover and picked up his aunt's old tennis racket that he'd rested against the gem cabinet. "You said you wanted to start playing again," he said, handing it to her.

He would have less room for storing his aunt's belongings after the move. Besides, she would have wanted Crystal to have it.

Crystal smiled with delight as she took the racket and bag from him, her magazine slipping to the floor. "Oh, you beautiful boy. Thank you. Now tell me why you're smiling, frowning, and then glowing."

Percy leaned on the table and massaged his head. "I have a big move today. Need to clean up my house."

"A big move? Today?" Crystal, bless her, looked startled and confused.

"I guess I sprang that one on you. But yes. Today. Don't be upset, this is a good thing—a wonderful thing. Turns out I do want to do this."

"What does Cal think?"

Percy bit his lip. "I don't want Cal to know. Not yet. I'll tell him in person this evening."

"Will this change things between you?"

"Yes. No. I mean, he'll be surprised, but it will make us stronger."

"Your horoscope suggested you'd have an emotional epiphany today." She picked up her magazine and peered at one of its pages. "Said Scorpio should rely on family to help you finally move on." She set the magazine between them on the table and patted his arm. "I trust you know what you're doing?"

"I haven't been more sure of anything in my life." Percy held his breath and looked her right in the eye. "I need your help. I need all the help I can get."

Help
transitive verb / help

DEFINITION OF HELP

: give assistance and support

: something Percy rarely asks of anyone else, though he often needs it

: what the cul-de-sac neighbors do for each other daily

EXAMPLE OF HELP IN A SENTENCE

Mr. Serna stared with narrowed eyes as Percy explained how he needed help moving, then he grabbed his keys and shut the door behind him.

"Let's get this done," he grumbled. "It's about damn time."

Chapter Twenty

Cal looked like a wreck when Percy picked him up from work. He sank into the front seat of the hatchback and gripped its vinyl upholstery. "Did you have a good day?" he asked tightly as Percy pulled away from the curb.

"It's shaping up to be quite emotional." He massaged Cal's shoulder, dropping his hold only to change gears. He wasn't sure when to tell Cal about the move. Or how. "Dare I ask how yours was?"

Cal leveled him a look. "Fraught with overthinking."

"About me?"

"Always."

Percy made a right turn, words catching in his throat. "It's not a mirage this time, is it?" He met Cal's gaze. "You're right here. No matter what? If I reach out, you'll reach back?"

"Good luck getting me to let go."

Percy nodded, and Cal relaxed into his seat, though his eyes barely dropped away from him. They picked up Ellie, Percy making a short stop to buy ice cream. Cookies and cream for Ellie. Chocolate mint chip for him. "French vanilla for you," he said, handing the cone to Cal.

"I hope this will become a thing," Ellie said, licking her ice cream.

Cal looked over his scoop at Percy. "I hope so too."

Percy's stomach twisted with nerves that no amount of ice cream could numb.

Almost home, Percy turned down the dead-end street that backed onto their cul-de-sac.

"Why are we parking here?" Ellie asked as Percy parallel parked under the weeping willow at the edge of the playground.

"You'll have to ask your brother."

"Cal?"

Cal snorted. "I might tell you later, El. For now, do me a favor and leave us alone?"

This was it then. The time had arrived to tell Cal everything.

When Ellie was out of sight, Percy looked out at the soft, late-afternoon light glinting off the slide and swings. He motioned Cal to follow him out of the car. Side by side, they sat on the swings.

Percy twisted the swing, chains clinking. "It took me a while, but I figured out all the gnome identities."

Cal's knuckles looked almost white where he gripped the chains. "I knew you would."

"Yes." What Percy hadn't pieced together until he'd read the mail from @cul-de-sac last night was a far heftier truth. It had hit him as he read "inaugural" and "making bellies flutter," but he should have seen it from the beginning.

Percy lifted his heels, untwisting the swing.

He stood shakily before Cal, gripping the chains above Cal's hands. "You are @cul-de-sac. You organized the game and rallied the neighbors to take part. You made up Sherlock Gnomes to help me fill my place—not to prepare it to sell, but to make it a home."

Percy studied Cal, absorbing the bashful twinkle in his eye.

The truth was obvious. Right there. If he'd only searched for it, he might have seen it since the beginning.

"Yes."

Chain links bumped over his palms as Percy bent and kissed Cal, their lips barely combing together. Cal stared at him with a hopeful twinkle in his eye.

It stole Percy's breath. "I love you, Cal."

S herlock Gnomes
noun / sher . lock/ gnomes

Definition of **SHERLOCK GNOMES**
: a game where members of the cul-de-sac secretly leave treats and surprises for each other. Those playing also try to solve the mystery of each gnome identity
: a game Percy is pretty good at

Examples of **SHERLOCK GNOMES** in a list
Gnomad = Percy Freedman
Gnomber9 = Cal Glover
Mrs. Gnomer = Crystal Wallace
Gnome de Plume = Champey Ong
Gnominated = Mr. Feist
Gnomega = Mrs. Feist
Gnome More Wood = Mr. Serna
Gnome Chomsky = Mr. Roosevelt
Real versus Gnominal Value = Josie Serna
I Don't Gnome = Ellie Glover

Chapter Twenty-One

They walked home.

Percy used Cal's green key to unlock the door, then he linked their fingers and pulled Cal inside, bypassing the lounge, heading straight to his room. The boxes that had been there this morning were gone and the room was tidy. "Take a peek in the closet."

"To decide how much I like you?"

Percy drummed his fingers impatiently on the doors.

Cal sauntered over and caged Percy, holding his arms up either side of his head. Soft lips touched his. So soft and tender and full of love that a knot tightened in his chest. He whimpered as he leaned into the kiss, his hand sliding over Cal's neck. "If we are heading toward our favorite word of the moment, I might warn you that we haven't finished talking yet. Also, dinner is in an hour."

"Plenty of time for stallions like us."

Percy laughed, and Cal pressed their foreheads together, looking Percy in the eye. "Say it again?"

I love you. "Open the closet." Percy set a hand on Cal's hip and steered him back.

Cal opened the closet door, keeping his eyes on him. He glanced inside and then did a double take. The quirk of his eyebrow was so surprised that Percy lifted onto the balls of his feet and kissed him right there.

"Where are your clothes?"

An unsteady exhale. "I moved today."

Cal cupped Percy's face and studied him. Only a flicker of worry clouded his expression before he shook himself of it. He searched Percy's eyes and seemed to find the answer he was looking for because his fingers stilled on his cheeks and his eyes widened. "You . . . you . . ."

Warm, trembling fingers wrapped around his wrist as Cal pulled him down the hall to Abby's room. His hold tightened as he approached the door and saw the tag hanging from the door handle.

No more Gnomad

He flung open the door and sucked in an audible breath.

Thanks to the help of their neighbors, Percy had moved all of Cal's things here and all of Ellie's things into Cal's basement.

This was his gnome surprise for the two Glovers he'd wanted to give something special to.

Cal's belongings filled Abby's old room: his bed, his shelves of books, his framed pictures, every single geeky T-shirt.

Percy had taken one of the watercolors Abby had painted and hung it above the bed, covering the sun-marked spots in the old paint.

"It's more symbolic than functional," Percy said, nervously seating himself on the bed next to the Glovers' bright yellow toolbox. "The shelves would have to be screwed to the wall, but we might want to paint first."

Cal shifted about the room, fingering a few of Percy's books on the shelves. He slipped inside the walk-in closet and breathed out some truly spectacular words. When he came back out, he sagged against the narrow stretch of wall.

Percy fingered the smiley faces drawn over the toolbox. "I thought about life-size Cal cut-outs to offset any remaining sadness."

"It could have been arranged."

"I wanted the more invasive method."

His thighs parted as Cal slid between his legs. Warm palms settled on his shoulders. Kisses feathered over his nose, cheek, mouth.

Percy snuck his fingers under Cal's sleeves at his biceps. "I like the T-rex ones the best."

Cal regarded him questioningly.

Percy pointedly pinched the T-shirt. "You're definitely breaking hearts wearing blue, but you break mine every time I see that pathetically short-armed dinosaur failing to reach *the stars, first base, a compromise,* and *the 1.*"

"Don't feel too sorry for him. A few well-aimed words convinced those things to come to him."

A laugh shot through Percy, and Cal swallowed it into his next kiss.

God, that did silly things to his insides. He nudged their noses together when they parted for breath. "When did you start liking me?"

"I've always liked you, Percy."

"When did you want more?"

Cal drew his thumb over Percy's bottom lip. "You snuck up on me. Every vacation, every weekend we crossed paths. I started craving our little bouts of banter. Started wanting to learn more about you. It came into sharper focus at Aunt Abby's funeral. You were hurting and you looked at me, emotions so raw, so open and I . . . I wanted to be the one you leaned on. I suddenly very much wanted to know all sides of you."

Percy hummed over the tip of Cal's thumb. "About the same time you broke up with Jenny."

"I recognized my infatuation with you, and it didn't seem fair to her."

"I was jealous of her yesterday. Unbelievably jealous."

Cal smiled a little too broadly, so of course Percy had to kiss it off him.

"When did you decide to stay?" Cal asked.

"It's been sneaking up on me too. But when you left last night . . ." Percy swallowed the lump of tenderness building in his throat.

He looked into Cal's eyes, preparing to ditch sarcasm for a whole minute. He wanted to be honest and direct—and it was safe to do that with Cal.

"The house still smelled faintly of smoke, and it reminded me of the panic I felt during the small fire. Despite how empty and lonely this place sometimes feels, I didn't want to lose it. And seeing those mugs Frank broke . . . it hurt, you know? I was staring at them and the truth was right under my nose. By moving, I was the one destroying all the good things in my life.

"I went to the house you found, and it was beautiful, Cal. It was so me. And it felt so wrong. I looked out the windows and you weren't there. This place is my home. I have memories here. Not only old ones with Aunt Abby, but new ones. I look at my couch, and I relive the moments you swept me over to it. The bay window, where I repeatedly spied on you. The bedroom, where you called me Percy for the first time. The backyard, where we camped with your sisters and hosted the Fourth of July barbecue. This room, where you distracted me, where we got jammed into a mattress, where we were so close to a flustered near kiss.

"Hell, even my house key made me think of the ones I gave your family after the funeral. It was meant for your family to bring in the mail while I wasn't here. But you brought more inside, Cal. You brought kindness and affection. You brought friendship." Heat pooled behind his eyes and he blinked hard, voice catching. "You brought me family."

Cal's kiss was crushingly sweet. Soft and slow.

Cal's gentle sigh turned into a moan, and their tongues tangled as Percy threaded his fingers in Cal's hair and demanded him closer.

Cal urged Percy farther up the bed. Percy wriggled back, clutching Cal's shirt and daring him to stop kissing him for even a second. He opened his lips, and Cal swiped his tongue along the bow. He crawled on top of Percy, a warm, thrusting weight as they deepened their kisses.

Light nibbles down the length of Percy's neck turned into a delightfully debauched kiss: teeth pulling at his skin, tongue sucking on him hard, Cal grinding rhythmically against him.

More aroused than he'd ever been, Percy clawed at Cal's clothes, stripping them until both their clothes came off.

Skin slid against flushed skin with an electrifying rush.

Cal nipped his collarbone. "You're beautiful."

"Ha. Right, yeah."

Cal stopped kissing him, propped himself up against Percy's chest, and frowned.

Percy poked his tongue out. "We can't all be unique like you."

Cal hummed thoughtfully. He dipped his head and tongued the rim of Percy's smallish ears.

An outrageously pleasurable shiver spiked through him.

"You're the only person in the world with these curves and ridges," Cal said. "I might know you by the feel of them."

"Please learn me very well, then?"

Cal's smiling lips moved over his jaw to his lips. "The little depression in your lip is like a signature." He flicked the tip of his tongue inside Percy's mouth. "Your voice is unlike anyone else's, mellow but loud. Your lilt, playful. You have this way of smacking your lips together on consonants. There are hundreds of things that make you unique."

Percy chased after another kiss. "I could hear another one or two."

A smile skated over his chest and stomach as Cal slid down. The friction against his cock had him biting his lip. Cal didn't stop there, though. He dropped kisses down the length of his leg until he reached the sensitive skin of Percy's toes.

Cal pinched both big toes. "You curl your toes when you're nervous, and I suspect your feet are made with coils. How else to explain the energy that always seeps from you?" Hands drifted to his ankle. "And this bone here juts out more when you walk backward, and"—Cal kissed him around the ankle—"I wanted to kiss this the day you sprained it."

Percy sat up and tugged Cal back on top of him.

Cal only let himself be pulled up so far, his hot tongue flicking over Percy's left nipple before lavishing it in attention. Percy arched, rubbing his cock against Cal's chest and feeling Cal's hard length hot against his inner thigh. Words of pleading tumbled off Percy's tongue.

He needed more of that invasive method—like right now.

Cal's laugh ghosted over Percy's sucked-on nipple. His nerve-endings blazed, and Percy stretched his arms under the pillows where he'd thoughtfully stashed supplies.

Another laugh slid over his hip, and Cal's fingers chased through the goosebumps. If that didn't launch him into a realm of sensation, Cal's hot mouth sinking over his hard cock did the trick.

Silver-tongue lashings of a different kind. Enough to render him speechless.

Cal could take that as a handy tip.

Hot breath trailed over his wet cock as Cal pulled back to lick Percy's crown. The light touch heightened his sensitivity, and Percy's leg jerked, bumping the toolbox at the end of the bed.

A moan ripped out of him when Cal looked up at Percy and sucked him into his mouth. Percy gripped the bedcovers and failed not to buck against Cal's hot tongue. Cal found an agonizing rhythm that pumped him toward an orgasm. When Percy thought he was close, Cal pulled off him.

Attention centered on his inner thighs and stomach, and then Cal sucked him deep again, fingers digging into Percy's ass. One wet finger slid over his hole. When and how Cal had managed to do that neat trick was beyond him.

Percy wriggled against the finger until the tip of Cal's finger nudged inside. Again, Percy felt the first throes of orgasm, and again Cal pulled away.

"Are you edging me?" This came out rather delighted.

Cal's lips curled, then he looked away. "I'm procrastinating. I'm not so practiced at this. Look at the mess I made of the bed."

A wet patch puddled the bedcovers where Cal had secretly lost his control over the lube.

Soft laughter seeped out of him, tenderness sweeping into his chest to replace it. "Come here. I'll teach you."

Cal took instructions well. A quick learner with enough natural confidence that he didn't like being told twice. He prepared Percy with a generous helping of lube, slicked on a condom, and steered his perky length right where Percy wanted it.

Cal shallowly thrust the tip of his cock inside Percy, his breath stuttering. Percy tipped his hips and pressed the heels of his feet against the top of Cal's ass, under the small of his back. "You won't break me, but please try."

That sent a groan rippling through Cal and he sank inside him, filling him up deliciously. Percy swiveled his hips and Cal's eyes rolled back.

With a few pointed words, Cal dipped down and thrust his tongue into his mouth.

Percy clenched his ass and Cal lifted his eyebrow, voice pinched. "You certainly like playing with my tools."

"You look like you'll throttle me if I make you come too quickly."

"You did say it'd be your favorite way to go." Cal inched out and surged forward again, making Percy gasp.

"That's more like it."

Cal rocked slowly, tortuously—and then drew back and snapped forward like a pro, hitting Percy's prostate with a sensual burn. Oh hell, consume him.

Cal did, thrusting in and out, sawing him into a begging mess. Percy pressed his palm against Cal's forehead, fingers sinking into his hair, legs wrapping around Cal as he arched hard into his next thrust. His cock leaked, painting Cal's stomach where they rubbed.

A grunt escaped Cal and his hips rocked harder until he was pistoning inside Percy. Like on the last stretch, he ditched the tortoise and went full hare. The bed rocked, headboard smacking the wall. The springs were barely audible over Percy's needy moans, and he loved every orgasm-building second of it.

Cal filled him up and rolled his hips. "I could learn you forever."

"Please do."

Percy sucked in a breath as his balls drew up. One slide of his cock over Cal's stomach sent his release pulsing through him. Cal choked on a gasp, pushing forward three more times against his prostate, lengthening the pleasure rippling through him.

Percy came over both of their chests. Cal's cock throbbed inside him as he spilled a delightfully garbled "Percy" on his lips.

Percy scratched his fingernails over Cal's shoulders to intensify his orgasm.

With choppy breathing, Cal collapsed on top of him. Short puffs of air tickled against Percy's sweat-laced skin at the crook of his neck. He bit his lip, not ready for Cal's blanketing weight to leave him.

His cock was slipping out of Percy, though.

A kiss met his temple, Cal's light stubble chafing his jaw. Percy curled his arm around Cal's neck and hummed his contentment. "Why I told your mom and sisters that we'd host dinner, I don't know."

"You did what?" Cal rolled off him, tying up the condom and tossing it into the wastebasket.

"I emailed your mom my plans last night and I figured, since it was all so sudden, the least we could do is offer dinner."

Lying on his side, Cal fingered the come over Percy's stomach. Percy couldn't hold back the ticklish laugh.

"What are we offering for dinner?" Cal asked.

"Don't know yet. What do we have time to make?"

"What's in the fridge?"

"I guess I could whip up pasta and a cheese sauce?" Percy rolled onto his side and grinned at Cal. "I do have cream cheese carrot muffins for dessert."

"We should hurry and shower then."

Percy bounded off the bed, snatched Cal's hand, and pulled him off the bed. "You know, I have this unhealthy obsession with us in the shower."

Cal shook his head, and said dryly, "Who needs dinner when there's dessert?"

Percy eyed Cal's gorgeous naked body as he propelled them into the bathroom. "I very much agree."

∽

THEY DRESSED ONCE MORE, WET HAIR DRIPPING ON THEIR T-shirts and smirks shifting between them.

Instead of leaping toward the kitchen to make dinner, Percy

backed Cal against his shelf full of model dinosaurs. "One more thing."

Cal's stomach rolled under Percy's caressing hands. "Are you going to tell me that I'll have time to resume my masters now because you'll be here to help with mom and the kids?"

"You thought that through."

"A man's allowed to dream."

"I'm glad to hear it. I will be here to help. You can count on it."

Cal smiled, and shifted to leave.

Percy firmly pressed him back in place with a cheeky smile. "That wasn't what I was going to say, though. Care to take another stab?"

Cal's gaze traveled to where their legs scissored together. He slipped his hands into Percy's pocket and pulled out his wallet. Then, from the other, he pulled out a roll of Mentos.

He flipped open the wallet and fished through Percy's cards until he found the shiny new library card. "Did you want to show me this?"

Percy smiled wider. "I was going to hand you that in the park and let you figure out it meant I'm staying. But again, that isn't it."

Cal pinched a Mentos and slid it between Percy's lips. "Were you going to tell me to take care of your—my—key?"

Percy sucked in the orange candy. "I'm not making any other copies."

Cal watched him chew and swallow. "What is it you want to say, then?"

A deep smile pulled at Percy's lips, and he stroked Cal's throat, right where it was red and raw from Percy's attention in the shower. "You've been living here an hour, and while we've been at each other's throats, you haven't yet slayed me with your words."

Cal gripped Percy's neck and walked him backward toward the door. "I have a few that will do it."

A warm blush bloomed over Percy's cheeks. "Going to tell me you love me, Cal?"

"No."

Percy almost tripped, and Cal's steady arm held him up. "Then what are your words?"

Cal leaned down and kissed him, cradling Percy's face as he looked him in the eye. "I'm *committed* to you."

The words fisted Percy's heart. He let out a hiccupping sob. "Committed?"

A gentle whisper hit his wet eyelashes. "I'm here. I'm not leaving. This is it, you're stuck with me."

Cal hooked him into an urgent, all-consuming kiss that Percy would always feel. When they pulled apart, Percy's voice cracked. "I guess we really are earth and water."

"Because together we're mud?"

"Together we stick."

C ommitment
　　noun / com . mit . ment

DEFINITION OF COMMITMENT
　: spending a lot of time together
　: buying mugs
　: Cal tying Percy's shoelaces
　: driving each other to work
　: taking turns caring when sick/ hurt
　: standing up when loved one is insulted
　: massaging and helping the Glovers
　: calling Percy out on their fake nemesizing.
　: trusting Cal to let down his defenses and speak sincerely

: CAL AND PERCY

EXAMPLE OF **COMMITMENT** IN AN EXCERPT BELOW

"There's only so many times I can sing 'Mary Had A Little Lamb', Oliver." Percy kissed the head of Cal's screaming brother, woolen hat soft on his lips. He breathed in the pleasant smell of baby shampoo as he continued walking down the cul-de-sac.

The houses glistened with the crispness of impending winter, and most neighbors were at work this time on a Friday. Which was perfect because he and Oliver had just completed a Secret Santa mission to drop off a self-made picture book using Aunt Abby's watercolor paints. They snuck in and left it on the Sernas' dining table for Josie's baby, Stefanie, under the guise of Jingle Jangle and Twinkle Toes (Percy and Oli respectively).

Rocked by his steps, Oliver stopped crying and nuzzled against Percy's chest.

"Are you complaining because you're stuck with me again?" Percy rubbed Oliver's back through the baby carrier he used at least an hour a day. Marg had had to start part-time work after six weeks' maternity leave. Percy offered to take care of him those ten hours, working his massaging clients around it. "Your mom will be home soon, okay? More Mary?"

He started a croaky repetition of Oliver's favorite nursery rhyme, then a familiar laugh caught at the back of his neck and Cal's arms slipped around the two of them.

Oli protested the moment Percy stopped moving.

"Hello to you too, Oli," Cal said and then dropped a soft kiss on the crook of Percy's neck under the collar of his thick jacket. "What are you two doing out here? It's so cold."

Percy turned in Cal's arms, eyeing his boyfriend

who wore a thin T-rex Tshirt under an open parka. "We're dressed for it. Mittens and everything. You not so much."

"I had to join Twinkle Toes here and"—Cal studied Percy, a caressing gaze sweeping over his face and lingering on his smile—"Chatterbox Cheeky? Rosey-Cheeks Kringle? Pointy-ears Pixie?"

"Heh. Chatterbox Cheeky is you, Cal. Though I like how you're trying to throw me off."

Cal lifted that brow of his, and Percy made no hesitation to slip a mittened hand behind his neck and steer his boyfriend down so he could kiss it off him. "How are your Jurassic Park studies coming along?"

Cal peppered a few kisses on Oli's head. "Just finished drafting a chapter, but I couldn't concentrate anymore."

"Because your mind kept wandering to how hot we were on the kitchen floor earlier?"

Cal laughed. "Because I heard you singing out here, and you're quite bad."

"You're lucky I'm carrying a baby right now."

Cal pinched one of Percy's mittens and sank his hand inside it with a soft smile that he only used around Percy. It touched his eyes with a mesmerizing twinkle, even though his lips only lifted a fraction. This smile was the secret that Percy had always yearned to fall from Cal's bottom-heavy lip. It whispered love and commitment. Promised that nothing else in the world mattered except them, and yet, the tiniest trace of sarcasm filtered through. As though he still wanted to stir him a little crazy.

Percy flashed a loving smile of his own, and started singing again. For Cal's obvious enjoyment.

THE END.

Acknowledgments

Writing a novel is no lone process. There are many people that work behind the scenes to make a story better.

My thanks go out to my wonderful husband for being my biggest support as I worked on Scorpio.

To Natasha Snow for the cover art! Every time, you knock it out of the park!

For beautiful chapter graphics of Scorpio and Virgo, thanks go out to Maria Gandolfo.

Teresa Crawford, thanks for helping me to develop this story. You're amazing, and I can't thank you enough!

Thanks to HJS Editing for copyediting. As always, your edits were brilliant! Thank you so much!

Devil in the Details Editing Services—thank you for proofreading!

Another thanks to Vicki for reading and offering valuable feedback, and to alpha reader Sunne for picking up the inconsistencies. Big smiles to my test readers for catching final slip-ups. And another cheers to Vir for helping me out at crunch time with a few final thoughts!

About Anyta

A bit about me: I'm a big, BIG fan of slow-burn romances. I love to read and write stories with characters who slowly fall in love.

Some of my favorite tropes to read and write are: Enemies to Lovers, Friends to Lovers, Clueless Guys, Bisexual, Pansexual, Demisexual, Oblivious MCs, Everyone (Else) Can See It, Slow Burn, Love Has No Boundaries.

I write a variety of stories, Contemporary MM Romances with a good dollop of angst, Contemporary lighthearted MM Romances, and even a splash of fantasy.
My books have been translated into German, Italian and French.

Contact: http://www.anytasunday.com/about-anyta/
Sign up for Anyta's newsletter and receive a free e-book:
http://www.anytasunday.com/newsletter-free-e-book/

Printed in Great Britain
by Amazon